Praise for *Year of the Bu*

"*Year of the Buffalo* is a brilliant testimony to how good Aaron Burch is, a perfect realization of what makes his writing so special. It manages that balance of tenderness and violence, finding beauty in the most unexpected places. At the heart of the novel, Burch looks closely at the nature of time, the way it pulls us backwards, then strands us in a present that we can't quite understand, and then makes us a little afraid to imagine what kind of future awaits. But Burch knows how to control time, to make it tell the kind of story that matters."

— **Kevin Wilson,** author of *Nothing to See Here*

"In *Year of the Buffalo*, Aaron Burch brings his considerable talents to bear in subtle and heart-stringing scenes that tell the kind of story that lingers long after last call, of the catch and release of late-night nostalgia and the love and distance between brothers."

— **Amelia Gray,** author of *Gutshot*

"Two brothers in a too-fancy rented SUV, driving towards Michigan and away from, what? Their past? Their avatars and alter egos? Their pet bison? All of the above? *Year of the Buffalo* by Aaron Burch is a poignant, searching tale of brotherhood and the personas we employ, both within the ring and without. It's a book about memory and the past refreshingly devoid of easy nostalgia. It's a book for anyone who'd pick Talking Heads as their walk-up song. It's a book you should read."

— **Danny Caine,** author of *How to Resist Amazon and Why*

Year of the Buffalo

by Aaron Burch

American Buffalo Books
Manhattan, KS

American Buffalo Books
www.AmericanBuffaloBooks.org

The Library of Congress has cataloged
the American Buffalo Books paperback as follows:
Names: Burch, Aaron, author
Title: Year of the Buffalo: a novel / Aaron Burch
Description: Manhattan, KS: American Buffalo Books, 2022
Library of Congress Control Number: 2022934965
ISBN: 9780578394015.

Printed in the United States of America
1st printing

"There were giants on the earth in those days."
Genesis 6:4

Part I:

WOLFMEN

How to ...

... Build a Habit?

... Break a Habit?

Be consistent.

Think about your motivation. Your goals.

... Make a Pattern?

... Build a Story?

Picture the distance between here and there, now and then. Think about it as actual distance, a literal picture. Draw it if it helps. Write it out. Talk through it with someone.

Let go of who you were. Let yourself let go of who you were. Become who you want to be. Let yourself become who you want to be.

... Turn Yourself into a Character.

I.

Scott couldn't get comfortable. He hadn't been to the gym since they'd bought the farm, but all through his body he felt the work he'd been doing—digging holes in the hard ground for oversized posts, throwing stacks of wood over his shoulder and carrying them to the far reaches of their acreage. Tired, a little sore, but it felt good too, his body carrying the ache of long evenings building The Fence. It was a two-man job, at least, but he liked the time alone, liked doing it himself. Liked the feeling of the work stinging through muscles he hadn't used in ages. It reminded him of when he'd first moved to upstate New York, when he'd started building his body. Re-creating himself. Making Mr. Bison. The kind of work that made him think of his father, the kind of work his father would have thought of as *real work*. He reached up, rubbed his right shoulder with his left hand, then switched, right hand, left shoulder. He remembered being on the road, the exhaustion of wrestling, traveling, wrestling again, traveling some more. Repeat. How, every couple of months, he'd spoil himself, splurge on the longest, most expensive massage he could find in whatever city he'd found himself.

Leaning over the arm of his chair, Scott sorted through his bag, flipping back and forth through the handful of CDs he'd brought with him, looking for his coffeeshop soundtrack. He knew almost no one listened to CDs anymore, knew he could just as easily burn CDs to his laptop and he wouldn't have to carry them around with him. But he didn't want unlimited choices. He liked preparing for each individual trip. He liked looking at his two tower displays of CDs before leaving the house and deciding which four or five he wanted to take with him. Holly made fun of him and he used to try to explain himself, but it never came out quite right and he liked his own argument less when voiced out loud than when it was just the way he did it. He just liked it.

There it was. He put the top disc into his laptop, and the media player opened automatically, started playing "Sugar on My Tongue."

Scott stared at the screen. He didn't really have anything to do. He'd spent the last decade going to work, sitting in his cubicle, getting his work done. He didn't love it, but he didn't hate it. He kind of liked it actually—the monotony of it all, the *regularness* of it after all those years on the road. He wasn't going to miss it ... but he still wasn't sure what to do with his days without it either. So here he was, getting his morning coffee, getting online, scrolling through his email because he kind of liked the routine, the mundanity.

Scott opened his email, stared at the long list of messages. All bold to let him know they were new, but all easily discernible as trash. Spam and mailing list emails that, technically, he'd signed up for but didn't actually care about and so were basically spam. Down at the bottom, same as it was every time he looked, was that first email from Michael. He'd read it so many times he had it memorized, and still, every time he checked his email, he started with it first, rereading and mentally walking himself through everything that had already happened since—talking it all over with Holly, quitting his job, buying the farm, starting to build The Fence.

Dear Scott Isaacson, Dear "Mr. Bison" (?),

Sorry, I never know how best to address messages like this. Apologies, too, for the informality. It was tricky tracking you down. (Trickier still, if this isn't you?)

The gist: I work for a small start-up game company. We've sold a couple games (to big companies. Companies who, unlike us, you may have actually heard of), and now, of course, as these things go, the game we built only for ourselves, for fun, is in the middle of a bidding war. And ... well ... the hero of the game is ... you. We hope you'll officially allow us to use your likeness, and will pay you accordingly. (Maybe, too, you might be interested in acting as some kind of official spokesperson? Like, in commercials and other promotional stuff? Those details are far from worked out though, just me thinking out loud here. Or, silently, I guess, but electronically loud.)

Anyway. Please contact me at your earliest convenience to discuss the details. I hope you're as excited by this prospect as we are! Go West, young man! (Too much?)

Sincerely,
Michael Leaf
Head Designer, CP Games

It still put a giant smile on his face. Every time.

He got out his phone, texted his brother again.

<Dying to share the news! Text or call me!>

Reaching down and putting his left hand on the back left corner of his seat and his right to the outside side of his left knee, Scott twisted his upper body to his left, then flipped sides and did the same to his right. Cracked his back five times one way, twice the other. "Sugar On My Tongue" became "I Want To Live" became "Love—Building On Fire" became "I Wish You Wouldn't Say That." The keyboards swirled and David Byrne half-crooned, half-chirped the title lyrics and Timmy "The Bully" Wallace sprang into Scott's mind. Timmy, who'd come out to "I Wish You Wouldn't Say That," an odd choice, maybe the oddest Scott remembered. Everyone thought so. It always caught the crowd by surprise, and the wrestlers, even having heard and seen the entrance countless times, would shrug, shake their heads and make faces.

Scott had a theory. A handful of theories actually, though all related.

One: Timmy had really wanted "Psycho Killer"—an odd enough choice itself but *better*?—but maybe another wrestler had already used it? Scott had never heard it used, but that didn't mean it wasn't possible.

Talking with Michael and some of the other developers had filled Scott with shock and excitement, but he hadn't stopped and actually recalled those days. He'd spent the first couple years after retiring playing and replaying old matches in his mind, replaying again. Thinking of his friends and feuds, picturing the matches that must be continuing to happen without him. Finally, he'd pushed all that to a corner of his mind, locked it away. Moved on. Made himself not think about it long enough to finally stop thinking about it without having to make himself. He'd done this once before, trained himself to forget.

In Scott's headphones, "I Wish You Wouldn't Say That" became "Psycho Killer" and, yes, it was definitely a better walkout song. Timmy wasn't a "Psycho Killer" though. He was "The Bully." Even if what exactly that nickname meant was never that clear. It sometimes seemed like Tim was a bully himself but other times like he'd been the kid who had been bullied growing up. Like he'd become a wrestler to seek revenge on his tormenters, to stand up for bullied kids everywhere. Maybe "I Wish You Wouldn't Say That" was fitting, maybe it echoed the cry of bullied little-kid-Timmy and the loudspeakers blared it before matches to remind Tim "The Bully" where he'd come from, to get him fired up for the match?

None of their personas had been *that* thought through. Scott had been confused when they'd first started dating and Holly asked about his character, who he was. "I'm Mr. Bison?" he said, not understanding. "Right. But were you, like, a buffalo trainer? A buffalo hunter? A buffalo reincarnated, a living embodiment of the spirit of a buffalo?" "I like buffalo," he told her. She thought about that. "Let's figure something out," she said. "Let's make it more than that."

Another theory: The song was supposed to have been "Psycho Killer," but the sound guy had queued up the wrong track.

Another: Maybe not even the wrong track but an altogether wrong CD. Something with screeching guitars, a rallying yell. Quiet Riot or Whitesnake.

Maybe it had been a match that The Bully had come in as an underdog and won and he'd kept the track thereafter for good luck. Maybe he just liked how weird it was. Did Timmy have a weird sense of humor like that? Scott couldn't remember.

He smiled at himself, his theories. Remembering the old days more fondly than he had in a long time. Scott got his phone back out: no new texts or calls. No reply from Ernie. He went to his messages with Holly, typed out, <Still no reply from Ernie. :(> Hit send.

Scott typed "Timmy Wallace" into the search box, found an accountant, an author of self-published model train books, a high school athlete who looked to have just set his school record for both the 50- and 100-yard dashes. Scott tried to remember his own high school track times to compare—to compare himself to this kid, to compare his own record of almost twenty years ago with this kid's brand new one. He wondered if his record still held, if his name was still up there on that board in his old gym. He'd gone back once when home visiting, a kind of nostalgia tour. The school had changed mascots since he'd been a student—the home of the Indians had become home to the Eagles, all mascot representations replaced—and the gym had gotten the most noticeable facelift, though his name was still up there on that board. That was years ago though. A lifetime, it felt like. Scott couldn't remember his track time posted up there on that board, but he was sure this kid had just demolished it. A certainty that meant there was no way his name was still up on that Eagles board either. Kids seemed to be getting faster every year—better shoes, better training, better diets. Everything more specifically researched, measured, and calculated. He pictured this Timmy Wallace's coach measuring his stride, the force of each push-off, re-training slightly up or down for most efficient, optimum results.

Scott highlighted "Timmy Wallace," typed "Timmy The Bully Wallace." A row of images popped up, and he laughed out loud before catching himself and reeling the laugh back in. Tim looked so ... ridiculous. So ... *'80s*, Scott thought, though these were all actually from the '90s. Like a weird fever dream of '80s flair and '90s edge, a mashup that left Timmy looking stuck between the two and belonging to neither, neither fish nor fowl in a purgatory of bad fashion. Maybe the pictures looked so '90s and Scott had forgotten how long ago the '90s were.

David Byrne sang about not having time for compassion, and Scott looked back at his screen, scanned down the ridiculous pics, and then a jolt. Scott felt it through his whole body, not just his eyes stopping their scanning but like a punch reverberating through his whole body.

Dead Wrestler of the Week.

He clicked the link before he'd even had a chance to wonder if he actually wanted to or not.

Timothy "The Bully" Wallace
Real name: Mike Sanders
Died: July 3, 2008. No autopsy, assumed drug overdose.

Scott skimmed the page, only half reading. It talked of Timmy's feuds, his tag team partners, his devoted fan base despite never crossing over into larger popularity. No mention of the Talking Heads, no clarifying story about the background of his "The Bully" character. Scott recognized most of the other wrestlers named for one reason or another. He didn't realize he was scanning for his own name until he felt a little pang of disappointment at not getting a mention. No mention either of Wallace's history of drug use, and Scott wondered if he'd known of any abuse at the time. A part of him wished for more info, wished the article more fully fleshed out what had happened, though another part was glad it was missing. Glad it primarily focused on the wrestling, the part of Timmy he wanted to remember, the high-energy "I Wish You Wouldn't Say That" Timmy, not Mike Sanders, drug addict. And, speaking of ... Mike Sanders? Had he changed his name to Timmy Wallace, or was that as much a part of the character as The Bully? Was that deemed somehow better than just Mike "The Bully" Sanders?

At the bottom of the page, Scott clicked the bold **Dead Wrestler of the Week** link to go to the homepage. A long list of pictures, names, dates, causes of death. Links to "read more." Scott scrolled down, kept scrolling. There were so many—names he recognized, some he didn't. A couple of the wrestlers were famous enough that he'd heard the news, but he'd been so uninvolved, for so long, he was unaware of most. Could he have been that unaware? All these deaths, all these men he'd wrestled with, against, heroes who had inspired him, likely some he'd inspired, and he knew nothing of their passing, their lives since he knew them, since he'd left the ring?

All this death. Scott remembered a conversation he'd once had with a friend. This friend had asked Scott if he ever felt guilty, ever felt like less of a man, because they hadn't been in the military. Hadn't fought in a war, hadn't served for their country like their fathers, their fathers' fathers before them. The question had surprised Scott—he had no guilt over it because he'd never before considered it at all, but it was obvious on the friend's face that he had. That he was burdened with this weight, that he carried it with him always.

It reminded Scott of his Uncle Paul. As a kid, Scott had been fascinated by him—Paul had long, dirty blond hair and a beard, where Scott and Ernie's dad, and nearly every other adult male in Scott's childhood radius, was clean-shaven, well-groomed. Paul's hands looked *rougher*, seemed to always be a little dirty, like he'd been working in his garage earlier and hadn't been able to get them wholly clean, or maybe he'd just gotten them so dirty, for so many years, had worked so much, this was as clean as they ever got. Paul rarely talked much when the family got together, but not awkwardly so. He measured his words carefully, didn't waste them. "Vietnam," Scott's father told him once. "I mean ... he wasn't a chatty Cathy before, but he hasn't been quite the same since. Tried to ask once, and he just shook his head."

Like, *no*, Scott thought now. Like, *no, don't ask. No, I don't talk about it.*

An inaccurate comparison, and Scott felt a little uncomfortable even noticing himself make it, but that was a little how he'd thought about his days wrestling for all those years since. It was how he'd been able to move on. *No, I don't talk about it.* How he'd been able to so compartmentalize those years. *No, don't ask.* How he was able to build a life for himself, away from wrestling. Why he was so far removed, why he was now so surprised by this list, the names included, the quantity, and likely not even comprehensive, he realized ... and shook his head at himself, sad at the thought, sad at himself for having it. But, too, it was possibly part of why he wasn't himself on the page. Why he was so sad to see all those names, all that news all at once, but there was also a kind of joy—for himself, his life, a reminder to give thanks to everything he had. All those deaths—so many drugs, so many health issues, suicides—so many seemingly inevitable outcomes for those unable to leave the sport behind. Unable to move on, unable to build lives and families and futures for themselves outside the ring. Wrestling wasn't like going to war, but it had been a kind of serving his country, hadn't it?

Scott realized the CD had ended, and then realized, too, he'd been focusing on keeping himself from crying. He wondered how long he'd been listening to nothing. His iced coffee was still ¾ full, all the ice melted. He thought of his brother, Ernie, that far-off, dazed look he'd sometimes get. Scott would often make fun of his big brother for being so spacey, but he'd never thought too much of it outside of the teasing. He wondered if that was why his brother seemed so sad, so often—spending too much time thinking of the past. Too much nostalgia, too little interaction with the present.

He added a bookmark to the page, clicked back to his email. Checked the boxes next to everything more recent than the email from Michael, deleted them all, leaving Michael's back at the top.

Scott ejected his CD, took off his headphones and wrapped them in their own cord. Put the *Sand in the Vaseline* disc back into its two-CD jewel case, the case back in his bag. He scanned his bookmarks bar, double-checking if there was anything else he wanted to check, though he knew all the links he had saved there, knew there wasn't anything else. He stopped at **Dead Wrestler of the Week,** almost as if forgetting it was there, as if forgetting how he'd spent the last ... half hour? Hour? Two? He couldn't remember what time he'd gotten to the café. He opened his bookmarks folder and moved the new link to the bottom, still saved but not at the top. Not so visible, not right there looking back at him.

Scott packed up everything, left his still mostly full pint of coffee in the plastic bin for dirty dishes, and got in his truck. Sitting there in the parking lot, before he even got his keys in the ignition, Scott started crying—he wasn't sniffling, it wasn't coming down in waves, just a sheen of tears, all down his face.

And then, sitting there on his passenger seat where he'd tossed it, his phone vibrated. He looked at the screen, a text from Holly.

<I have an idea. Hope it's ok!>

2.

Ernie stood in front of his open sliding glass door, staring out into his backyard. He hadn't been out there in nearly a year, hadn't done any yard work or upkeep in two or three. He tried counting by remembering what they'd done each summer: every vacation they'd gone on, every vacation they'd postponed due to one promotion or another. Ernie always said—and believed, or at least thought he believed—that he didn't even care about the job or working his way up or career advancement or any of it, but the upward momentum felt inevitable and then unstoppable, each incremental move up the ladder coming with just enough more money to not be able to turn it down. More money meant more hours, meant more responsibilities, meant more demand on his attention, all of which meant less time for the rest of his life, less attention paid to anything that wasn't his job, less prioritizing vacations together, never mind yard- and housework. Could it have been four years? Five? Had it been *five* years since he'd done anything out there but mow? And even that he gave over to a neighborhood kid last year to earn some extra money for ... whatever kids saved money for these days?

Ernie leaned forward, let his face push into the screen door. The mesh netting crisscrossed his nose, his lips. Down by his side, he absentmindedly swung his morning coffee back and forth. Two fingers hooked into its handle and his thumb on the top lip, the mug swung gently and upright enough for it to keep threatening but never quite spilling over.

A dull pain sung from somewhere almost behind him, oddly more absence of headache than ache itself, like a ghost pain of a migraine, and Ernie rubbed the back of his head. He squinted his eyes, crossed them. Somewhere down there, hidden in the overgrowth but nearly visible when he relaxed his gaze, when he *Magic Eyed* everything through the screen and blurred vision, was the well-groomed garden he and Becca had immediately fallen in love with. The house was the twenty-third they'd walked through—not including the open houses they'd randomly stopped in just to peek, nor everything they'd walked through virtually, the hours and hours of Internet searching and browsing. Not that Ernie had been counting. They'd fallen in love as soon as their Realtor unlocked and held open the front door, letting Ernie and Becca walk in first. Neither had even thought they believed in love at first sight. It had taken them weeks of dating (*months*, the stories sometimes went, depending on who they were telling, how much they were drinking) to feel the same about each other. But there was no other way of describing walking into the house. The beautiful backyard had sealed it, insofar as they'd needed anything sealed.

A sudden sound jolted Ernie out of it. *Sentimentlust*, Becca called it, her term for when her husband slipped into a kind of nostalgia dream, teasing Ernie for his own teasing of his father's *wanderlust*.

Ernie stood still for half a second, somewhere between daydream and reality, his face pressed into the mesh of the screen door. It felt oddly pleasing. Then the sound happened again, and this time he felt its accompanying vibration in his pocket. Ernie took a step back, letting his vision unblur, refocusing on the scene of his backyard. He waited, let himself believe in the possibility of who the texts might be from, what they might be about. Like maybe Becca was ready to talk. Like maybe now they were going to work through all this after all.

Outside, the snap of something clicking into place, a rush of release. Almost like cocking a gun, but more fluid, more plastic. The sprinklers. Ernie thought about going to the basement and turning them off, though he didn't move. He probably should have turned them off a week ago when it had started raining and the forecast called for more, rain every day for the foreseeable future. A week of gray skies and everything wet and a closed house, the opening up of which had led to this current staring out into his backyard, this moment of breathing in the fresh air. He pictured, now, the sprinklers turning on every day throughout the week of rain, just watering the wet. He thought of the waste of water, the waste of money. He thought about how he shouldn't have had to turn them off for the rain because he never should have even turned them back on anyway. He'd let it all go so much, all he was watering was weeds. But it was habit: the days got warmer, there stopped being frost on the ground when Ernie woke in the morning for work, a couple of days in a row came and went without a need for a jacket, winter finally felt like it had passed, taking with it the fear of pipes freezing, and Ernie went into the basement and turned on the sprinklers, his own annual acknowledgment of and symbol for spring, one of his favorite moments of the year. It always spurred memories of growing up, of running through sprinklers with his brother, Scott, and his best friend, Benjamin. Setting up the Slip 'N Slide. The feel of wet grass on his bare feet, between his toes. At least until his allergies kicked in, sending him into a sneezing fit, one after another after another, endless, like he was going for some kind of Guinness World Record. Ernie realized he liked the sprinklers themselves too. He liked the sound. It was soothing, hypnotic. He wondered if the sound machine that Becca used to fall asleep to and had taken with her had a "sprinkler" setting.

Ernie pulled his phone out of his pocket, hopeful for Becca, even while *knowing* it would be Scott. Scott, who never texted him. Ernie never texted Scott either, but he only ever thought about how Scott never texted him. And now, out of the blue, for the last three or four days, a sudden pileup of attempted conversation. Every day, a single call and then a text. Never a voicemail, always just the missed call, a follow-up text.

<You OK?> And then, a second, with the same time stamp. <Kinda dying to share the news!> Today was the first day with two texts, the added "OK?" check-in. Was he just wondering why Ernie hadn't yet replied? Was he concerned? Did he know something? Had he heard? Via who?

As Ernie stared at his phone, rereading the texts—*You OK? Kinda dying to share the news! You OK? Kinda dying to share the news!*—and wondering what Scott might be dying to tell him, the phone vibrated in his hand.

"Ernie?"

"Fuck!" He didn't even realize he'd answered the phone until the voice came out the other end. He looked down, saw he'd spilled his coffee. "Shit."

"Ernie? Hello?"

Ernie stared at the phone in his hand like he'd never held or used one before, like he had no idea where this voice might be coming from.

"Shit," he muttered again and bent down, placing the mug on the ground.

"You there?"

"Yeah, sorry." Ernie looked at his phone, saw a number rather than a contact name. "I'm here. Ernie speaking."

"Ernie! It's Holly." She waited for a beat for a response that never came. "Scott's wife."

"Right, right. Of course. I know who you are, Holly, duh," though he hadn't immediately made a connection.

"Scott's been trying to get you—"

"Right, right. I keep meaning to call him back. I've been so busy—"

"It's OK. I'm glad I got you! "We have some news!"

I *know*, Ernie thought. *Scott's been vague-texting me about it for days*. Even only thinking it and not saying it out loud, he felt guilty. It felt meaner directed at Holly than it ever did at his brother, even though it was still meant to be directed at his brother.

"Scott's going to be so jealous I finally got you. He's been so excited to talk to you!"

Ernie wondered if that was really true or Holly's embellishment. He wondered the last time Scott had been excited to talk to him. He thought about how Scott talked when he got excited. Other than when they were kids, it was usually when he was talking about wrestling. And that had been … had it been a full decade since that phase? And then, having just *thought* the word jolted Ernie, made him remember one of their last big arguments, Scott's anger and frustration and exasperation when he'd referred to wrestling as a "phase."

"Two pieces of news," Holly continued. "Some news and an idea. An offer."

"OK, OK!" Ernie said, as he went and grabbed a hand towel hanging on the dishwasher and dropped it on the ground. He'd noticed this in himself more and more in recent years, this lack of patience with his brother. Or: Becca had noticed it. She'd pointed it out, and Ernie had to acknowledge, had to admit to himself his own role in the minimalism of his relationship with his brother. It was odd—Scott was a good guy, they had no actual problems with one another, though they seemed to have no relationship at all; meanwhile Becca's brother was a world-class asshole, and she and he couldn't have been closer. She'd admit herself every bad tendency in him but wouldn't allow it spoken from anyone's mouth but her own.

"Sorry," Ernie said, suddenly aware of the silence Holly had left for him to respond. "It sounds exciting!" He smiled, remembering Becca telling him that people can hear your smile even when they can't see it. "Is it like a good news, bad news thing? Which to tell me first?"

"No, no. Good news, good news. Good news, crazy news. Something like that."

"OK …"

"You haven't talked to Scott at all? He hasn't said anything about his news? You don't know?"

"No!" he said with more edge than he meant, but he just wanted her to say it already.

Only a few weeks before, the entire backyard had still been dead or dormant, the perennials just starting to push up through the ground. The yard had looked like a clean slate. That was what he needed. A clean slate. He'd let himself believe this would be the year. He'd clean out the beds, pull any and all weeds as soon as they showed themselves. He'd be a new, better version of himself; he'd do the things that in the past he'd only gotten as far as intending to do. He'd use his new extra time productively. He'd resod the lawn. Was that the right word? Sod? *Re*sod? Was that what the grass needed? Or just more water and a little care? There were bare patches from the weeds stealing the sunlight and water and whatever other nutrients fed the grass, and also from Bulleit, from that scurry of kicking that seemed cute when out on walks but had turned their yard into a dirt field.

This all before the night Ernie went for a few drinks with coworkers and left the gate open. Bulleit wasn't outside when he left, but the gate stayed open until

Rebecca let him out before bed; until she'd waited longer than was normal for Bulleit to run down the stairs, go to the bathroom, run around some more, after a squirrel or something imagined or just to run off energy, and then back up the stairs and inside; until she finally stepped outside, closing behind her the screen door Ernie was now daydreaming through; until she went outside herself, leaned over the railing and looked around the yard, calling, "Bulleit! Bulleit!!" to no response; until she went around the railing, down the steps—"Bulleit!"; frustration starting to turn into panic, while either pulling and cinching her robe tight against the chill in the air or letting it flap open, billowing out behind her like a cape, panic overriding even the instinct to brace against the cold—sometimes Ernie pictured her one way, sometimes the other; until finally Rebecca turned the corner off the last step and, seeing the gate swinging wide open, her heart sank.

There was the phone call to Ernie—*multiple* phone calls, the vibration of the first not felt, and then the next couple ignored, Ernie assuming it could wait until he wasn't *in the middle of listening to Steph's story*, until the repeated calls, one after another, the constant, unending vibrations finally convincing him it must be urgent, something must be *wrong*, by which time Rebecca was already in her car, already driving slow circles around the neighborhood, watching and calling out her window and wondering why her husband wouldn't fucking answer his fucking phone when their fucking dog was fucking *missing*. This all came to Ernie between tears and hiccupped explanations, and anger and panic, and more calls out the open window, every quarter-block or so, "Bulleit? Come 'ere, Bulleit!"

Ernie's first thoughts, the thoughts that pained him later, when Bulleit didn't, in fact, find her way home and return, and that pained him now as he stared out into his backyard: *She'll be fine. She always finds her way home.* They'd taken her in when Becca's brother was in the hospital—the shelter had called because she had a chip; Becca answered thinking she should, not knowing what else to do, thinking anyone who called her brother might want to know he was in a coma. No one had called except telemarketers and the animal shelter. And Bulleit had adapted immediately; she loved both Ernie and Becca, loved the yard they paid a handyman extra to jump ahead in line and come build a fence around, agreeing they'd take care of her as long as they had to. She seemed to love to escape and run, but she always came back. More often than not, they'd find her sitting on their welcome mat, looking like she didn't understand where they were, why no one would let her in—both out circling the neighborhood, already designing *MISSING* flyers in their minds, making note of optimal posts and trees for taping (or staple-gunning? They should get a staple gun, Ernie would think each time, before returning home and finding Bulleit sitting there on their porch, waiting, and he'd forget all about trips to Home Depot and tape vs. staple guns, until the next time she got out and the pattern repeated).

Ernie's second thought, sitting there at the bar, Rebecca crying and hiccupping her worry about Bulleit getting out: did Becca somehow know? Some wifely sixth sense tell her he was being ... not inappropriate but flirty. Flirtier than his wife probably would have thought appropriate.

These thoughts came together with a third, all three happening as near to simultaneous as possible, but this being the order in which he always remembered them: First, *she'll be fine*; second, *am I in trouble?*; and then, finally, *what if this had happened in the past?* In his parents' generation, or even only a few years ago, when he and Rebecca first started dating. Before cell phones, before constant reachability. Before the *ability* to respond immediately meant everything was *required* to be responded to immediately. She might have called the bar? Maybe? He would have likely told her where he was going, she could have looked up the number in the phonebook, called and asked to speak to him. Would she have? Would he have told her the bar they were going to? Would he have lied? Would that have become another part of their fight?

"Right," Holly said, reeling Ernie back from wherever he'd gone. "So," she said again. "Scott got this email. A few weeks ago. From this guy at a video game company. CP Games. Have you heard of them?"

"No," Ernie answered and then wondered who had heard of specific video game companies. Other than the systems themselves and, like, Capcom. Tecmo? He thought he'd somewhere heard of Rock Star Games maybe?

"They actually have a couple of games I really like. *Forever Space* is pretty great. Have you heard of that?"

"Nuh-uh."

"Sure, yeah. Scott hadn't heard of them either. Anyway. They make video games, and this guy, Michael, he emailed your brother because they made one where he's the hero."

"What?"

"Like, the *main* guy. The guy you play as."

"*Scott*?"

"Well. Wrestler Scott. Mr. Bison."

"So ... It's a wrestling game?"

"No. That's the thing. It's real weird. It's like this post-apocalyptic adventure game."

"And Scott—wrestler Scott, alter-ego Scott, Mr. Buffalo—has survived into the future?"

"Mr. Bison."

"Right. That's what I meant."

Outside, the sprinklers switched off. Or: not *off* but to another station, out of sight around the side of the house. Ernie could still hear them. The familiar *ch-ch-ch* reminded him of having to set up sprinklers in his yard when he was growing up. Spiking it into the ground, positioning it to spray the yard but stopping before it hit his dad's car or watered the street or shot into the house—which it sounded like was happening now—unkinking the hose if the water didn't look to be coming out full force.

"We haven't seen or gotten to play it yet or anything. But that's how they described it. It's like part post-apocalyptic, part Old West."

"And part wrestling?"

"It's exciting, right?"

Ernie wasn't sure that's what he'd been thinking, but sure.

Holly stayed quiet.

"Wow." It was all Ernie could finally think to say. He thought of Becca reminding him sometimes to slow down. To take a deep breath. To refocus his attention.

Ernie stopped and tried to picture it. His brother as cartoon, as video game character. He had always thought of that phase as kind of ... *cartoonish* anyway. *Not a phase*, Ernie again self-corrected. That period? Those years? Maybe it made sense.

"Yes," Ernie finally agreed. "Yes, exciting! But ... I don't mean this rude. I'm excited! I am. I'm excited for Scott. I just... Why are you telling me?"

"Sorry. Right. Of course! I'm getting to that. That's the background. That all actually happened a little while ago. Anyway. What that means is that they're paying Scott to allow them to let him be their hero."

"Likeness rights," Ernie answered, glad to finally know what to say, to have a concrete answer amidst the crazy.

"Yes! Exactly. Likeness rights."

"They can't use your name or, well, *likeness* without your permission. It's usually invoked for athletes in sports games. That kind of thing."

"Right! Exactly! Scott didn't know the phrase or anything about the idea. You know how he is."

Did he? Did Holly think he did?

"How much are they paying him?" Ernie asked, knowing it was rude to ask about money but curious. And also not sure what else to say.

"A lot."

The way Holly's voice shifted a little grabbed Ernie's attention.

"Really? What do you mean? Is there really that much money in video games?"

"There is! A ton actually. It's crazy! I feel stupid even saying the number. It's ridiculous. It's ... it's a lot."

More silence, from both. Ernie was dying to hear the number—he'd only half-cared when he'd asked, but now that Holly wouldn't say, he couldn't stop wondering.

"Ahh!" Ernie yelled, breaking the silence as his phone vibrated into his ear.

"What's that?" Holly asked, but Ernie was holding the phone away from him, looking at the screen. It was Becca. It was the call he'd been hoping for in the first place. Before whatever was happening with this whole conversation.

"I'm sorry. I gotta take this, Holly. Real quick."

"Everything OK, Ernie? Do you wanna call me—"

"Hi, Becca."

"Hi, Ern."

"How are you?"

"I'm OK. I just. I don't know. I'm not really OK, I guess. Bryan died."

"What?" Ernie asked. He thought about how else to respond. He was sure there was a right response, something obvious, but he just couldn't think of it.

"Yeah. Last night. I guess I just thought I should let you know."

"No, I'm glad you called. I—"

"Samantha's coming over. I actually need to finish getting ready. Like I said, I just thought you should know."

I'm sorry, Ernie realized he should have said. *Are you OK? Is there anything I can do?* But it was too late. Becca had hung up, the line was dead.

Ernie realized his head hurt again. It hadn't, or he'd been too distracted to notice.

The sprinkler stopped hitting the side of the house. Next would be the front yard, Ernie thought, though he wouldn't have bet on it. He could still hear the sound of the water, the slight mechanical clicks of that water being distributed but only barely.

3.

Holly checked her phone, put it back in her desk drawer. Looked up at her classroom. Mark and Susan were heads down, doodling; Regan and Johnny were on their phones; but everyone else's attention was on the movie. A pretty good percentage. Early in the year, Holly would have made an example of them—something with a little humor, a lightheartedness so as to not lose the class for having singled them out, but also direct enough to not just be a joke, to let the class know she saw, and it wouldn't be tolerated. "Look," she'd maybe add. "I know, I get it, I understand the pull of distraction, the magnetism of technology, being in constant contact with someone, anyone, is strong, addictive even, it's hard to pause for even just the fifty-three minutes of my class ..." Actually, she'd definitely not say all that. But she'd imply. The students paying attention would pick up on it. But that was for the beginning of the year, when she had to set the tone and rules for her class, letting every year know anew what would and wouldn't be tolerated, what they could and couldn't get away with, lest the class fall into a chaos that she'd not be able to recover from. And she led by example—she'd make a show of putting her phone in airplane mode and locking it away in her desk, only checking it at lunch, during her study period, and then finally at the end of the day. She sometimes thought fondly back to her first years teaching, before most people, much less every single one of her students, had a cell phone. *If I'd only known how good I had it*, she'd think, her way of allowing herself to "kids these days!" but in her own way, allowing her to both have the complaint and to look down on her colleagues when they'd use the teachers' lounge or their occasional Thursday happy hours to complain.

Now, though. Now it was the end of the year. Time for ... not total resignation, but. Leniency? Appreciating the little victories? Showing movies in class and not saying anything if only two kids were on their phones, winging lesson plans, and occasionally checking her own phone too.

She pulled her phone back out of her desk, reread Scott's text. Typed, <Really? He's in? Is he sure?>

This was her third year showing *Stand By Me*, her fourth year teaching Stephen King's "The Body." Three years, three-to-five times a year, depending on her class schedule, not to mention all her own viewings, pre-teaching. She had it pretty much memorized. It was possibly her favorite movie, led to some of her favorite conversations with her students.

Every year, when it gets to the scene when the four boys finally find Ray Brower's dead body—his face bloodied and pale, both grotesque and not—she pauses the movie and draws attention back to the novella. There was blood, but not a lot, Holly notes. She reads a sentence about Gordie staying up all night and then asks the class to return to the first page, reads again the end of the first chapter, about how time seems to collapse for Gordie, about how he wakes from dreams and sees hail falling in Ray's open eyes. She nudges the class off-script, delicately guides the conversation through things that keep you awake at night, things that wake us up from dreams. Every year or two, at least one student will push the conversation somewhere darker and more personal than she or the rest of the class expects, and every year she is surprised anew at the class's empathy and ability to be respectful. She knows there are exceptions aplenty, that some of her students can be horrible assholes and worse, there are exceptions throughout the year in her own very classroom no doubt hinting at what outside the classroom is surely manyfold worse, but never at these moments of barest honesty. Sometimes she wonders if it is the depth of revelation that allows such classroom respect, or if somehow "The Body" itself acts as a kind of talisman of compassion, but unlike with countless examples throughout other times of the year, Holly never leads by example, never digresses with a story of her own.

Holly looked at her phone, reread what she'd typed. It read different than she'd intended. She'd meant it excited, but reading it on her screen, something about the sterility of text made it seem rude. Like she didn't believe it, though whether it read as disbelieving Scott or Ernie, she wasn't sure. She thumbed back, deleted the final question, added a smiley face. <Really? He's in? :)> She hit send. Put the phone back in her desk and looked out at her class. Smiled at Korey, who was looking at her, both of them acknowledging she'd been caught.

She'd had Korey's older sister, Steph, in her class just a couple of years ago. As always happened when she had siblings across multiple years, she felt an extra kinship with Korey; she loved asking how Steph was doing at university, being able to continue following her life, even if only minimally and secondhand. Holly heard her phone already vibrate a reply into her desk drawer. She focused her attention to the TV she'd wheeled into the room for the day, trying to forget about her phone.

On the screen, Gordie Lachance watched a deer near the train tracks, first thing in the morning. *Teenager* Gordie, Wil Wheaton, watched the deer, while adult Gordie, Richard Dreyfuss, narrated that he never told his buddies that he saw the deer.

This, in particular, was maybe her favorite scene. She liked to ask her classes what the scene made them think about. Not what it meant, or what the deer *stood for*, or why the scene was included in the book and movie at all, but just if it reminded them of anything. She'd start by telling them it reminded her of her husband. Of this roadtrip they'd gone on together, before they were married. Sometimes she would ask who among them had been on a roadtrip. Where had they gone? With family, or something else? She and Scott had driven across the country to see his brother in Michigan and they'd stopped in the Badlands. They sat in his car together, and then on the hood, leaning back into the windshield, holding hands, like they thought they were in a movie or something. Just watching the buffalo. How hypnotic they were. They had each other and so weren't alone, and they talked about the buffalo, both at the moment and over the years, and she'd tell any friend who would listen. She wondered if she loved the scene in *Stand By Me* because it reminded her, albeit unconsciously, of watching buffalo in the Badlands with Scott, or vice versa, or if they were unrelated but just touched the same nerve.

And then this year ... with a video game in the works, starring her husband, Mr. Bison, and his pet buffalo; with Scott having asked for and been granted a year leave from his job; with a text waiting for her on the phone that she was trying not to think of; with her conversation with Ernie from just an hour ago while on her lunch break, she thought about the continuation of that roadtrip for the first time in years.

They hadn't yet been dating long, but they'd wanted to take a trip together—ideally, somewhere neither had been before, a tricky restriction due to Scott's travel, though he tried to tell her none of those cities should count, his time in each limited to the ring and his hotel room. Every city seemed the same when touring, he'd told her. He remembered cities via hotel carpet pattern, bed-desk-bathroom configuration. They volleyed ideas back and forth. Philadelphia, Florida, Texas, Savannah, Boston, Maine? "I've been to Michigan but have never actually visited Ernie," Scott mentioned without even realizing he was saying it. He'd never before had the thought, and already Holly was running with it. "That's it!" she exclaimed. "A roadtrip!" And it was settled. She planned their route, highlighted maps, algebra'd miles and miles-per-hour, how often they'd want to stop and how many hours together in the car at a time she figured to be optimal, getting as much progress made as possible without pushing into wanting to kill each other, each variable inexact but important. She planned that stop in the Badlands special for Scott—*to see the buffalo!*—skipping over Yellowstone as too touristy, too obvious.

When they arrived, Ernie was nothing like she'd expected. Nothing like what Scott had warned of. He was mostly good-natured, a little more introverted and quiet than Scott; he was awkward, sure, but who wasn't? And he and Becca were in full tour-guide mode—a night on Mackinac Island, wine tasting in Traverse City, all their favorite restaurants, the dive bars, the local arboretum. One day, they took a trip down to Ohio, where Becca had grown up.

Malabar Farms. A long drive for a daytrip, but she wanted to show off. She wanted to share with her future brother- and sister-in-law one of her favorite places in the world. Becca had grown up only a couple of towns away, had gone there all the time with her family when little. It held a magical place in her mind—part memory of her childhood, part pride of the most famous resident of any small, neighboring Ohio town.

A wave of movement and backpack shuffling and rearranging crested through the room, and as soon as Holly noticed, the bell rang. She grabbed the remote, hit pause. "I'll see you all tomorrow!"

She opened her desk, checked her phone.

<In-in :)>

How to Punch

Make a fist. Curl your fingers in tight, each knuckle forming a ninety-degree angle. Look at, and remember, your fingers coiled in on themselves like that. Admire how they look like that was their intended purpose, fist as Fibonacci spiral.

Tuck your thumb under, not inside. Like it's holding your fingers down and in, not vice versa. Lock your wrist. Hold your fist so the back of your hand is flat, is parallel with your arm. One long, straight line. Power is in straight lines.

Most people don't really think about it. Most people think it's pure strength. Brute power, maybe a little desire or will or drive. Then again, most people never punch anyone.

Aim through your target. Behind it. Your target isn't what you're punching; your target is two, three inches behind what you want to hit.

Use your whole body. Twist your shoulders into it for torque. Use the power in your hips, your core. Use your legs to plant and to push off. You'd be surprised how much arm strength is really leg strength.

Like a pitcher pushing off the mound, increasing pitch speed not just with his arm, his upper body, but all the way down through his legs. (See: "How to Pitch.")

Practice. Visualize. Practice again. Know and remind yourself: it is harder than you think to throw and land a punch with full strength. You'd be surprised. Your mind doesn't want to let you. It does all these calculations, figures out how hard it thinks you should punch, and calibrates. Know that this is usually for the best. Know that sometimes body overrides mind.

4.

Over the loudspeaker, Ernie heard them call that his flight was delayed. He sighed, looked at the board for confirmation, hoping he'd misheard. He'd only been half-listening. Half zoning off, daydreaming, probably, though he already couldn't remember what about. The board confirmed: his flight, supposed to depart at 7:12 was now scheduled for 8:21. He sunk in his chair, looked away then back at the board, like maybe he'd misread or could will the number into changing back. 8:21. Ernie sat up so he could reach into his pocket to pull out his phone to check the time. He now had an extra hour to kill. Texted Scott, <Plane delayed an hour.>

By the time his phone was back in his pocket again, he felt it vibrate and wondered why he hadn't just kept it out.

<OK. Thanks.>

<No prob. Keep me updated!> came a second text, while Ernie was still reading the first.

Ernie looked back over his shoulder, at the terminal and its restaurants and stores. Figured he'd have a drink, at least. If he had some time to kill.

By the time the plane finally boarded—after three hours, two slowly nursed bourbons, two more delays, at least two questions to the bartender about how many delays or how much time of delay had to pass before they canceled the flight—it was almost 10.

He'd texted Scott, said they were finally boarded but at this rate wouldn't get in until midnight, why didn't he just stay at the airport hotel. Scott argued, said he didn't mind. Three in the morning my time, Ernie'd reminded, he'd be exhausted, crabby. They'd get a fresh start in the morning. And Scott had finally, reluctantly agreed just before Ernie turned off his phone.

"Can I get you a drink, sir?" the flight attendant asked.

Ernie looked up, smiled. "Um," he stalled, thinking. "Yes!" he overanswered. "Please. A … bourbon? Bourbon and Coke?"

"Of course. We have Jack Daniels, Canadian Club, Dewar's, and ..." she pulled out her cheat sheet, double-checked. "Woodford Reserve."

"That one," Ernie answered. "Woodford Reserve. Please." Thinking, *I didn't ask for scotch. Or even whiskey. I said bourbon*, then he gave her another smile, added, "thank you," as apology.

Ernie stretched his legs, looked out the window until the drink came. He touched the screen on the chair in front of him but nothing happened. It must not respond until they were in the air.

"Excuse me, sir. I'm going to need to take that, for takeoff."

Ernie considered his drink, still half full. Hadn't she just given it to him? He'd been nursing it, letting the full experience settle in.

"Oh, of course," he answered, trying to sound like he knew how this went, that she'd have to take it before takeoff. He'd never before flown first class. He picked it up off his armrest table, held it for a split-second, then tipped it back and finished it in two big swallows.

For the next couple of hours, Ernie alternated between sleep and fighting to stay awake, watching out his window, nodding for another drink every time the flight attendant asked. He wanted to get the most out of the occasion, though he was unsure what counted more: enjoying the comfortable, oversized chair, with actual legroom to stretch out, for sleep; or staying awake, taking full advantage of the free drinks, not wasting any of the experience on sleep.

"Heading home?"

Ernie turned and looked at the businessman sitting next to him. The voice had surprised him. He'd forgotten the man was there.

"No."

"Work? Vacation?"

Ernie thought about that. He could have just said yes, end the conversation before it got any further. It wasn't work, wasn't vacation. Washington was kind of home. He'd grown up there, that counted.

The attendant came by, asked which meal each would prefer. Chicken salad or cheeseburger? Ernie couldn't believe it. Not only a free meal, but a choice too?

"Burger, please," to the attendant, and then, to the business man, "I'm visiting my brother and his wife. Or maybe moving in with them. Or maybe just visiting? I'm staying with them for a while."

Business Man looked confused but smiled. Ernie couldn't tell if the guy was sorry he'd asked or curious for more. Either way, the seal had broken.

"Yeah," Ernie continued. "It's kinda weird. They bought this farm, and they asked me if I wanted to come out and live with them? I don't even really talk to my brother. It's kinda weird. I don't really know why not. Actually, now that I think about it, *they* didn't even ask me. His wife did. That's kinda weird, right?"

"I don't know. Sibling relationships can be kinda weird. My wife and her sister—"

"Have you ever heard of Malabar Farm?"

"What?"

"Louis Bromfield?"

"I don't think so?"

"Yeah, I hadn't either. He was this writer, back in the ... '20s and '30s, I guess? He was friends with Hemingway, Faulkner. He won a Pulitzer! At some point he bought this farm in Ohio. He was kind of a big deal. He was friends with movie stars! They'd come to this middle-of-nowhere farm in Ohio to visit. Humphrey Bogart and Lauren Bacall had gotten married there."

"Is your brother a big fan of this guy?"

"What? No. My wife was. My ex-wife. Well, she isn't my ex-wife yet, but it seems inevitable? You know. We're separated. I guess that's why I'm flying out to visit my brother. What's tying me to Michigan, right?! Not my wife! Not anymore. Not my job. I mean, my job's fine. It's kinda weird though. I had this fling with a coworker. Not really a *fling* fling. I don't know what to call it. It's weird around the office now though. And weird at home, being alone. What am I doing, you know?"

"Chicken salad," the attendant said, placing a meal down in front of Business Man. "And cheeseburger for you, sir." Ernie handed back his empty glass in return, smiled and *yes-pleased* for another.

"Thank you."

"Thank you."

Both men unwrapped their napkins, twisted their plates around a little in front of themselves to get them just right.

Ernie stared at his food. He'd already forgotten where he'd been, what all he'd said and hadn't. He wasn't sure if he should say something to wrap up, but then he looked at Business Man, and he was already eating, paying Ernie no mind. Ernie picked up his burger and took a giant bite. It was the best burger Ernie could remember having in years. Because it actually was? Because of something about being in the air? Because it felt special, the privilege of a first-class burger? Because he was so tipsy? Maybe it didn't matter.

After eating, Ernie went back to alternating between closing his eyes and staring out the window, and then the pilot announced the arrival temperature, reminded them of the time change, announced their new time, and a flight attendant followed by asking that all tray tables please be up, seats returned to their upright position. Ernie couldn't believe they were already there. Because he'd slept more than he'd thought, or flights were just more relaxing, seemed quicker, when drinking—staying awake for the free drinks and full enjoyment of the comfortable chair having mostly won out—or maybe even flights were just somehow *shorter* when in first class?

They landed, and Ernie noted his final perk, being one of the first few to deplane, not having to sit there, anxious in stale airplane air, waiting for his turn.

Walking through the sliding *No return beyond this point* glass doors, he saw a group of people waiting for loved ones and, beyond them, another group: older men, all in suits, each holding a sign with a name. Ernie did a double take when he saw his own. *Vernon Isaacson*. He noticed the weird officialness of Vernon instead of Ernie before he realized the one guy holding the sign with his name looked not like the others, was the one smiling guy in regular clothes among a group of straight-faced dark suits, the one guy who was so much bigger than the straight-faced, dark-suited drivers around him, bigger, maybe, than anyone else in the airport.

Scott was already laughing by the time they made eye contact. He folded up the paper, put it in his back pocket. Opened his arms wide for a hug and waited for his big brother to come to him.

"You check a bag?"

Ernie held up his small bag that held his laptop and a book for the flight, though he hadn't taken out either.

"Right. Of course you have more than just that," Scott said. "Wait." Scott looked Ernie up and down. "You have a couple on the flight?" He smiled conspiratorially.

Ernie smiled, a little guilty.

"Good, good! You know what's underappreciated? A good airplane drink. Toss a couple back, relax."

"It did seem to make it much better."

"Exactly! Of course it did. Might as well enjoy the flight, right?" Scott looked up at the board above them and then pointed toward number three, like he hadn't already figured it out, hadn't been waiting for who knows how long, checking the board every few minutes to be sure it hadn't changed since he'd last looked. "Looks like you're down here."

They moved together, neither talking, and stopped at the luggage carousel, stood waiting.

"I'm glad to see you," Scott said. "I'm glad you're here."

"Thanks. Thanks, Scott. I am, too. You didn't have to come. I was just going to find a hotel room, crash."

"It's no problem. In fact, I've got a surprise!"

They stood in silence, anxious among the crowd of travelers anxious for their luggage. Ready to get home after a long trip, or ready to hurry up and start their long trip so they can hurry back home, or, like more and more it was seeming, just anxious to get from one task to the next, no matter what it was they were currently doing but always ready to move on to whatever was next, an airport full of perpetual anxiety machines.

Scott looked to be more relaxed than most but anxious in his own right, like he would have preferred to fill the silence but was holding back, consciously trying not to overwhelm Ernie with too much talk. Already Scott was more talkative than Ernie remembered him ever being. Was he nervous? Excited? Had he just grown more chatty since they'd last seen each other?

The carousel buzzed, a light flashed, and the track started moving. Scott and Ernie had been two of the first to arrive, had staked out a spot where the luggage came out, but now half the plane was standing around, waiting too, and half of them had crowded in as tight as possible instead of just spreading out around the track.

"What are we looking for?" Scott asked, and Ernie waited to answer, watched, and then pointed, his luggage already breaching up the ramp, down onto the main track. It came as a shock, seeing it so soon. Ernie couldn't remember ever not having to wait until the very end, his flights somehow always at the furthest gate in the terminal, his luggage always seemingly last to appear. He made a move to shoulder in between the two men who'd shouldered their way in front of him, but Scott was faster, was already filling that space.

"I got it, I got it," Scott called, not so much pushing through the crowd as moving through the lane that magically parted for him. "Let me get it."

Ernie stopped, standing awkwardly for a beat in between the two men he'd been trying to get past. "Thanks," he said, for his brother, but also like maybe for the two men, and he waited another beat, letting the awkwardness set in, wanting to give the two men some kind of message for being rude, for being impatient, even while not knowing what exactly that message might be other than a maybe-sarcastic *thanks.* Finally, he took a couple steps back and waited in the empty area just outside the ring of travelers scavenging for their bags.

Scott met him there a second later, luggage in hand, not giving the sea of people any thought, as they all parted to let him through.

"Thanks," Ernie said, reaching for his bag.

"You *sure* this is yours?" Scott asked. Before Ernie could answer, Scott held up the PRIORITY tag stickered to the bag. Gave his brother a teasing look.

"Yeah, yeah, it's mine. I traded in the two tickets for one first class." Ernie shrugged, tried to say it as nonchalant as possible.

"Nice. Good thinking."

"Yeah—"

"Plenty of time," Scott waved him off. "You doing alright?"

"Yeah. I'm good."

"Good. Good. You're gonna love the farm. It'll be good for you, I bet."

Ernie realized Scott must have known as soon as his brother saw him coming out of the terminal alone. Wondered if, somehow, he'd known even before then. Scott had bought the tickets, against Ernie's protests. *I insist*, Scott had said. *I invited you. Not even invited really, right? Requested. It's the least I can do.* When Ernie got to the airport alone, two tickets for one passenger, he'd asked when checking in. Was an upgrade possible? An exchange? Two coach tickets for one first class? It seemed like something he'd seen happen in a movie or something, figured he may as well ask. No harm in asking. There was a small charge, upgrade fees plus travel-change fees equaling more than the original ticket price, but he wouldn't tell Scott that.

Now, Ernie appreciated Scott's nonchalance, his lack of questions. He'd been worried—more worried than he realized? a subconscious reason for all the drinks?—about how to tell Scott. He still hadn't, but he kind of had, without having to. They'd talk about it when the time came.

Scott led the way, pulling Ernie's rolling suitcase—he'd insisted—out of the terminal, stopping to pay for parking.

"The surprise?" Ernie asked.

"Well," Scott said. "It's a surprise! But I had this idea ... something I've been meaning to check out. You're gonna love this place. I mean, you're gonna really love the farm, it's so great. But a quick reroute first?"

"Reroute?" Ernie looked at his brother. The reason he'd offered to stay in the airport hotel was because he knew he'd be exhausted, which he now was, and Scott wanted to go the long route, to *add* something to the itinerary?

"You'll see," Scott answered. "It's closer than the farm. We'll be there before you know it. This little place on the water. I guess that's the surprise. You can sleep on the drive, if you want; you can fall asleep as soon as we get there. And then in the morning ... we'll wake with a fresh start! We'll get you some of this West Coast sun that you've been missing. Bouncing off the water? A view of the mountains? A fresh start! Just like you said about staying in one of those boring traveler hotels at the airport, but better."

Had he? Ernie didn't remember saying that. It didn't really sound like Scott either, and then Ernie found himself annoyed, either that it didn't sound like Scott or that Scott had said it at all, he couldn't say. This was always how it went with Ernie's complaints about his brother; every time he'd tried to describe any annoyance to Becca he knew he came across poorly, unable to really put it into words for her, and Ernie guessed, in the end, Scott just drove him crazy in that way siblings drive each other crazy.

"A new start in the morning!" Scott said again. It felt almost as if he was rubbing it in, scratching his fingernails down the chalkboard, but he was smiling, sincere, excited. Ernie nodded, smiled back.

5.

"Morning."

"Morning," Ernie answered. Scott sat by the window, reading. Ernie couldn't remember his brother being much of a reader.

"I ordered a big pot of coffee and some fruit and muffins. Help yourself." Scott pointed, and Ernie saw the room service tray sitting on the desk. Ernie thought of their dad, the few times growing up they'd stayed in a hotel when traveling. They never would have splurged for room service. He wondered if Scott had had the same thought when ordering, if his brother had grown up and allowed himself this luxury or if this was a new perk of the video game money. He looked outside and then clenched his eyes shut, his eyes not yet ready for the day, much less the brightness of sun, water. He held his eyes shut a moment then opened them extra wide and realized how tired he'd been, how deeply he'd slept. He hadn't heard room service knock for delivery, he'd slept who-knew-how-much-longer than Scott.

"Thought I'd go on a walk here in a bit. You interested? Want to go on a little hike?"

His eyes a little more prepared, Ernie returned his gaze out the window at the water, the mountains beyond. The sunlight bounced off the water, shattering itself into a thousand different directions; the water was perfectly still, broken only by the occasional duck or seagull water-planing down to rest. The silence of it all echoing off the water and held in by the mountains sounded almost overwhelmingly quiet. It looked like they were in a commercial, but better. Rejuvenating, like he could be his best self here. Like he wouldn't be able to help but be some kind of idealized self, here in this idealized setting. Maybe that's why so many commercials looked like just this, trying to sell you this feeling. Selling you optimism, the promise of a better life, a better self. He took a deep breath in through his nose and smelled both the coffee and the crispness of the air, but it also unlocked the slight pangs of a hangover. But it felt, he realized ... *good*? He'd had a slight headache for weeks, but this was different. This, he could already tell, would go away in a few hours, leaving in its wake a clarity like the current blue of the skies outside. Maybe Scott was right, maybe it would be good for him. Maybe Scott had known what he was talking about after all, with his "fresh, new starts" and whatever else he'd preached on about.

"I could walk." Ernie held up the pot of coffee like he needed a prop, like Scott might not know what he meant otherwise. "Can I have some coffee first? Get dressed?"

"Of course. No hurry. Have some coffee! We can even get another pot if we want more. Or just drink what we have and get some more on the drive. No hurry at all." Scott smiled, picked his book back up and started reading.

Ernie grabbed a slice of pineapple, popped it in his mouth while pouring himself a mug of coffee. He'd gotten in the habit of getting a large coffee with cream at the drive-thru on his way to work but liked the mug. The feel of it in his hands. He ate another slice of pineapple and took his coffee and a muffin to sit in the chair by his brother. Scott looked up, smiled.

"Don't rush. No hurry," Scott repeated, looking up, and Ernie nodded.

Ernie wasn't sure what more to say. *Thanks? This place really is great? How'd you sleep last night?* Finally, "I like these mugs. They're nice." He held it up in the air, his right index hooked through the handle but cupping the bowl of the mug with both hands. "It just ... feels good, you know?"

Scott made a face, like, *interesting*, and nodded. He looked at the small table between them where his own mug was resting; he picked it up, kind of bounced it in his hand to remind himself of the feel. "I hadn't really noticed, but I guess you're right. It does feel good. I hadn't really thought of it before."

"Oh, a good mug ..." Ernie trailed off, like he didn't even need to finish the thought. "It's underrated. Half of the joy of coffee is the experience of it, and half of that is the mug itself, the feel of it." Ernie took another sip, still cupping the mug in both hands.

Scott rolled his eyes in thought, considered the philosophy. "That makes sense. But, you know ... that kind of sounds more like something I'd say." He looked at his brother, and they both laughed. Though, that wasn't quite it either. It sounded like ... like Holly, actually, Scott realized.

"I guess it does," Ernie agreed. "Maybe it's the setting. Or maybe that disqualifies it? Maybe that's how you know it's bullshit." He laughed and then pushed himself to keep laughing an extra beat or two to be sure Scott knew he was teasing. They didn't normally give each other shit like that.

"Maybe," Scott returned. "That makes sense too."

They sat in silence, Scott reading, Ernie staring out at the view. He was comfortable, sitting still and quiet. Enjoying the *act* of drinking his coffee. He didn't want to disturb this shared moment with Scott but also the serenity he was trying to lower himself into. If he went to his room, he'd check his phone. He'd be disappointed at the absence of message, just as he had been when his plane landed and he'd turned it back on, when he'd looked at it last thing before falling asleep last night, when he'd grabbed for it first thing in the morning, his eyes not yet awake and adjusted, probably still unable to read anything but able enough to see there wasn't anything to read.

One of his goals for this trip was to wean himself off constantly looking at his phone—because he wanted to not always be checking for word from Rebecca, but also just to get away from the phone itself some. To be more in the moment, and again Ernie remembered his idea from only moments before, this idea of an idealized self in this idealized setting. He closed his eyes, lifted his face to the sun. The small tilting and angling immediately made it feel ten degrees warmer, like he'd moved a sunlamp directly onto his face instead of off to the side. He raised his mug to his lips and took a sip with his eyes still closed, and the sun, the coffee, the silence, the fresh air ... a warmth washed over him, a calm, an acceptance and excitement and a kind of newfound energy, all of it.

Growing up, they'd spent their summers outdoors. Their dad spent the winter and rainy days in preparation, collecting and studying topo maps, campground brochures, cutting pages out of magazines and tossing the rest, amassing boxes and boxes of ideas, possibilities. His *wanderlust* boxes, their mom called them, the word sticking with Ernie even before he knew what it meant, liking the sound of it to tease his dad about.

When the weather got nice, weekends got blocked away for camping trips, backpacking, fishing. The boxes put to use, every trip somewhere new, every birthday and Father's Day gift card spent on some new toy. As often as not, Ernie would have rather stayed home, playing video games and watching TV, while Scott went along with it, maybe loving the trips, maybe wishing the same as Ernie but, at least on the surface, always excitement and ready-for-anything attitude.

Ernie hadn't gone hiking or camping since, didn't own a fishing pole and wouldn't remember how to tie on a lure or hook, or which was called for in which situation, but these memories were maybe the most common of his own *sentimentlust* go-tos, either because of his romanticized memories of those trips or because Becca's teasing and name-borrowing had forever linked the two. A meal out of a bag, cooked over a fire he'd helped build, tasting like the best thing he'd ever eaten at the end of a day hiking. Swimming in the middle of an ice-cold, glacier-water river, feeling energized and like he couldn't even feel the cold. Reeling in that first fish of the day, hooking his finger through the gill to hold it up, proud, his smile way bigger than when watching TV or playing video games.

"You daydreaming over there?" Scott asked.

"What? Why?"

"That smile on your face. You look like you're off in Ernie's World!"

Ernie looked at his brother, confused or surprised, and then laughed, and Scott followed. Ernie had forgotten their dad used to call it that, this daydreaming tendency apparently going back even further than he'd remembered. He hadn't thought of that in years, nor had Scott, for that matter, before it fell out of his mouth as if he hadn't even known it had been in there.

"I guess so," Ernie said. "You know. It's beautiful here. Made me nostalgic, I guess."

"It is." He looked around anew like confirming his agreement. "You about ready? Wanna go check out the area? Before we head out."

Ernie had forgotten this was just a quick detour, that they still had to head to the farm, the *actual* reason he was here. "Let's go!"

Not a hundred yards from their room was the gnarliest roadkill either Scott or Ernie had ever seen. They'd each noticed it from afar, but neither said anything, both unsure if the other had seen it until they were right on top of it.

"Wow," Ernie said. "Right?"

They'd stopped, arranged themselves on either side of the thing. Each of them staring, like at a car crash, like at something cut open and dissected that they had to now diagnose or find and name the parts of. A baby deer or a small doe? It was small but maybe looked smaller than it actually was with its insides removed, body all folded and tangled. The more they stared, the more confusing it seemed. The body was torn open, half a ribcage visible, branching up and out from the body, what barely seemed right to describe as a body.

Scott closed his eyes, put his fist to his mouth. He turned and didn't open his eyes until facing away, having taken a couple steps toward the side of the road. He kept walking, stepping over the ditch between the road and woods, tucked himself behind a tree too skinny to actually tuck himself behind and folded over, hands on knees.

Ernie watched his brother wander off, and then tried to look as much *not* at Scott as possible. On the road, all around him, he noticed shit everywhere. But, not *shit*. Excrement. Ernie had never before thought much of the difference, one just seeming a more vulgar name for the other, but there suddenly seemed a definite distinction. This hadn't been expelled but had come out through the body being ripped open, turned almost inside out.

Ernie circled the deer, what used to be a deer, and re-inspected from his new angle. He was still trying to figure it out when Scott returned, said, "Let's keep walking."

"What do you think happened?" Ernie asked.

Scott shrugged. "Hard to know."

"You ever see anything like this? Around here? Or anywhere?"

Scott shook his head. They stood silent another minute and finally continued walking. Scott set the pace and Ernie kept up, but without either saying anything.

A mile down the road, the path forked and they took the trail that followed the water. The canal tucked into a small reservoir and a small bridge crossed a stream that fed it all. The brothers stopped, both leaned over the railing and stared into the water below.

"This stream's fresh water," Scott said. "It comes down from the mountains, and then out there's all salt water."

"Crazy." Ernie looked one way, up the stream that disappeared into the forest, and then the other, out into the open water, the canal looking like a giant lake. It seemed crazy, this intersection. At what point did it turn from fresh to salt? It must happen gradually, not a line like *on this side: fresh, on that side: salt*, but at what point did whoever made that distinction decide?

They both stood, silently staring into the water again.

"You ever go fishing anymore?" Scott asked.

Ernie tilted his head back, looked up into the sky and scratched at the couple of days' worth of stubble on his chin, his neck. Like he was thinking about it. Like he had to think about if he did or not. "No." He shook his head. "No, I guess I haven't been since Dad took us."

Scott nodded. "You ever miss it?"

Ernie kept staring out at the water, still not turning to look at his brother, paused like he was thinking about that too. He wasn't sure. He never really wanted to go fishing, but he did miss the idea of it.

"I think Holly will really like it here," Scott said, pulling Ernie out of it. "It's beautiful. Really serene and relaxing. I want to throw her a surprise shower here."

"Yeah, it really is beautiful." Thinking, *it really is.* Thinking, *I bet she would.* And, finally, *oh!* Ernie looked at Scott, a big, cheesy grin waiting on his brother's face. "Shower?"

Scott nodded, let loose his smile. "Probably in ... November? I hope it won't be too cold then. It's perfect out right now." Another big smile.

"Wow," Ernie answered. "Wow." He looked at Scott for another second, opened his arms to give him a hug. "Congrats! That's great. So exciting!"

"Thanks, man. Thanks. I don't know ... I wanted to tell you in person. I'm glad you're here."

Ernie knew Scott didn't mean anything by it, but also couldn't help but feel like it was a slight pry. Or: not a pry. A nudge? A little, *I told you what I wanted to tell you in person, don't you have something to tell me?* He didn't know if he was frustrated that Scott wouldn't just come out and ask or if he appreciated the lack of questions. Was not prying his way of prying, some kind of passive aggressive reverse psychology tactic? He was nearly sure Scott hadn't meant anything by it,

95% sure, at least, it had been completely innocent, he was sure. Still, Ernie now felt put on the spot, and intentional or not, that was kind of Scott's fault, no?

"Rebecca's been gone a few months," Ernie blurted, like it came out without him meaning to say anything, but also consciously saying Rebecca when he only ever called her Becca or even Beck. "I think it had actually been a long time coming. And then Bulleit ran away. And there was this thing with a woman at work. I mean, not a *thing*, but—"

Scott turned, put both his hands on his brother's shoulders. Ernie always thought of his brother as *big*, described him to friends always in hyperbolic terms, but still most of the time forgot his actual size. Or: not so much forgot as took for granted. But standing face to face, Scott's hands felt huge on Ernie's arms, and the bulk in front of him seemed suddenly surprising. The intent was comfort, and Ernie appreciated it, but his kneejerk was to realize it felt almost intimidating. He wouldn't have been able to move no matter how much he'd wanted. He pushed his mouth to the side, shrugged his shoulders as much as Scott's grip let him, all as if to say, *it is what it is. So it goes.*

Scott didn't respond with questions about what had happened or why Ernie hadn't said anything earlier. Didn't ask why Ernie had let him buy two plane tickets only a few weeks ago if Rebecca had already been gone by then, or where she was, or why she'd left. "Like I said," Scott finally said. "I'm glad you're here," and left it at that. Gave his brother a smile and squeezed his shoulders, and Ernie tried not to give any signs that it had been a little too hard.

"Thanks, Scott. I am too. Thanks."

They turned back to the water, again stood in silence for a few minutes. Ernie wondered if Scott was also taking in all this new info, or was he maybe just looking out and enjoying the view, mind blank instead of nearly overflowing with questions and what ifs, what else should I say, what am I going to do with my life?

"Head back?" Scott finally said.

"Sounds good."

They turned, started walking. "You know," Ernie said. "A part of me doesn't want to see that dead deer still there at all. But another part of me kinda can't wait."

Scott closed his eyes, nodded.

"I mean ... what the hell happened? I've never seen anything like it."

Coming from the other direction, unlike before when they'd approached with no idea what to expect, both Ernie and Scott could nearly perfectly visualize the scene as soon as they saw the dark object on the road in the distance, so clearly had the image been burned into their minds. And still, it surprised them.

"It wasn't hit by a car," Ernie said.

"Doesn't seem like it."

"I'd thought maybe, but no tire tracks," Ernie went on, like Scott hadn't already agreed. "Its ribcage looks intact, not broken or anything. Wouldn't a car hitting it break those bones?"

It was grisly, but clean—there was no blood anywhere, no part of it pancaked to the road with tread marks. Had no cars passed since they'd walked to the bridge and back, or had everyone driven around it? And how so gruesome but also bloodless?

Scott counted the deer's legs, counted again. "I don't get what's going on with its body," he said.

"What do you mean?"

Scott pointed. "Look at its legs." He waved his hand around like tracing something in the air. "I don't get it."

Ernie considered the body. "Well. Those are its back legs, right? Obviously. Then, this. This is its front ... left? But kind of wrapped around its shoulder. It's just bent around backward."

Scott grimaced, imagining the action of Ernie's description. He thought of wrestling, some of the other wrestler's leg holds. He didn't really have a signature one, would do a basic leg move when called for, but one skill he always prided himself on was selling. He thought of all the times he'd help his competitor twist his leg back behind him, grimacing and pounding the mat, trying to squirm his way out of it.

He thought what it would have taken to get his leg, or someone else's, all the way wrapped up around a shoulder, like this deer's. It made him cringe anew, and that was part of it, the leg pointed in the opposite direction than would seem to make sense. But on the other side of its head were what looked like two more legs. Scott pointed—

"I thought maybe one was just its tail, but no. That's back there. You can kind of tell. Not really, but kind of. So ... does it have five legs, you think?"

Ernie looked at the seemingly three front legs, the back two. The front three again. Tried to make sense of it.

"I think ..." Scott made a face, picturing it as he talked it through. "I think maybe the bone's come out of the ... what would you call it? Skin? Fur?"

"Hide?" Ernie shrugged.

"Sure. So, that's one leg, maybe? Just taken apart?"

"Maybe," Ernie agreed. Wanting to believe both that explanation but also still the possibility of five legs. Could that be why they were now witnessing this scene? This deer had been born with a fifth leg, making it weaker than the others, easier prey?

Ernie wandered off to the side of the road, staring down at the ground and moving slowly, like he knew what he was looking for. At the gravel shoulder, he found a small tuft of fur, and then the shoulder banked up before dipping down into bushes and thorny berry brush all the way to the rocky beach. Hanging from a thorn was another small tuft of fur. Ernie looked from one piece of evidence to the other and saw a couple small marks in the dirt.

"Scott! Check this out!" He waved over his brother, then arced his hand out in a big C, signaling him to walk around.

Scott approached wide, following Ernie's arc around the evidence while looking down where Ernie was pointing to look.

"Look," Ernie said. "There's some fur, here and over there. And it looks like some drag marks." He smiled, proud of his investigative skills. "I bet it got attacked, down in the brambles down there somewhere"—the word 'brambles' appearing out of nowhere, as he spoke—"and it either started to get away or they wrestled a little bit, it hobbled or got dragged from here to there, then was finally killed, right there in the road. The … what do you think? Wolf?"

"I bet."

Ernie nodded. "The wolf took it down right there in the road. Picked it clean, ran off."

Scott looked at his brother, back at the scene in front of them, wondered if that might be right. If everything could be so relatively easily traced back and figured out. A chill shot through him, something he hadn't felt or even thought of in years. He looked around like someone might be watching, like someone—his brother, someone else out on a walk, someone who'd magically appeared and had been keeping watch—might have noticed the memory on him, but Ernie looked lost in his own world again and they hadn't seen anyone else all morning, not on the walk, not even at the hotel other than the guy who'd brought their room service.

Ernie started staring off into the woods around them, looking for the wolf or maybe trying to think like a wolf himself—*Where might it have gone? What prompted the attack?*—until indeed slipping into Ernie's World or *sentimentlust*.

The last week of elementary school, Ernie and his best friend, Benjamin, had stood in line together with all their classmates, waiting to return to class after an end of the year assembly. "What do you want to be when you grow up?" Benjamin had asked.

"I don't know." They were in grade school; the only jobs Ernie was really aware of, he either wasn't interested in (doctor, lawyer, teacher) or was already too sensible to think he had a chance (athlete, rock star). "I don't know," he said again.

"Want to know what I'm going to be?"

Ernie shrug-nodded.

"A wolfman!" Benjamin's eyes lit up, and he smiled big, excited. He put his arms in the air, bent his elbows, curled his fingers into claws. He snarled.

"What do you mean?"

"You know … a *wolfman*!" Benjamin repeated the pose. "I'm not ever going to cut my hair or shave or anything. I'm going to let my hair grow long and become a wolfman!"

It had seemed crazy but also made a weird, perfect sense.

A few weeks after that assembly, Benjamin moved, and Ernie never saw him again. Ernie knew Benjamin's dad got a job in Chicago and had moved in the middle of the school year, but he hadn't considered the logistics for the rest of the family, that Benjamin and his mom and sister were just waiting for school to end to follow. The next year, Ernie started junior high by himself. They'd been each other's best friends and hadn't hung out with too many others, but Benjamin was the more outgoing and Ernie knew that if he were still around, they would be meeting and making new friends. A new beginning. Instead, he walked the halls with his head down, kept quiet in class, ate lunch by himself. At home, he started locking himself in his room, coming out rarely other than for food and school, communicating with his brother less and their parents almost not at all, only grunts and single syllables. He watched horror movies by himself instead of WWF with Scotty, kept an eye on the news for any word of a wolfman. Every now and then, he'd see something about a wolf sighting in a major city, people assuming it had come in from the mountains looking for food, or just lost, and he'd think, *Maybe?*

"Yeah," Scott finally said, to shake Ernie out of it, or maybe himself. "Yeah, that makes sense. That seems about right. It all looks pretty fresh too. What do you think, just a few hours?"

"I bet. If that," Ernie agreed, as if either had any idea what an animal carcass would look like after an hour, a few hours, a day. As if either knew at all what they were talking about. "Shit. Can you believe it? We couldn't have missed a wolf attack by more than a couple hours! Probably less than a hundred yards from our room!"

Ernie felt proud—proud, for some reason, to have been so near a wolf attack, but even moreso for his detective work. To have been given a puzzle and solved it.

6.

Ernie stood frozen, disbelieving. Only minutes before, they'd been almost running through the house. "It's amazing!" Ernie said, as soon as they pulled up, and then again when they walked through the front door, and then they were off, moving through the house like they were little kids again, playing tag or on a scavenger hunt, Scott showing off every room, pointing out everything he and Holly had already done since they'd bought it. And then all of a sudden Ernie stopped, stared. If he wasn't seeing it with his own eyes, he'd think it tall tale.

The drive from the hotel at the canal to the farm had been quiet. Ernie wasn't especially tired—he'd slept well, maybe the best since Becca had left—but he made himself yawn, closed his eyes every now and then to give Scott the impression he was tired and not just awkwardly silent. When they pulled off the last main road and onto a long dirt driveway, Ernie shook it off and sat up straight, ready for the big reveal. Which didn't disappoint. A barrier of neatly trimmed shrubbery, like moat around castle, and then the farmhouse itself—big wraparound porch, banisters and awnings. It looked exactly as expected, everything matching Scott's descriptions and the pictures he'd forwarded, but also surprising. The pictures had looked *too* perfect—like a postcard, like boringly staged and listed on a real estate site—but here in front of him, it all looked so ... *real.* The white paint was chipping in places, sun-faded in others. The deck, so welcoming, could probably use to be fixed up if not completely replaced. Its slight fixer-upper-ness, Ernie realized, made it all the more lived-in, more welcoming, all the more perfect than presumed perfection. And then they were walking from truck to house, up those steps (indeed, Ernie felt a couple creaks, nodded at his own summing up), a couple strides across the porch, and Scott was opening the front door, Ernie noticing that it hadn't even been locked. Scott had sent so many photos—the online real estate listing with virtual walkthrough; his own cell phone photos that looked more or less the same as those online but of lesser, albeit slightly more personal, quality—Ernie would not have thought he'd be so surprised, but here he was, surprised anew with every room.

Ernie realized he hadn't seen any photos post-decoration, anything that looked real and lived in. But there was also something about the size, the layout, the openness of everything—the high ceilings, all the windows, the view of the fields and the forest beyond them—that wasn't capturable in photos. And, maybe most of all, there was the simple reality of it. It was no longer a house described over the phone or pictures on his computer; it was somewhere Ernie could see himself living. Somewhere new and apart from Becca. Somewhere she'd love, if she came back, but also somewhere, unlike home, that wasn't theirs. They hadn't lived here together; the bed, the pillows, the comforter, every plate, every glass, every light bulb that needed to be replaced, every corner that collected dust and that would have driven her crazy ... it didn't already all remind Ernie of Becca.

If anything, it reminded him of those first couple of seasons of *The Real World*. When it was Eric Nies, pre-*Grind*, and southern belle Julie, and poet/activist Kevin all walking into the coolest apartment in New York 1995 could imagine. Judd and Pedro and Puck in San Francisco, choosing rooms and choosing roommates, everyone running around their house like a Disneyland for adults, or at least for 20-somethings, which in high school seemed so grownup and adult and now, in his thirties, seemed so young, almost indistinguishable from teenagerdom, a lifetime ago. Ernie kept remembering seasons, remembered watching every Monday night on the TV in his bedroom, fascinated by these people, these houses. In high school, when the show had debuted, it all seemed so hypnotic, so amazing. Like maybe this was what his life could look like in just a few years when a 20-something himself. He'd graduate college and get a job good enough to pay for his own apartment-Disneyland, or maybe he'd even be on his own season. *The Real World: Whatever-City-They-Were-In-In-Five-to-Eight-Years.* He wondered why he and Scott had never really watched TV together, not *The Real World: New York*, nor *San Francisco*, nor *London*, nor any other show, not *MTV Cribs*, or *Dawson's Creek*, which Ernie wouldn't have admitted to watching, believing it to be for girls, but somehow had found himself addicted to, nor even *Boy Meets World*, which Ernie wouldn't have admitted to watching either, believing himself to be too old for, but watching with his brother could have bridged that gap, could have been the perfect excuse, he realized now.

<The sale went through!> Michael had texted, a few weeks ago.

Then, a second later, <Time to celebrate! You deserve a bonus! What do you want? Name it.>

Scott pictured Michael and his team celebrating—opening champagne bottles, shooting corks at the ceiling and one another, spraying it at each other like athletes who'd just won a championship. The mental picture surprised him; he wasn't sure why he expected such over-celebration. Purely because of Michael's exclamation points? Because that was how much *he* wanted to celebrate?

Scott figured he'd get an email the next day, something more official. An attached press release, maybe a link to an announcement already posted on some video game news site. Or maybe he'd just get another check in the mail, the amount a surprise upon opening the envelope.

He didn't really want anything. More money? It already seemed like they were giving him too much. Not that he wouldn't take more, if they gave it. But he didn't need more. He wouldn't ask for it. It didn't seem like he deserved what they were already paying him, much less more.

<A buffalo?> Scott texted back. Then he called Holly at work, was surprised when she picked up.

"What's wrong?"

"What? What do you mean? Because I'm calling?"

"No," Holly said. "Well, maybe a little. You sound like something's wrong, I guess."

"I was just surprised you answered."

"You know it's my study period. Every day, same time."

"Right. I guess I forgot."

"You want to call back, leave a message?" Holly laughed.

"No, no. You just surprised me. I'm glad you answered though! That's why I called. I wanted to tell you I just got a text from Michael. They sold the game!"

A longer pause than Scott was expecting. "Didn't they already sell it?"

"Well." Scott's turn to pause. "Yes." He'd wanted a bigger reaction, more excitement.

It *had* already sold, yes. In fact, now that Holly mentioned it, he wasn't sure of the distinction between Michael's text news and what they'd been told previously. They'd already celebrated each of the announcements along the way—the initial email, the contract, the first check ("And how many of these are we going to get?" Holly had asked, knowing the answer but no less amazed to now be seeing the number on an actual check, made out to her husband's name, the check itself looking designed by a teenager. "Each for this amount?"), the news that Michael and CP Games were taking it to auction, the news that it had sold at said auction. They'd even already used that first check for a down payment on the farm. Thinking through all the stages now, Scott remembered Michael telling him about the auction and that it was "done," but everything just needed to be made official, numbers vetted, the boring parts of the contract ironed out, all of that. CP Games had paid Scott his first installment right away regardless, a "sign of good faith" or because it helped negotiations on the particulars of the contract, or something like that, Scott couldn't remember exactly.

"I'm sorry," Holly said. "I didn't mean to undermine your excitement. I'll be extra excited when the farm sale goes through. When everything *there* is official."

Holly had been anxious, ready for the sale to be final and have all the paperwork and realtors and lawyers behind her. She wasn't nervous, nor especially unhappy or frustrated with the process, everything was going smoothly, she was just ready for it to be over. Scott, meanwhile, had been enjoying every little step of that process too. They'd bought the farm, but it wasn't yet quite theirs, and Scott was enjoying this odd homeownership purgatory. Every day, waiting for the final paperwork to go through, he'd visit and tour the house, walk the grounds, enjoy the contradictory feeling of being both admiring visitor and proud new owner.

Then, the day after the something-of-a-joke and Holly's underexcited reaction, Scott arrived for his daily walkthrough and the house had a musty smell. Not a *bad* smell, and not unlike what he imagined a farmhouse might smell like, but it surprised him. Not enough to draw attention to itself, but enough that made it seem new, like it definitely hadn't been there before. Every time he retold the story, the smell grew a little stronger, more vivid, Scott himself more aware of it and also of his own surprise. In the moment, however, there was the smell and the surprise of the smell, but neither gave him pause, and then he made his way from front door, through open kitchen and dining room, down the hall and around the turn into what would become his and Holly's master bedroom, and there it was. *He*. Billy. Though not yet "Billy," of course—just a huge, brown, pile of fur. This massive beast curled up on the floor, its sleep breathing visible from its heaving chest, looking like the biggest, cutest sleeping puppy he'd ever seen.

Then they were in the backyard, and Ernie stopped. Frozen in place, more surprised than he'd been by anything about the house. A buffalo stood still, staring back at him.

"You want to pet him?" Scott asked. "C'mon," he said. "Come meet Billy. He's friendly. The friendliest. You're about to fall in love, I guarantee it."

Part II:

THIS MUST BE THE PLACE

The Legend of Mr. Bison

In 1985, the Year of the Ox, Scott "Little Scotty" Isaacson turned seven years old. Coca-Cola changed its formula and released New Coke; within mere months, it was deemed a failure and Coca-Cola returned to their "original formula." Sally Field, winning Best Actress at the 57th Academy Awards for her role in *Places of the Heart*, famously exclaimed, "You like me, you really like me!" Only, what she really said was, "The first time I didn't feel it, but this time I feel it, and I can't deny the fact that you like me, right now, you like me!" The first WrestleMania was held at Madison Square Garden. *Moonlighting* debuted. Also: Windows 1.0, the Nintendo Entertainment System (NES), and *Calvin & Hobbes*. *Tetris* was released in Russia the year before (1984), and in the U.S. the year after (1986), but didn't, however, reach its full popularity potential until paired with Nintendo's Game Boy at the end of the decade. Mike Tyson knocked out Hector Mercedes in the first round of his first professional fight. *Super Punch-Out!!* was released as an arcade game. Two years later, Nintendo would release the game for their home system with Mike Tyson's name attached and his likeness as the World Heavyweight Champion, the final fighter to beat to win the game. That was the version Scotty would play and grow attached to, although he'd never beat Tyson, he'd never take Little Mac quite all the way to becoming Heavyweight Champion. The main event at that first WrestleMania was a Hulk Hogan-Mr. T tag team match against Roddy Piper and Paul Orndoff, for which the special guest referee was Muhammad Ali. A little over a year and a half later, in November 1986, Tyson would break Ali's record as the youngest boxer to take the title from a reigning heavyweight champion.

The Isaacsons' neighbor, Mr. Shafer—the corner house, across the street and at the other end of the block—brought home a goat. Immediately, Scott fell in love. Every day, he longed and begged to go down the block to the Shafers', to visit and pet Pony the goat, kept on a leash connected to a wire strung between two trees until Mr. Shafer could build a proper pen. He'd named her Pony as an anniversary gift for his wife, Emma, who'd wanted a pony when she was little.

By the end of the year, however, they'd moved. Mrs. Shafer had passed away; or they'd divorced and sold the house and each moved away, in their separate directions; or she'd passed away (or they'd divorced) the year before and Pony had been intended as companion during mourning (or post-divorce) and not gift, and who knew where the name had come from.

For months, Scott continued to visit—out of habit, forgetting Pony was gone; or hopeful, just wanting to visit the empty pen, a place now of sadness but also one of memories of joy.

Scott spent nearly all of his non-school hours either at Pony's pen—seeming lonely now and weirdly out-of-place without Pony to give it context, but also familiar and like his alone—or in his bedroom, watching movies and playing video games with his big brother, Ernie. *Back to the Future, Gremlins, Goonies, Stand By Me. Super Mario Bros., The Legend of Zelda, Street Fighter II ...*

7.

"Ern. I gotta run some errands. You wanna come with?"

Ernie closed his book, holding his place with his finger. "Where you going?"

"Home Depot. Maybe some groceries."

Ernie waited to reply, like trying to decide whether or not to go. He wasn't sure why. He wasn't doing anything, just sitting on the couch, reading, feet up on the coffee table.

Ernie hadn't really figured out his role or purpose in the house, how to spend his time. His role or purpose in life really—without Becca, without his job, staying at his brother's home instead of his own. Was he guest? Roommate? Boarder? He spent his days sleeping, sitting around, reading more than he had since it had been required for college. Walking long laps around the property with Billy.

"Sure," he finally answered. "Just let me ..." What did he need to do before leaving? He was dressed, and it was warm enough that he didn't need his jacket. His keys? Scott would drive. Wallet? Sure, though he didn't need anything. Unless they stopped at the liquor store, though he hated asking. He preferred to stock up on his own occasional trips into town, when Scott couldn't see how many bottles he bought, how quickly he went through them and needed more. He'd sneak them from car to room, trying not to think of it like *sneaking* but always conscious of when neither Scott nor Holly was around or paying attention. Or he'd take long walks, setting out through the woods, good for his health or being one with nature or remembering hiking trips growing up or whatever. He'd nearly always end up in town, and if he was in town, he might as well pick up a bottle.

"Just let me get ready real quick," he repeated, not needing to ready up but not wanting to feel rushed.

"Course. I'll tell Holly we're heading into town, make sure if she needs anything. Meet you outside?"

Ernie nodded, found his bookmark and traded it in for his finger. He went to the bathroom, brushed his teeth while peeing, suddenly realizing it was getting on midday and he hadn't yet. He flushed, spit in the sink, rinsed off his toothbrush and stared at himself in the mirror. Turned a quarter turn one direction, then the other. Took himself in. He didn't look great, but not like shit either at least. Better than he'd feared.

Outside, Scott was already in his truck, radio turned to the station that had been alternative rock when they'd been growing up and still played almost all of the exact same songs, only now as nostalgia. *Classic alternative*, it called itself now, and Ernie wondered how long before it was just *classic rock*, how old they would be when it was just *oldies*.

The brothers walked the lumber aisles, Ernie half a step behind, following Scott's lead.

"What are we looking for again?"

Scott had explained what he was looking for on the drive, what he wanted to build, but Ernie hadn't really been paying attention. He'd been staring out the window, watching everything wash past. Staring out, he'd focus on the foreground while the background blurrily floated by, and then vice versa, watching every individual telephone pole and tree dart across his vision while the background behind them all washed by in a blur. "What you see out there in *Ernie's World*, driver," their dad liked to say when they were all in the car and Ernie got that look. He had the habit of nicknaming both sons "driver" whenever he himself was driving. Neither was sure how it had started, but they liked the nickname; it sounded cool, kind of grownup. Ernie had half-expected Scott to ask the same at the beginning of their drive, teasing him, sharing in his memory of their father and being kids. But then he'd so zoned out, so slipped into *Ernie's World*, he might not have heard even if Scott had asked. Staring out into the nothingness of trees and farms, this great expanse of land between their own farm and the nearest town, Ernie had drifted off into considering all the deer that must be out there, hiding, living in the forest. He imagined a wolf pack, a wolf attack taking down a young deer that had gotten too far from the rest. Did deer live in groups? Packs? Families? A pack of wolves, a pride of lions, a murder of crows, a ... of deer? How did he know lions but not deer? He'd pictured a whole reenactment of the scene from the canal. Did wolves live out here? Could a wolf take down Billy? It didn't seem likely, certainly not soon, he seemed to get bigger by the day. Horns couldn't be too long away, Ernie assumed. But maybe now, during this short window of time when he was still only barely larger than that deer whose carcass they'd found on the road? Not likely ... but possible? He should look into it. Maybe ask Scott. The possibility of wolves in their area, the possibility of a wolf attack. *Another* wolf attack. And what was the relationship between buffalo and deer? Ernie hadn't realized they'd slowed down through town, parked in the lot, until Scott looked at him, shook him out of it. "Ready?"

"Lumber for planters," Scott said. "I have in mind those planters dad built out in the backyard, but I guess it doesn't have to be the same."

Ernie looked at his brother.

"You know," Scott said. "In the back, but off to the side of the house. I don't remember when he built 'em. I was ... I bet we were six and ten? Seven and eleven? Mom tried to grow some vegetables for a couple, three years, then gave up."

Ernie shook his head. He didn't remember but didn't want to actually say. He didn't remember planters in their backyard, didn't remember dad building planters, didn't remember mom growing vegetables. He shrugged his shoulders, shook his head again.

"Well, they were ... They were kinda red, but I don't know if some kind of red wood or just stained? They would have had to have been stained, I guess. And they must have been ..." Scott put his hands together but apart, paused a couple of inches from clapping. "Two-by—No. Four-by-fours?" Scott moved his hands around, back and forth, but holding them parallel to one another, spreading them further apart then collapsing the distance between the two. "And rounded on the sides. So, you know, flat top and bottom, and looking like round logs on the sides. But we don't *have* to build the same thing. That's just what I remember."

"Works for me," Ernie said. "Your call."

"Maybe we just get whatever? Build our own planters, make it up as we go?"

"Can't be that hard."

"Exactly! Right? Stack a few logs up in a square, fill it with dirt."

Ernie nodded. They stopped where they were, looked at the stacks of wood up and down the aisle around them.

"Shit," Ernie said. "Wood's expensive!"

"Can I help you?"

Ernie and Scott both turned, synchronized. Saw the employee standing there, orange apron, walkie talkie clipped to his belt, looking too eager to help, too happy to be working at Home Depot.

"Looking for some lumber for some planters," Ernie answered, before Scott could *No thanks, we're good* him.

"Well. Anything specific in mind?"

Ernie thought, for a second, of describing the same cut and stained logs his brother had just described but stopped himself. "Not really."

"OK." The guy nodded enthusiastically, smiled. "Well. You're probably going to want something treated. Otherwise, it'll rot out in the rain. Other than that, it really just depends on what you have in mind—how big you want it, what you want it to look like. What the *wife* wants it to look like, right?" The guy smiled, almost a full laugh. He took a small step toward Scott, like he was going to nudge his shoulder—*What the* wife *wants, right, nudge, nudge*—before stopping himself.

"Right," Scott answered, straight-faced, not turning toward the guy but keeping his focus on the wood stacked right in front of him.

"I mean," the guy said. *Kyle*, his nametag said. "These four-by-sixes you're looking at right there would work. Think you made a good call, if that's why you're looking at 'em," Kyle said. "If you want the planters a little bigger, a little bulkier."

Ernie thought Kyle put a little emphasis on *bulkier* for Scott's benefit, or maybe even subconsciously. Or maybe he hadn't and only Ernie's subconscious had emphasized it.

"Great," Scott said. "These are perfect. That's what we were thinking"—Scott gave a little nod to Ernie—"just as you got here. Guess we'll need ..." Scott motioned with his hands while thinking it through and counting in his head—*four for a square, maybe four rows tall, four, four, sixteen, times two for a couple of planters*—"Thirty-two?"

"Sounds good! You two want to take them today? We could have them delivered?"

"Today. We've got a truck."

"Great. Want me to grab a cart to stack them up on ... or you just want to toss them over your shoulder, carry them out?" Kyle stood up straight, puffed out his chest, made like he was picking up a beam in each arm and pantomimed throwing them up onto his shoulders. "I'm kidding, I'm kidding. We'll get them for you. Need them cut or anything?"

"Nope," Scott said. "We need a couple more things though. We'll go finish getting everything while you get these ready?"

"Of course! Take your time, get everything you need."

Scott turned, started walking away.

"Thanks," Ernie said, gestured a little wave and hustled a few steps to catch up.

A couple aisles away, Ernie asked, "That happen often?"

"What?"

Ernie stopped, waited for Scott to notice he'd stopped and come back to him. Ernie rocked from one foot to the other, puffed out his chest, pulled his chin into his neck, made like he was flexing. He mimicked the guy's little mimicking of Scott picking up logs like sticks, tossing them around. Scott watched straight-faced, then the two broke into sudden laughter at the same time.

"Yeah," Scott finally said, through his trailing-off laughter. "Pretty much all the time. *You work out?*" Scott asked in a funny voice, like a million people had asked him over the years. "*Bet buffets don't like you!* Or, just flat out, *How much you bench?* Or even—" and now Scott puffed out his chest, stood up a little straighter. He raised both arms to his sides and flexed, like years' worth of another million dudes flexing at him over the years—as comparison? as request to see Scott flex without actually having to ask?—three or four degrees of impersonation now, a full circle back into itself.

Ernie recognized the ridiculousness of his brother's ability to instantaneously make the middle of a faucet aisle in Home Depot look like a bodybuilder's competition, but damn if it wasn't impressive, too. It was the first thing Ernie said when describing Scott to his friends—*big*, he'd stress—and even still he realized now he'd taken for granted not just *how* big, having said the word and described his size so many times to the point of the words no longer meaning anything, but also the impressiveness of it. Ernie was impressed anew, *actually* speechless. He wasn't sure if that had actually happened before or if he'd just assumed it an exaggeration, a saying without actual meaning behind it. Ernie remembered, years ago, he must have been 27, give or take, making Scott around 23, one of the few times they'd hung out together as adults. Had that been before Scott and Holly's trip together? Had Scott actually visited twice over the years? Yes, Ernie realized he must have. Scott had been in town for a match, hadn't told Ernie he was going to be in town until the last minute. Ernie didn't make the fight, but they'd gone out that night, drinking with some of Ernie's coworkers. A few hours, and more than a few beers, in, one of Ernie's coworkers—what seemed "older" at the time, but probably only 35, *maybe* 40, Ernie realized now—out of nowhere wanted to make a bet with Scott.

"Ten years," he'd said. "Ten years, and I bet you've got a gut the size of mine. At least."

Scott had tried to shrug him off, *yeah, yeah*.

"I'm telling you guys," the guy kept going. "I used to have a six pack!" Everyone at the table laughed. "For real! I'm serious! Age turns that shit into a keg!" The guy laughed, big and hearty. Put his hands on his belly, which he was now pushing out for full effect.

Ernie couldn't remember who that had been. Someone he hadn't kept in touch with, or even thought about, since, just another guy he'd worked with and forgotten. Probably they'd never hung out outside of work other than that one night, the guy wanting to come out and meet the wrestler brother, maybe make fun of wrestling, though not to the wrestler brother's face, just to his buddies later, sitting around and telling tales. Now, Ernie wished he could remember the guy, wished he and Scott could call the guy up, prove him wrong, collect their money owed.

Ernie looked at his brother, thought for an instant about asking if he remembered that night too but let it go.

They continued through the aisles of bathroom displays, lighting fixtures and ceiling fans, plumbing. Scott stopped and considered bins of nails, and Ernie wandered up and down the aisle, like he was looking for something in particular or comparison shopping or who-knows-what-he-was-doing.

"Got 'em," Scott said, holding up a bag of big lumber nails, and they moved on, toward the saws.

"What kind of saw you think I need for this stuff?" Scott asked, walking up and down the aisle like Ernie had been a minute or two before, half-considering what he might need, half-embarrassed he didn't just know.

Ernie shrugged. "You have anything already?"

Scott shook his head.

"Man," Scott said, after a minute of silence, each pretending like they were comparing the selection not only against other options but also against their expectations, against what they were hoping to find, as if they'd had anything specific in mind only a minute before. "Too bad we don't just have all of Dad's old tools."

Ernie nodded, though without necessarily wanting to. Scott and Ernie rarely talked about their father, seldom mentioned him to one another. They never shared stories or reminisced.

They again walked up and down the aisle, in opposite directions, away from and then back toward each other. Slower, a little more carefully.

Ernie stopped in front of the circular saws. He tried to imagine holding the handle of one, his other hand holding the end getting cut off, keeping it level and steady. He thought he could; that seemed right. "One of these?" he called, pointing.

Scott came to him, checked out the selection. "You think?"

"Yeah," Ernie said. He made the motion of holding one, cutting through one of the pieces of wood they'd picked out, then felt a little embarrassed. "That seems right, right?" he asked with something of a shrug.

Their father had gone in for a routine surgery, but there'd been complications. A two hour surgery became four, six. Neither brother had come to the hospital with him, so routine was it supposed to be, but as his hours in the hospital grew, their father's girlfriend called both brothers. Scott was there within the hour, though only to sit in the waiting room until the doctor finally came out with the bad news. Ernie was in the air at the time; he landed and turned on his phone to see a single message waiting for him. He didn't call his voicemail to listen. He knew it was Scott. Knew it was bad news. Knew he didn't want to hear it over the phone, waiting there for him as a message. Knew he'd make the comparison later, when telling the story, to those twin brothers on *G.I. Joe*, how they knew when the other was injured or in trouble, a kind of fraternal psychicness. Scott and Ernie had spent hours and hours playing *G.I. Joe* growing up. *G.I. Joe* and *Star Wars, Transformers* and *M.A.S.K.* Maybe *Transformers* was their favorite, but *G.I. Joe* was a close second. They'd take their action figures outside and try to find the most action-scene-like setting in their yard, often wondering how the kids in the commercials seemed to have yards that perfectly echoed the terrain of the movies and TV shows, not considering until years later that of course they did. Those weren't the kids' backyards. They were *commercials*. Over time, guns and accessories were lost, arms and legs broken, torn completely off, or locked up due to dirt in the joints, or the rubber bands that held them together would break, leaving the appendages dangling loose, no longer able to hold themselves in place or be positioned. And when they tired of the action figures, they'd recreate the wrestling moves they'd been turned onto in part via one of their favorite *Joe* characters, Sgt. Slaughter. Until Ernie started feeling too old for toys and *fake* wrestling, started collecting baseball cards, memorizing the stats on the backs, meticulously keeping track on graph paper, organizing the cards by set number, by team, by value, getting a new *Beckett Baseball Card Monthly* in the mail every month, and every month refiguring worth, reorganizing sets, reevaluating which cards belonged in a box according to set, or smaller plastic boxes for teams, or sleeves in one of his binders, or individual hard plastic cases for the most special and/or valuable (1989 Upper Deck Ken Griffey Jr., 1987 Topps Mark McGwire), though there was seldom, if ever, any actual change in those. Scott tried to follow his older brother's interests, but it felt too much like school and he didn't understand and couldn't match his brother's fascination with the minutiae. He started playing baseball instead, so they could talk about the sport, maybe play catch together in the backyard, but he was immediately good at it, better already than his older brother, and so Ernie doubly never wanted to play with his younger, more athletic brother. Those were some of the last times Scott and Ernie had been close.

After Ernie got to the hospital and saw the look on Scott's face, confirming what he'd known at the airport but hoped had been wrong; after they sat in that waiting room for hours, silent except for Scott's occasional hiccups of held-back crying, each staring at the ground, at their hands, at the ceiling, at anything at all that didn't matter; after they finally went home—Scott to his own house, Ernie to the hotel nearest their father's, neither wanting to actually stay at their father's home without their father there, without the other, alone in a house that wasn't their own, a visitor in the home of a man who was no longer with them; after all that, for the next few days Scott commuted the hour drive back and forth between his own home and his father's while Ernie made himself a hotel coffee, enjoyable in its own kind of shittyness, and flipped between morning talk shows he never watched except when in hotels and the morning *SportsCenter*, which he typically, when home, watched the late-night airing. Funeral and burial plans were easy and smooth, most arrangements premade by their father, always preferring to be organized, planned, *ready* for any outcome, both for himself and, now apparently and obviously, for others, or at least for others when it came to himself, and whatever wasn't pre-organized was spelled out in simple but specific directions, leaving Scott and Ernie little to second-guess or have to make decisions about or argue with one another about what might be for the best, or what their father wanted, or whether any decisions might be one and not the other. Ernie's only decision, actually, insomuch as it could even be called that, was that he needed to buy a suit, having feared for bad news—otherwise, why had he been called, why was he flying across the country on a moment's notice?—but not having *prepared* for bad news, because preparation would have meant admittance of, and not just fearing, the worst; or maybe preparing for bad news wasn't the same as preparing for the worst; or maybe it was, but no amount of preparation meant much when it actually came to a parent passing away.

Through all this, Scott and Ernie cleaned and packed up the house. Ernie bought a paper shredder at Office Depot and shredded boxes and boxes of paperwork, while Scott hauled truck-bed-fulls of junk to the dump. Finally, after they had the house nearly as bare and empty as possible, looking empty as an open house ready for walkthrough, Scott and Ernie had to deal with what they'd been avoiding. The garage.

The coffee tins and mason jars full of nails, screws, nuts and bolts were the easiest to throw away, and even those came with hesitation. Growing up, Ernie had always made fun of his dad for the collection—there were so many containers, none with any attempt at organization, perhaps the only thing in Mr. Isaacson's life left disorganized, that whenever something was needed, it was so unfindable in the mess that he still made a trip to the local hardware store, and more often than not the containers sat there, unused, untouched except for when something was taken apart and new nails or screws or nuts or bolts were added to the collection. Still, as much as he liked to tease, the collection always felt to Ernie like a symbol of adulthood. Of home ownership, of being prepared to work on and fix anything in or related to your own house. Of being a man. He'd always assumed that, as he grew up, moved out, bought a house, he'd start and grow his own collection, one jar multiplying into two, four, a full row of tins and jars full of nails and screws, nuts and bolts, none of them being used but there *just in case*. There for when he needed them. Of course, he'd never started the collection, knew how to do almost nothing around his house. And now he was being given the opportunity at a readymade collection, or even the possibility of taking just one, a starter jar, but he didn't really want them when it came right down to it. He wanted the idea of them. Maybe. The idea of wanting them. He didn't need nails as weird keepsake of his father. Didn't need a reminder that when something broke he called someone to fix it before even trying himself. Definitely didn't need to carry any home with him, and shipping jars of nails and screws and nuts and bolts across the country was so ridiculous he never actually considered it but liked to think about himself going through with it just to make himself laugh. Meanwhile, Scott thought nothing of them—didn't remember thinking anything of them growing up, didn't have room in his house for what seemed like an example of pack rat behavior in his father's otherwise so organized life.

The next and hardest to know what to do with were the tools. Maybe the sons'—*both* sons'—biggest symbol of their father. The collection of hammers and screwdrivers and wrenches, all in every size, for every job; the level passed down from their grandfather; the wall of tools neither brother even knew the purpose of, much less names for. And then the power tools. The drills, the nailgun, the sander. The circular saw they were now looking to buy a new model of. The table saw. A part of each brother had wanted them all, the whole lot of tools, but neither had the room nor practical use for them. Finally, they'd had a yard sale, sold everything but a toolbox's worth of smaller tools that Scott kept. It had pained them at the time and pained them each doubly so now, each remembering the day of the sale, the diminishing size of the collection over the course of the day, each piece their father had purchased and used and kept good care of over the years, hopefully now receiving similar care in their new homes, their father's life's worth of being a man.

Neither Scott nor Ernie said as much now. Neither wanted to voice the memory, neither wanted to share, to break their self-imposed but shared silent memories of their father. But it's what both were thinking.

"You have a handsaw?" Ernie finally asked, breaking the silence, the spell.

"I don't," Scott answered. "Don't really have anything."

"I'm gonna go get one," Ernie said. He started walking away before Scott could say anything or volunteer to go with.

8.

Holly was happy to have the house to herself. Happy Scott had taken Ernie with him into town, happy to see the brothers doing something together. Happy to have had the idea to invite Ernie, happy he took them up on it. She'd remembered that at least some part of Ernie and Becca had dreamed of living on a farm, that had been the one conversation that had stuck with her from the time she and Scott drove across the country to visit them in Michigan, and here she and Scott had been blessed with this opportunity, this money from nowhere, a kind of life freebie, and so why not share the goodwill? Isn't that what you're *supposed* to do? Then Ernie showed up depressed, even more quiet and uncommunicative than normal—what she projected, and Scott confirmed, as "normal" from the only couple of times they'd met—but sans Becca. It seemed all the better that they'd had the offer to extend, like it could be just what Ernie needed, to get out of that house, out of town. *Out of himself*, her husband might say. She'd hoped for the best and not necessarily feared the worst but worried they might all drive each other crazy—Ernie would wedge some kind of tension into her and Scott's relationship; or the proximity would bring to light why he and Scott weren't that close to begin with instead of bringing them together, or who knew what to possibly expect—but that hadn't been the case at all. He was no extra burden; he largely just kept to himself, and as often as not she forgot he was even there with them.

Some days, Holly would be watching something on TV and Ernie would join her, thinking maybe she wanted the company, or trying to be social, or just needing a break from his room, the same impulse that had usually driven Holly to watch TV herself.

Some of those times it was nice having someone to watch with, making the activity more social and less like she was just wasting away time, and other times they'd both quietly read, immersed in something or other, or faking immersion for the other's benefit, but other times still, Holly would look over at Ernie and he'd be neither watching TV nor reading but staring off into nothing. Something about it made Holly slightly uncomfortable and then a little guilty for feeling uncomfortable for no reason.

But most days, Ernie kept to himself in his room, or he'd help Scott with The Fence or other farm or buffalo duties that Scott seemed to just make up as he went, and Holly did the same, keeping to herself and making up tasks to keep herself busy in her room. Officially the "baby room," Holly had sanctioned it as half-baby-room, half-office, not especially needing an office but liking the idea of having one. She spent time decorating and reading books for expectant mothers, and books for new babies, and when those got overwhelming, books on gardening, which the yard wasn't yet ready for, but Scott and sometimes Ernie were working on it, so she was preparing for that too. Or vice versa: when the gardening books and thinking of farm life overwhelmed her, she prepared for the baby.

And, finally, coming as a surprise even to herself, she journaled. She'd never been big on the idea, hadn't kept a diary other than very sporadically, here and there, in grade school, nor had ever really looked back and wished she had. It might be fun to have a record of her and Scott's drive across the country, or to have a near-official "record" of Scott's days wrestling maybe, she'd sometimes think, but never with regret that she hadn't nor with an *I-wish-I-had* sentiment, and she'd just as easily let the thought go. But having a baby felt different. She wanted to not just cherish but *hold on to*, to have some kind of record or memento of each small moment along the way. The stores overwhelmed her with books to keep track of firsts—first crawl, first step, first word, first tooth ... a million different firsts Holly had never thought of, but maybe she would when they happened? She liked the idea. Liked the idea of starting at day one and having a record going forward, liked the *narrative* of it. And so, she'd think of these last couple months of pregnancy like practice. Getting into the habit now so the routine would be formed and in place by the time the baby was born.

And what better practice than her life around her—not just her first baby, first pregnancy, but her first farm, her husband's first video game, their first buffalo. One day, she wrote *The Year of the Buffalo* on the outside of her notebook, a kind of joke, and she laughed to herself, but then she liked it, the sound of it, the way it made it feel less like journaling and more like a project.

They'd done their research—*some* research, at least—and had agreed that they would keep Billy for a year and reevaluate their situation at the end of the year. They'd be new parents, Scott's Mr. Bison game would have been released. It would be a big year. And Billy would be a big pet. As big as he was already, this time next year he'd be huge, unmanageable by all measures. It would be time for him to be somewhere more equipped to take care of him, somewhere he could be with other buffalo. Or, who knew, the year would pass and their lives would be even better for Billy being there with them—maybe they'd figure out how to best accommodate his size, how to best take care of him by then, maybe they'd grow their farm into something of a ranch, get another buffalo, raise a whole herd. The latter option had really only been presented to make it seem like there would be a decision to make, like there was some kind of other option, though it had only been a few weeks and already she couldn't imagine ever getting rid of him. She'd never imagined she'd become this attached to the animal, to love and care for this buffalo as much as she did, and she swore Billy loved them back, same as any dog or cat or any other pet whose owners swore loved them.

Every day, she looked forward to spending time with Billy, giving him treats—Scott fed him his meals, hay first thing every morning, before Holly woke—and walking the grounds together, Billy following at her side, sometimes nuzzling his head into her arm, wanting her hand on his head or back. She liked that her clothes took on the buffalo scent, and she loved sharing stories, telling others about Billy and seeing their faces grow in surprise. She even kinda loved that, in town, she was thought of as the "buffalo lady." She thought about if they had a boy, maybe giving him the middle name William, though hadn't yet told Scott the idea.

Every few days, Scott would go into town, shopping or to the coffee shop to get online. He liked holing up in the coffee shop, a habit he'd picked up when on the road. He'd liked the time away from the ring and the other wrestlers, losing himself in the hypnosis of his laptop and enjoying the mundane, everyday activity around him, or so Holly imagined. Same as he liked carefully choosing a few CDs to take with him every time he left the house, despite Holly's endless teasing of the ritual. He'd leave the house and just drive—"We find God in our cars," he'd tell her, Holly assuming it was something he overheard at some point, on the radio or TV in a hotel room, or maybe even half-remembered from one of the few college classes he'd taken before dropping out; hell, maybe even it was that professor in that same art class that had turned him onto Wojnarowicz—and as much as Scott said, and Holly believed, that he liked the coffee shops and the driving, Holly loved knowing Scott knew her well enough that another small reason for the every-few-day ritual was for Holly's benefit. She liked having the house to herself. Not for any specific reason, not because there was anything she did while Scott wasn't home, nor because she got so sick of him that she needed the occasional break, though some small degree of both was true, but primarily just because she liked it. The solitude, the quiet and independence, the *feel* of the house with only her presence in it, the same way she assumed her husband enjoyed being in his truck by himself, rolling his windows down, turning the volume up on whatever CD he'd painstakingly chosen for the occasion, and driving far enough, and taking enough random turns, to get himself lost, to give himself that full feeling of not knowing where he was, becoming a kind of explorer or pioneer, the cowboy looking for a new life that she kind of liked thinking of him as, the prospector going west for gold that she sometimes pictured Mr. Bison to be. "Go West, young man," he'd told her on their first date that he was playing with as a kind of motto for himself, for Mr. Bison, and they'd together tried to think of a larger narrative tying together strands of buffalo persona and Old West prospector, but they couldn't quite figure anything out that either believed fully worked, and so he'd dropped it, just like that. No motto after all.

Now, with the men off at Home Depot and the house to herself, Holly turned on the stereo. Scott hated the radio—hated most *popular* music, hated all the commercials, hated hearing the same six songs cycled over and over—but Holly loved it. She loved the randomness of turning the radio on and being surprised, though Scott would tease her about this "surprise," give her his whole "it's only the same six songs at any given moment in time" gripe, but she'd tease back that even that was more of a surprise, at least, than listening to the CD he just took ten minutes deciding to listen to. And, anyway, she usually loved at least four of those six songs, so all the better. "They're *popular* music for a reason," she'd tell him.

Holly turned up the radio, turned it up again, started dancing around with the stereo remote in her hand, kept turning it up one click at a time. She had the conscious thought that maybe there *was* a more specific reason than just enjoying the *feel* of having the house to herself. She danced and danced, stopped when it went to commercial and felt her heart racing, her legs not quite burning but feeling the warmth, the pre-soreness of a good, long walk with a focused pace. She felt good. Relaxed, happy. She hadn't realized she hadn't been, or she had, a little bit, but had attributed it to the pregnancy or maybe missing the classroom. She couldn't even remember the songs she'd just been dancing to, but her body felt loose, alive. Sun beams shone through the window, lighting her dance floor, giving the whole room a movie-like tint. She could feel in her cheeks that she must have been holding a smile on her face the entire time. The DJ welcomed her back from commercial and cued up the next track, and Holly was at it again—spinning, circling her hips, moving through the house. She turned up the radio a little more again, found herself dancing to the door, swinging it open like a dance partner, holding the knob like a hand and swinging herself in toward it, then out, let go and twirled herself, kept going through the doorway, outside. She felt the warmth of the sun wash over her and closed her eyes and tilted her head up to feel its full effect, then opened her eyes and saw Billy out across the yard. She put out her arms for him, like calling *C'mere, Billy!* Like calling, *Come dance with me!* But then also like he was already next to her, in her arms, leading her, them. She held her arms out like that, again closed her eyes, and swayed with the moment. She pulled her hands to her side, pushing them up toward the sky above her, pulled them down over her body, the music making her feel not just alive and happy and energized, but *sexy*. She never thought she'd have moments of feeling so sexy while being pregnant, but these moments came nearly more frequent than even before she'd gotten pregnant. She thought about stopping to text her husband, tell him how great she felt, tell him she was horny, electronically wink at him, but at the same time, she didn't want to stop.

But then there was a short pause, between song and commercial break—again? already?—and Holly thought she heard something. She instinctively tried to turn down the stereo, to be sure, but she was well out of the remote's reach, just pointing it at the house. Then another dip in volume in the commercial and, yes, the phone was ringing. She hadn't noticed before a few seconds earlier and wasn't sure she heard it until just now, but she suddenly realized some part of her had been hearing it ring for a while, long enough for its insistence to imply importance, or the sudden ringing of their landline recalled some childhood instinct to run for the phone, or the synchronicity of the call and her thoughts of texting Scott collided into an urge to get to the phone before she missed him, and so she gripped the remote tight in her hand like a baton and ran through the door that only a moment before had been her dance partner, grabbing the phone with her free hand.

"Hello?" Holly asked, too heavy-breathed.

"Bison?" the confused voice on the other end said nearly overtop Holly's *Hello*.

"Hello?" Holly asked again, confused herself. "Excuse me," she added, starting to catch her breath.

"Sorry. Scott. I meant, is Scott there?"

"No—"

"Holly? Hi, Holly. This is Michael. Sorry. At CP—"

"Right! Of course." Holly tried to remember if he had called the house before. Not that she remembered at least, not when she'd answered the phone. "How are you? Is everything OK?"

"Yes, yes. I'm great. Everything's great. I was calling to ask the same actually. Scott hasn't returned my last few calls or emails."

"He's actually in town at the café right now." Holly was pretty sure Mike knew they didn't have Internet, that they went into town every few days to get online. "I bet he might even be ... wait. No. I'm sorry. He and Ernie went to Home Depot. I think they're getting some stuff to upgrade the fence for Billy."

"Oh! He must be getting big, I bet!"

"Huge. Is it urgent?"

"Urgent*ish*," Mike hedged. "Has he told you about Detroit?"

"Like, in general?" Holly smiled to herself, at her own little joke, but Mike didn't catch it.

"No, no. There's this video game conference there. They have this conference every year, every year it's in a different city, this year it's Detroit. That doesn't really matter though, I guess. *More* important than where it is is that we're going to make the first big *Go West!* reveal. It's going to be a pretty big deal. And I was hoping Scott would come. You know ... shake some hands, stand there and look awesome. It sounds dumb, but it'd make a pretty big impression. Pun intended. I think?"

"*Go West!*?"

"Yeah, that's what we're calling it. Did Scott not tell you?"

Holly wondered how much Scott had told him—just the motto itself? the small run of merch? their whole first date?—and shook her head, stared out the door she'd left open. She could see Billy out across the yard. Faraway but a little closer than when she'd been out there, air-dancing with him.

"I mean ... I know you're pregnant. And I'm asking a lot to steal him away. This is going to be my one request. I mean ... you know, until my next one." Mike laughed at himself now, but it sounded overdone to Holly, like he was forcing it, like he'd caught her laughing at him and was trying to match her energy. He sounded—either now, in this moment, or something about being on the phone, or maybe it had always been there, but she just hadn't noticed it before—a little sleazier than she'd previously pegged him to be. Then again, maybe that was part of how CP Games talked their way into so much money for the game. "We could fly him there one day, home the next," Mike continued. "Keep him away from home as short as possible, I promise." And there it was again, something in the way he said he promised. But, even aware of it, the promise and pleading had its desired effect. Which is probably why she was already in her mind figuring out if it might be possible. Her parents *had* been wanting to come visit. And it *could* be good for Scott and Ernie to go together. To make a trip of it. They could have some travel time together, and she could have some family time.

"I'll talk to him," Holly finally answered. "I think it could work. I bet we could figure it out and make it work."

"Holly! You're my new favorite. Not that you weren't before. You've always been my favorite!"

"Maybe Scott and Ernie could do it together," she offered, sure it would be fine, and not wanting to explicitly ask, but also making sure Mike wouldn't shoot down the idea, claiming they need Scott undividedly.

"Yes! Even better! The Brothers Bison!"

The oddness of the phrase struck her. She would have said The Bison Brothers, but as she rolled it over in her mind for a second, Mike's version did sound a bit better. Because this was what he was good at, his talent, or because he'd already thought it through, had been waiting to drop it at just the right moment.

"I'll talk to him," Holly said again.

"Yes! Thank you, thank ..." and Holly hung up. She stared out through the door at Billy again, realized they'd have to teach her dad how to feed him every morning, go over all the basics. She pictured a handwritten sheet of *Buffalo Care Instructions* and laughed out loud now, letting loose what she'd kept reserved to a smile when on the phone. She turned the radio back up, went back to dancing.

How to Forget

Start, counterintuitively, by remembering. Not trying to remember but not trying to forget either. Let it happen. Like throwing a punch, like taking a punch: allow it to happen.

Think of the memory not like a memory to remember or forget, but like any other. One in a series. Not first, not last. Not as integral to making the series complete. One piece that, as part of the whole, becomes negligible. Think, here, of a metaphor of your choice: one blade of grass in a lawn, one screw in a jar full of screws, one uneventful, non-holiday day of the year. Metaphor in place, forget the whole lawn, the entire jar of screws, the entire year. Forget the metaphor altogether.

Keep moving forward. An object in motion stays in motion. A rolling stone gathers no moss. A shark that stops moving dies.

Remember: most people don't want to forget. They want to want to forget. Think of yourself not as this kind of person.

Remember, too: there is such a thing as trying too hard. Find your rhythm; let yourself embrace the natural action, the natural reaction; be in the zone. Be the bowler working on 300, the pitcher in the middle of a perfect game, John Henry working his way down the line.

Practice. Visualize. Practice again. (See: all.)

Don't force it.

9.

"This is nice," Ernie said. He assumed Scott would ask "How so?" and he could tell him how it seemed like something out of a commercial or something. How he'd sat like that almost as a joke, like an ironic mimicking of a commercial, but the mimic had turned into the real thing. Instead, Scott simply agreed. "It is." It was just a moment, but Ernie was feeling more comfortable here.

"Did you always know you wanted to end up here?" he asked.

"On this farm?"

"Back in Washington, I guess. Or maybe I meant on this farm. Or … *a* farm. Something like this. If I got a bunch of money … I don't know what I'd do with it, but I don't think I'd buy a farm. Invite you to live with me, build planters together. Get a buffalo."

Scott laughed. "The buffalo was a gift."

"Right. Still."

Scott watched Billy walk around, graze. He put his arms back behind him, leaned back like kickstanded and looked up into the sky. "No, no. None of this was planned. I don't even really know how it happened." He looked, to Ernie, like he was thinking about it for the first time, like he hadn't actually stopped and thought about how it had all happened.

"I used to like to walk around cities a lot," Scott said. "When I was traveling. When I was wrestling."

Scott paused, seemed to be gathering … himself, or maybe his story. Like he wanted to figure out what he wanted to say next before saying it.

"When you travel a lot—tour-travel, not like *travel*-travel—you don't actually get to see much of where you go. You can say you've been to all these cities, and it's fun, but you haven't really *been there*. You drive to some new town, you find the place where you'll be wrestling, you find your hotel. You check in to your room, try to get a little rest, then head to the match, then back to the hotel and crash. Then you get up, do it all again in a new city. You work out in the hotel workout room, if it has one, or sometimes the high school gym or wherever we're gonna be wrestling would let us use their workout room, you bring into your shitty, cheap motel room the dumbbells you've learned to always keep in your car, everywhere you go, and you lift weights until you've made yourself tired enough to pass out on the shitty, uncomfortable motel bed. Maybe you go out drinking, your impression of the town is whatever bar you happen to find or stumble into. It's fun, but … It's fun until it isn't. It's lonely, it gets exhausting. At some point I realized I was really looking forward to settling down. Putting down roots. Once I realized that, I started looking at everything a little different. Every city, I'd think, 'Could I live here?' I realized I was always comparing everywhere to here. You know? Not this farm, but kind of? Washington, in general, something like this."

Ernie nodded like he understood, though he wasn't sure if he did, and Billy walked over while the two were quiet and nuzzled up against Ernie's leg.

"See? Billy wants you here. It's pretty great, right?" Scott pushed himself back upright, sat quiet.

"It is," Ernie answered without thinking about it and then thought about how instinctively he'd answered that it was.

"You ever get in a barfight?" Ernie asked.

Scott sat silent, and Ernie wondered if his brother had heard him or not.

He'd been thinking of Scott traveling, wrestling, stopping and drinking in all these different towns. He remembered the guy at Home Depot, *Kyle*, and how he'd reminded Ernie of the one time Scott had visited, the coworker who'd gotten too drunk. He worried the question seemed out of nowhere, and now his brother's continued silence only made him feel worse. He wasn't sure if he should ask again or not, if he should stay quiet and wait or maybe say something else, redirect the conversation as if he'd never asked in the first place.

"Not really." Scott took his huge hand and rubbed his face. His forehead, down his cheek. He rubbed his neck. He shook his head a little. "I shoved a few guys. I mean, they had it coming, or were asking for it, or whatever, but …" Scott trailed off again. He patted his leg, calling over Billy. "I never really got in a *bar*fight though, no. At first, especially … the first few times it happens, you don't know how to let it go yet. But then you realize there's some jackass in every bar, every town. They see some big guy, and maybe somehow they find out you're a wrestler. They get hung up on this idea that everything we do is fake. But we know what we're doing. *I know* what I'm doing. These guys … they don't know how to throw a punch. A *good* punch …"

"What do you mean?" Ernie asked right away, not letting Scott's trailing off linger into silence.

"There's a secret to a good punch." Scott looked at his brother. "Make a fist."

Ernie made his hand into a fist in front of himself, held it up for Scott to see.

Scott shook his head. "See? That's what I mean." He held up his own hand now, made a fist. Billy looked at the fist, got attentive like Scott was holding out a treat. Scott tried to brush him away. "No, Billy. *No*."

Scott's fist looked to Ernie like a club, a weapon. Ernie looked back at his own, still floating out in the air in front of them—it looked like a hand and then an arm, not even really a fist, certainly not like it had transformed into something else, something more.

"Open your hand." Both brothers did, Scott by way of example, Ernie following his brother's lead. "Now curl in just your fingers. Make it tight, each knuckle forming a ninety-degree angle." Scott turned his hand ninety degrees so Ernie could see. "Coil your fingers in on themselves like a spiral. Like a ..." He traced his exposed finger with his other forefinger. "Like a Fibonacci fist."

The phrase caught Ernie off guard, but Scott didn't catch the look of surprise. Instead, he was still looking at his fingers, huge and wrapped in on themselves, and Ernie's look went from surprise at Scott's language to appreciation, admiration. He hadn't ever tried to pick a fight with Scott, to show off or just to prove anything to himself, but he'd looked down on his brother. He'd harbored decades' worth of that same sense of "it's all fake" sizeism, or intellectual superiority, or whatever it was. But how many things did he put as much thought and appreciation into as Scott did into making a fist?

Scott finally looked back at Ernie. "*Now*," he finally added. "Tuck your thumb under, not in. Like it's holding your fingers down and in, not vice versa." Ernie did as told, made himself cognizant of what that felt like. He opened his fist, remade it like he had before, and then pulled his thumb out from under his fisted fingers, and again made his fist as directed. He could feel the difference, how much better his brother's way felt, how much stronger.

"You want to lock your wrist," Scott continued. "Hold your hand so the back of your hand is flat, is parallel with your arm. One long, straight line. Power is in straight lines."

Ernie made both hands into fists, held them out in front of himself to get the straight lines just right. His hands felt more like the clubs of his brother's, the strength spreading all the way up his arms, proper fists making his biceps feel stronger, his shoulders more like what he presumed a fighter's shoulders felt like.

"See? You're already more ready to throw a punch than half these jokers in a bar. Maybe three-quarters."

Ernie took those fists, threw shadow punches out in front of him. A couple jabs, what he presumed was more of a hook. Billy watched for a moment, unfazed, and then wandered off, neither brother looking to give treat or affection.

"When you punch," Scott interrupted, "where are you punching?"

Ernie kept throwing punches at the air, nodded out at his fists. *Where does it look like I'm punching?*

Scott held out his palm, and Ernie tapped it with a right jab, a left.

"Punch through your target. Your target isn't what you're punching; your target is two, three inches beyond what you think." Scott held his other hand a couple inches behind the one he'd already been holding out, and shook it. Like, *this is your target, back here. Punch here.*

Ernie kept punching, with his right, his left, right, aiming for further and further behind the hand he was hitting. The punches landed harder, felt better, the slap of knuckles on palm got louder. Ernie's punches finally started not just landing but moving Scott's hand; Ernie was sure they must be leaving at least a little sting. He had to lean his whole body forward, he was finally aiming so far back behind Scott's palm.

"There you go. You can already feel it through your whole body, right?"

Ernie kept punching, harder, in agreement.

"Use your whole body. Twist your shoulders into it for torque. Use the power in your hips, your core. When you're standing, use your legs to plant and to push off. You'd be surprised how much arm strength is really leg strength. Like a pitcher pushing off the mound, increasing pitch speed not just with his arm, his upper body, but all the way down through his legs."

Ernie finally stopped punching. He was a little out of breath, surprised how much it took out of him.

"Most people don't really think about it. Most people think it's pure strength. Brute strength, maybe a little desire or will or drive or whatever name you want to give to that unknown element." Scott watched Ernie catch his breath, smiled. "Then again, most people never punch anyone."

Ernie stopped. "No?"

Scott shook his head. "Nah."

"I figured I was more the exception. Like most guys had gotten in one fight at least."

"I don't think so. Most guys want you to think they've been in a fight. Most guys like the idea of getting in a fight a lot more than the idea of getting hit themselves. Most guys, in their mind, a fight is them throwing a couple punches and being victorious. And then there's just enough of the hint of an idea of not just throwing a punch, but taking one too, and so usually guys like to make like they want to fight while waiting for someone to hold them back."

Ernie laughed. "I thought it was just me," and Scott smiled, both nodded and shook his head.

"I think it's everyone. Most everyone."

Ernie thought about that, about all the unvoiced ideas and worries he thought were only his own but were actually universal.

"But ..." Ernie started. "I don't want to ..." He considered how to word his question, whether or not to ask at all. "You're talking about, like, boxing punches though. You guys ... You didn't really throw ... *punches* though, did you?"

Scott smiled. "Exactly. So, first, there's basically two kinds of guys who will pick a fight in a bar. Two mindsets. The first are the guys that don't think about it at all, it's all instinct. Maybe they recognize us—me, or all of us together, or whatever—or maybe they don't. They see a big guy, and they want to prove something. Then there's the guys that definitely recognize us. Or they hear someone say something, or they even ask what we do and we tell them. And you can even kinda see their thought process. They go, 'oh, he's a wrestler, wrestling is fake, this guy *looks* big but probably can't actually fight, I bet I can take him and it'll look good and be a good story.'"

"You *see* them think all that?"

"More or less." Scott shrugged. "You see it often enough. Some guys, some of the wrestlers ... They wouldn't provoke it, necessarily, but ... They'd let it play out. This guy Joe. *Mightiest* Joe. He would never incite anything, but he wouldn't discourage it either. If the other guy actually wanted to hit him, if some guy pushed past that phase where he just wanted to *look* like he wanted to fight, until his friends held him back, if he could tell a guy was going to take a swing, Joe would brace himself and let the guy. He'd take the punch and, no matter how big the other guy was, no matter how hard he swung, I never saw Joe even flinch. He'd just stand there like a statue, smile, and then counter with his own. And Joe's punch ... it would drop the other guy. Every single time." Scott smiled at the memory, kept thinking about it and started actually laughing. "Fucking Mighty Joe. *Mightiest*."

"But. That's what I mean. You were trained to punch?"

"Yes and no. Not like *trained* trained. There's no *real* training at any of it, or at least not what I saw. Not at our level. We were all self-trained, making shit up as we went. That was the fun part actually. Some guy would come up with a new move and then that would kinda ripple through. Other guys would come up with reverses, or would add something, put their own spin on it and make their own version. Sometimes we'd get together and just ... I don't know what you'd call it. We didn't ever really have a name for it. They were never planned or anything. Just ... if we had some down time and were in a gym, we'd spar or grapple or whatever. That's where you'd really learn this shit. We'd practice how to most make it look like we landed a move and also how to best sell someone else's move. But sometimes we'd really land something. We'd want to see how it felt to really bring an arm or leg down on someone. How much force it took to take them down to the mat, what it sounded like to actually connect, not just to slap the mat or yourself *like* you were connecting. You'd be surprised ..." Scott trailed off.

Ernie let it sit there. He wasn't sure if his brother was pausing to give Ernie a chance to nudge the story, almost as if they were themselves now sparring, or because he didn't want to go on. Ernie thought about those differences in intention, how for most of his life he'd assumed the latter, and so would usually not say anything. He'd almost always erred on the side of inaction, and he thought about how often he'd regretted that. He thought about that cliché, it being better to regret something you did than something you didn't do. Something he'd heard in a song or something, a song or movie he'd forgotten, but a line he remembered. He thought about all this. Were some people less self-conscious about just asking something as simple as what Scott had meant by surprise, or were they just quicker in thinking through this whole process and pushing themselves into action ...

"Surprised at what?" Ernie asked. Made himself ask.

"What?"

"You said, 'you'd be surprised ...' and then just kind of trailed off."

Scott nodded. Ernie wasn't sure if it was a nod of thanks, for the reminder of where he'd trailed off, or just in agreement that he had indeed done so.

"All of it," Scott said. "You'd be surprised how hard it can be to actually let yourself punch someone with full strength. Your mind doesn't want to let you, I don't think. I think it does all these calculations, figures out what it thinks the person you're hitting could take, and calibrates. You'd be surprised, too, how much you can take. How hard of a punch. The body is tougher than you think. It'll shake off more than you think it might."

Scott looked off into the distance. Not at Ernie, not like he was orating, not like he was in the middle of telling a story to anyone at all.

Then, just as suddenly, "Or it doesn't. The body can take more than you think it can ... until it doesn't."

Scott pushed himself and hopped up off the truckbed, stood. He walked around to the side of the truck and reached over, grabbed one of the logs, and slung it over his shoulder as easily as Kyle had the imaginary piece of lumber.

"Let's unload."

"Scott!" Holly's voice came calling, and both brothers realized she was repeating herself, that they'd heard her calling though it hadn't registered—Ernie too busy listening, on the edge of his seat; Scott telling his story, and thinking, and off who knows where.

"You guys gonna sit on that truck all day?" she asked. "No 'I'm home!'?" Her smile could be seen purely through her voice, the smile that Ernie knew was part of what was already making the farm feel like home. "Mike called. I told him you'd call as soon as you got home."

10.

Ernie stood on the deck, stared out into the yard. Acres of yard. Off in the distance, barely visible, visibility at this distance as reminder of size—size of yard, size of animal—stood Billy. *Billy*, Ernie said to himself—not so much whisper as more audible representation of what was intended to only be thought, Billy's size not only shrinking distance across the yard between them but able to turn thought into speech. Or maybe Ernie often said things aloud without intending, a kind of talking in his sleep, only are people self-aware when talking in their sleep? And, if he's self-aware enough to recognize, to question, then he's here, on the deck, on Scott's farm, not zoned-out, not dreaming, not off in *Ernie's World*.

And then, the confession: had he said it aloud hoping Scott or Holly might hear him? Might peek outside, ask, "What was that?" Might come out and join him, share the moment, either in silence or posing some kind of thought or question, though he had no specific ideas for what that may be. They'd have to fill that in themselves.

Then, with confession, admission: he was standing on the deck, arms half resting on the railing, half holding himself up, body leaned at a noticeably relaxed, nonchalant eighty, maybe seventy, degrees, looking out into the distance—at Billy, at the entirety of the farm, at *life*—at least in part hoping to be seen. Hoping, in fact, to be joined, to be posed a thought*ful* or thought-*provoking* statement or question, but also equally hoping not to be joined so much as just noticed. For Scott and Holly to see him—how at peace he looked, how at one with nature. How he was looking out at Billy before leaving town because of how fond he'd grown of the buffalo. How he was looking out at the farm itself, maybe not even thinking *Scott and Holly's (and Billy's) Farm*, but maybe in part *his*, too, this place he'd taken to calling home. Self Portrait as Zen. Still Life at Home.

Holly sat on the couch, watching TV. Out on the porch was Ernie, probably not wanting to be disturbed. Down the hall, in their bedroom: Scott, who she didn't want to disturb. Scott was self-aware enough to be able to joke and laugh about himself, but not until later, once it had passed, never in the moment: he could kind of be a dick when packing. That was probably putting it too strongly but was more than likely the word Holly would use after Scott—stressed, short-tempered—would snap at her. *Why are you always such a dick when packing? It isn't anything to stress over.* A question that would help as much as presumed. And so they'd realized this was best: he packed, she left him alone. Everyone won.

Yesterday, they'd had the cable company come out. The idea of the farm had been to embrace its *farm*ness—a general simplifying of life, minimizing down to necessities. They'd read more. Watch more movies. Even their favorite television—awards shows, occasional dumb morning shows or sitcoms in the evening, *SNL*—were all network, could be watched with rabbit ears. But, Holly had presented, cable would be great while Scott and Ernie were gone. Meaning: great for while her parents were there. Great to help keep them entertained, great as personal distraction, as reprieve. So Scott called, had someone come out.

"You want me to set up Internet too?" the guy had asked.

"No thanks."

He'd looked at her like he didn't understand. Like the sheet of paper on his clipboard that had cable TV checked but not Internet must have been a mistake.

"We have a special, TV plus Internet—"

"That's ok. No thanks."

"You sure? It's just ... It's actually *cheaper* with—"

"I *don't* want Internet," Holly cut him off, a little harsher than she'd meant, only maybe not. It seemed the guy wasn't going to get it until she really put her foot down. She didn't add that even the TV they were probably going to just call and cancel in a month or so anyway.

The guy finally shrugged it off. "Alright. Was just making sure. But whatever you want."

The guy smiled, and Holly sighed a bit. When was it that *The customer is always right* became only said sarcastically? Maybe always?

Scott stared down at his suitcase, flayed open on the bed like for inspection. He couldn't remember the last time he'd packed for a trip. Somewhere with Holly, both packing together, two suitcases side-by-side on the bed at once, Holly asking if she could put a few of her things in his bag, she was running out of room, only he could see that she wasn't, she just didn't understand how much could actually fit in a suitcase, didn't know how to best pack a bag. They'd gotten in a fight, Holly storming out of the room, returning only when Scott had come and found her, had apologized, had said he was all done packing and did in fact actually have plenty of room leftover, the room was hers and he could, of course, add whatever she needed him to to his bag.

During the height of his travels, Scott had it down to a science. Could look at his calendar, see how many days he was going to be gone, what cities he'd be in, what weather and activities he should plan for, and picture exactly what all to pack. Further, he'd visualize everything he was going to pack and then could see it all fitting together, like when he used to play *Tetris* for hours and then, long after he'd stop playing, would continue seeing pieces falling, would play level after perfect level in his mind. Same as, even long after retiring, the way he was able to see complete matches, start to finish, as clear as if he were watching them on TV or even in person. He hadn't pictured a match in years, hadn't played *Tetris* for even longer. Hadn't had to pack with any kind of regularity for longer than he'd realized.

Scott wondered if Ernie was done. If he was ready, waiting on Scott. Last he'd seen, Ernie was out on the deck. Because he was ready to go? As final procrastination, and Scott was the one closer to being ready?

There was a video game conference in Detroit that Michael wanted Scott to go to. Scott had found it easier to avoid than to turn down (*that sounds more like me*, Ernie had joked, at Scott's telling, and Scott had nodded, agreed), but Michael had convinced Holly, Holly had convinced Scott, and so what did Ernie think? Head back to Michigan together for a few days? Roadtrip? How about it?

Scott looked down at his suitcase, surveyed everything he'd already packed. Closed his eyes, tried to visualize everything he'd need—everything he'd already packed, anything he might be forgetting.

Holly flipped through channels. So many channels. She thought of that Springsteen song. How many channels, and nothing on? Ninety-nine? No, she thought. Fewer. Fifty-something? Ha! If only he'd known.

"What was that," Scott asked from the other room.

"What?" Holly called back.

"I just asked, 'What was that?' Thought I heard you call for me."

"Oh. No. I just laughed out loud, I guess."

"You sure?"

"Sure I laughed?"

Silence. Holly wasn't sure if Scott had moved on or was just waiting a moment before replying. He counted sometimes, only out loud instead of to himself, couple-joke.

"Never mind," Scott finally called back. "I just thought you'd called for me is all."

Holly smiled, went back to channel-flipping. Reminded herself anew that this was why she was watching TV, not in the bedroom trying to help.

Finally, Billy noticed Ernie out on the deck, watching him. Stopped grazing and slowly started moving toward the house.

Lumbering, Ernie thought, but that wasn't right. Lumbering implied an awkwardness, but Billy was smooth, graceful. Though Ernie knew the buffalo had an ability at speed rarely used, Billy nearly always moved slow, with a fluidity that almost seemed like floating, all of it belying his size.

A part of Ernie wanted to turn around, look into the house. See if either Scott or Holly was looking at him. But trying to look would ruin how he wanted to be seen—not looking for Scott or Holly, not even thinking of them. Looking, only, at Billy, at the farm, his whole body radiating an inner peace he wanted to project even more than he wanted to attain.

Instead, he turned, looked at the gate, at the SUV Scott and Holly had returned with earlier that morning. It looked, from here, plainer, more boring than he thought a cross-country roadtrip warranted, but he knew from throwing in his bags and a few pairs of loose shoes, a jacket, how nice it was inside. Navigation, Sirius, everything electronic—seat adjustments, entire console—and a screen for a backseat passenger to watch DVDs.

"We'll rent something nice!" Scott had said as soon as he proposed the idea, asked if Ernie was in.

On the other side of the SUV, Scott's truck. Ernie realized he didn't actually want to drive across the country in that thing, the SUV was going to be immeasurably more comfortable, but when he pictured the drive, that's what he'd been picturing. On the road together in that beast of a truck—uncomfortable, sure, but more looking the part. The truck looked like his brother. The truck was Mr. Bison.

"You ready?"

Ernie's body jumped, a sudden feeling like falling just before drifting off into sleep.

"Sorry, didn't mean to startle you."

Scott stood towering behind Ernie, suitcase in hand, big smile on his face.

Ernie wondered if he had in fact slipped off into the kind of zen state he'd been hoping to project. Scott probably would have called it *Ernie's World*, though Ernie was glad he hadn't. Though maybe that was indeed where he'd been. Maybe they were the same, at least more or less.

"You put your suitcase in the van?"

"Yep."

Scott watched as his brother turned around, nodded and smiled.

"I threw most everything I needed in, yeah."

Scott stopped himself from asking what that meant; or, at least before he could ask, Holly's hand was on his back, rubbing his shoulder.

"You guys about ready?" Holly asked, moving her massaging hand to her husband's neck, smiling with her whole face.

"Yep!" both brothers answered at once.

"I made you guys some sandwiches for the road."

Holly held up their father's old lunchbox, a surprise. He'd taken it with him every day of his working life. Ernie hadn't realized or noticed, but Scott must have taken and kept it when their father had passed and they'd cleared out his house; Scott had brought it home and tucked it away he-couldn't-even-remember-where, had forgotten about it entirely, had no idea when or from where Holly had retrieved it.

Both brothers smiled big, unrestrained, and Holly felt a wave of relief. She had been looking forward, was excited to present the lunchbox as roadtrip bon voyage gift, but was nervous too, unsure how it would be received. Neither brother talked about their father much, almost never unsolicited, but she knew the love and reverence both had for him.

"Go East!" she called, putting her relief into exclamation. She'd thought of it a few days before, was nearly as excited to use the phrase as to gift the lunchbox. Scott could tell from her face, she was proud of the phrase. "Young men," she added with a smile.

Part III:

SOUNDS LIKE THE OCEAN

The Legend of Mr. Bison (part 2)

The second quarter of his freshman year, Scott signed up for Art History 104. Art History because art seemed interesting enough, that section of 104 because he'd heard Professor Lynch was easy. In the Fall, he'd taken a variety of survey courses—Economics 200: Intro to Microeconomics, Sociology 110: Survey Sociology, Chemistry 142: General Chemistry—thinking he would find something he liked or at least something he was good at, ideally maybe even both. He'd talked to a counselor long enough to understand that pretty much any class freshman year would fulfill one gen ed requirement or another. Instead, he disliked each as much as he was horrible at it. So, winter quarter, he swung as far in the other direction as he could figure—Drama 101: Intro to Theater, Music 162: American Pop Song, and Art History.

In Drama, they rarely referred to their textbooks and never had quizzes or tests—mostly they helped prepare the lighting and build the sets for the graduate student plays. Music was more boring than he'd anticipated—all Tin Pan Alley and ragtime, it was interesting enough, Scott admitted when pressed, though it sounded frustratingly similar, the difference between Eddie Cantor and Jimmy Durante nearly indistinguishable to his ears, whether it was written in 1920 or '23, impossible to remember. By the time they got to the kinds of stuff that most of the students had in mind when registering for the course (The Beatles, Hendrix, Zeppelin), it was a welcome revelation, but they'd also nearly all, Scott included, checked out. Professor Vine had been teaching the same class, with the same syllabus, the same multiple-choice "pop" quizzes every Friday, for an eternity, and those multiple-choice answers had spread through the campus as thoroughly as the rumor that if the teacher was at least ten minutes late (some versions even had it as short as five), then the students could leave, class "officially" cancelled. Scott got an A because everyone got an A.

Art History proved the most difficult of the three. It presented the same struggles as Music—an endless stream of names, years, dates—but without the cheat sheets. Unlike Music, however, he found almost none of it boring. Scott could remember and recite the stories behind each painting, each new style and movement, the characterizing traits, why it was important, but rarely whatever specifics the tests called for. All the more frustrating were his classmates who seemed to pay no attention, seemed to not care at all, and yet when tests were returned, Scott spied nothing but A's and B's where his were cluttered with red X's and points marked off. A month in, Scott gave up. He paid attention in class, followed along with the assigned reading, but more for entertainment than studying purposes. He stopped highlighting his textbook and taking notes, gave up making flashcards and studying at all. It was what it was.

Week five, Professor Lynch introduced photography. "Works of Art in the Age of Mechanical Reproduction," it said on the course calendar. Skimming through the chapter to look at the photos before going back to read, Scott was immediately struck by one image in particular, near the end of the chapter. It looked familiar, though Scott wasn't sure if he'd seen it before or it was like that once- or twice-a-summer pop song that sounds, the first time you hear it on the radio, already like you'd heard it a million times before, so perfect is its "pop song-y-ness." Scott looked to the caption. *Untitled (Buffalo)*, 1988-1989, David Wojnarowicz. The name didn't look familiar. He tried to say it to himself, Wojnarowicz, wondering if it might sound familiar out loud where it didn't on the page. He pronounced it half a dozen different ways, none of them triggering any memory or recognition. He stared at the photo until he didn't see anything else on the surrounding page, until it looked like it was moving—the buffalo tumbling over and off the cliff at once beautiful and tragic, horrible and inevitable—and he remembered the U2 music video for "One," the one with the running buffalo, before MTV pulled it for something more traditional, Bono just sitting on a couch, singing into the camera, being Bono. Scott had never understood why that had happened, why the need for two videos for the same song and why the latter got all the airplay when the former was so obviously the better of the two, though he'd only seen it a couple of times before it was pulled from rotation. He'd only seen that one other time, two videos for the same song, for George Harrison's "Got My Mind Set on You." One was the typical guy vying for a girl narrative; the other featured only Harrison, in a den, playing the song while the furniture and various taxidermy slowly came alive and sang and danced along. When Scott had asked his dad why this song had two music videos when every other song seemed to only need one, his dad replied only that music videos were expensive but Harrison had been in The Beatles and so had "more money than he knew what to do with." So he paid to have two videos made just because he didn't know how else to spend his money? And if more artists had "Beatles money," they'd maybe all make multiple music videos? Just because?

Scott returned to the beginning of the chapter, read through it but hurrying to the end, feeling pulled toward the falling buffalo. Finally, three pages before the end of the chapter, on the page before the photo itself, three sentences about Wojnarowicz and his work.

> Wojnarowicz was a painter, photographer, writer, filmmaker, performance artist, and activist, prominent in the NYC art world of the 1980s. *Untitled (Buffalo)*, specifically, was one of the decade's most haunting artistic responses to the AIDS crisis. A photograph of the Old West diorama from a Washington, DC museum, the work depicts stampeding buffalo plummeting off the edge of a cliff to certain death.

Scott turned the page, again looked at the photo. Held it up to his face, looked closer. A diorama, of course. He hadn't stopped and thought of the logistics of it—someone being there, with a camera, to record the event. In 1988? But some subconscious part of his mind had thought it amazing, just that, that someone had been able to record the moment, with such beauty no less. He wasn't sure if it being a photo of a diorama made it more or less beautiful, more or less important or epic. It didn't matter.

All week, Scott waited for Professor Lynch to get to this photo. To spend a whole day talking about Wojnarowicz, about photos of dioramas, the capturing of a capturing of something, but it never came. There was something about "camera obscura" and the "transparent truth" and "culture of light," and then the week was over and the next it would be on to "Representation, power, and the art-historical discourse." Maybe they would talk about Wojnarowicz then? What was *Untitled (Buffalo)* but representation and power? Instead, they forged ahead to the next chapter, giving Wojnarowicz no due, and Scott couldn't believe it.

And with that, he was done. Done with school, done trying to study shit he didn't care about, done getting frustrated with himself for not being able to remember every single name and date his teachers threw at him.

The more Scott stared at that photo, the more he analyzed it, the more he related to it. He felt that same momentum, pushing them, pushing him, over the cliff. Not to "certain death," Scott wasn't that dramatic, but still. Certain disappointment? Certain college failure? He went to the library and found what he could on Wojnarowicz and skimmed it all, pretending to care, but really it was just that one photo. The falling buffalo. Though one small piece of info stood out: Wojnarowicz attended the High School of Performing Arts for a brief period, until dropping out of school.

Scott took a week off. Sat around his dorm, skipped classes, played video games. He unpacked and hooked up his old Nintendo and Super Nintendo that he'd boxed up and brought to college, not sure why at the time but feeling pulled to. He played through the classics, all his old favorites. *The Legend of Zelda*, original through number 4, *Ocarina of Time*. He instinctively remembered nearly all the 1-ups, warps, and other hidden secrets of *Super Mario Bros.* and played speed rounds, seeing how fast he could beat it. He still couldn't punch out Mike Tyson. He remembered the hours, days, months' worth of hours playing fighting games with his brother. *Street Fighter II* was a particular favorite. Ernie always liked playing as the "good" guys, Ken and Ryu, sometimes Guile, but Scott liked the bad. Blanka, Zangief. He liked M. Bison, liked his "psycho crusher" special attack, liked that the mythology went that he had killed Guile's best friends, and so there was a personal vendetta between the two. He liked the narrative of it.

Scott called Ernie, hoping to talk it through, get some kind of brotherly advice, though they quickly fell into what had become their pattern when not in front of a TV together, controllers in hand, of awkward small talk and nothing more, until Ernie apologized but said he had to go. Ernie, four years older, was in the first year of his post-college job (something with computers, Scott wasn't sure what exactly) and already talked about working his way up, the growth potential for his kind of job.

At some point during this week of drinking and playing video games that Scott was calling "soul searching," he remembered Hilary. He couldn't remember her last name, only that she spelled it with only one l. *Hilary with one l.* She showed up to Scott's high school out of nowhere, a striking beauty, the kind of mature perfection that hadn't existed anywhere in middle school the year before. Moved from another state, transferred from another school? Some in the school seemed to know her, or at least were less intimidated than Scott, made faster friends. Scott admired from afar, wondered where she'd come from, invented stories and histories and then fell in love with those. Finally, a month into the school year, he approached her at lunch. Just walked up to her, put out his hand and introduced himself.

She laughed. "You really don't know?"

Scott looked confused, wasn't sure what she meant.

"Hilary," she finally said. She took his hand, shook. "With one l. We had Algebra together. *And* English. Mr. Bradley."

Scott stood frozen, even more confused, a little embarrassed. They'd stopped shaking, but he hadn't let go her hand. He pinched in his eyes, his forehead, searched for any sign of recognition.

"It's okay," Hilary with one I said. "I had a growth spurt over the summer."

"Well," Scott stammered. "You look great. Really. Wow." He let go of her hand and took a step back, looked her up and down. He couldn't help himself, then he did, and he grew red, more embarrassed. Hilary smiled, and everyone else at the table broke out in laughter.

Even when it finally clicked, Scott still couldn't completely recall what Hilary had looked like the year before. Like this new version had completely destroyed the old. She'd gone through a growth spurt, sure, but there was more to it. She'd lost weight or maybe stayed the same and the spurt had just stretched her out? She was maybe the tallest girl in the school, but with an accompanying grace and beauty that almost no one else her height had at that age, boys and girls alike. Had her hair changed too? Or she'd figured out how to style it to complement the rest of her? And how to laugh—did she laugh different now, or more, or did it just look more attractive on the new her, making everyone around her funnier, trying harder to make her laugh? And how to dress, her make-up, how to walk and speak and carry herself with a confidence but not arrogance.

Scott imagined it as part nature—there was the growth spurt itself, of course—but another part nurture. Effort. He envisioned a summer of Hilary devoting herself to this transformation. Not only learning how to style her hair, but then combing it that way over and over, every day, training it to do what she wanted, similar, he thought, to the way he shaved—daily, sometimes twice, even three times a day, though he barely needed to once a week—trying to encourage the beard growth he believed would make him look older, more manly. He pictured her in her room, devouring fashion magazines, cutting out favorites and building scrapbooks of inspiration, flipping through them as often as he looked through his notebooks of plastic-sleeved baseball cards, trying to collect full sets and as many of his favorites as possible. Griffey, Rickey Henderson, Roger Clemens. Nolan Ryan, the Bash Brothers. They weren't all that unlike one another, Scott and Hilary, he convinced himself.

Remembering Hilary, her transformation, having known the before to now be able to fully appreciate the after, made her all the more attractive. Even more than attractive, *impressive*. Scott called the office of the registrar, dropped his classes, asked that any tuition refund be sent in the mail. He wrote Ernie a letter explaining that he'd been offered an amazing opportunity to work on a farm on the Canadian border. He'd write or call when he was there and had an address or phone number. Scott gave the stamped letter to his roommates and asked if they would please mail it for him, but not until the semester was over.

The next time Ernie or their parents or anyone else who knew Scott saw him was almost fourteen months later. He was forty pounds heavier, all muscle. Almost unrecognizable. He answered to Scott, but sometimes referred to himself in the third person as "Bison."

II.

Scott spotted it on their first loop through, but Ernie asked if they should keep going. "Just to make sure there isn't something better up ahead?" Scott nodded, smiled an *of course,* and kept going, and Ernie spent the second half of the loop staying quiet but knowing nothing else was going to be as good, worrying the first site was going to be taken by the time they came back around. It was going to be his fault they'd missed their chance. He let out a sigh when no one had taken it and it was still free.

Scott parked on the flattened-grass parking space, turned off the SUV.

"She's nice, right?"

"What?" Ernie asked.

"She's nice, I said. The car. The SUV. Drives nice, right?"

Ernie shrugged, smiled in agreement.

"Can I tell you a secret?"

Ernie made a look like he was thinking about it. Overemphasized drawing his hand back from opening the door, like making a show that the secret would stay in the car. "Sure. Yeah."

"Holly's idea. Renting the SUV, I mean. She's better at those kinds of ideas." Scott smiled, but Ernie wasn't sure what *those kinds of ideas* meant. He couldn't help but wonder why that would be a secret, and then he wondered why didn't they go all in, get an RV or something?

"Good idea," Ernie finally agreed.

Both got out of the car, stretched their arms as if in some kind of synchronized driver routine. Scott walked forward to check out the spot, patted the hood. "Good girl." He smiled and looked around, surveyed their home for the night. Tucked into a corner and not *on* the water, but next best: river-accessible without having to go through anyone else's site. Close enough to hear the water. The kind of site their dad would have chosen. The kind they'd stayed in countless times growing up.

It reminded Ernie of Becca, of her sound machine, of standing in that house they were now headed toward, staring out into the yard, listening to the sprinklers. He realized how much better this was, thought it silly he'd considered a sprinkler setting to fall asleep to.

Scott walked back toward Ernie and again spread his arms out in presentation. "It's perfect!"

He double-clicked the remote on the car keys, and the back automatically opened. He handed the tent, still in its box, to Ernie, and went to moving stuff around, reorganizing. By the time Scott grabbed their sleeping bags and egg-crate foam pads, Ernie had already tracked down the flattest plot of ground, had the tent out of its box and spread out.

"This is it?" Scott asked, approaching. A big, simple square of material and two poles.

"Rain tarp and stakes are still in the box. Probably don't need them?"

Neither brother had been camping, had had any need to set up a tent, in a decade at least, and though Ernie had gone a few times in high school and college with friends, both of their most vivid memories of tents was still their first: the Army-issue-like, antique monster they'd used with their dad growing up. Its construction had required near-perfect teamwork, actual craftsmanship, a number of mumbled bursts of swearing, and at least one forfeit and then starting over again from the beginning, before they could finally prepare it for the night and then play in it, while their father recouped with a beer and the promise of silence and being left alone until the beer can was empty and discarded. Ernie snapped the poles together and Xed them across the flattened out square of a tent, and each brother tucked an end into a corner pocket, attached a handful of clips from tent to pole. *That's it?* The tent looked the same as on the box, all in less than five minutes. Everything with Scott seemed so easy.

"What next?" Ernie finally asked.

Tent set up, still not yet dusk, they weren't sure what to do. They'd splurged on the tent and sleeping bags and sleeping mats but hadn't bought any cookware or anything else to pass the time.

Scott shrugged. "Build a fire?"

"What about firewood?"

"You think we're allowed to just pick it up off the ground? We don't have to buy a bundle from ... somebody?"

Scott gave his brother a funny look.

"I don't know," Ernie answered. "Don't they have park rangers or something? Or ... what are they called? People that stay in the campground and sell you firewood? Hosts? I'm gonna walk around, check it out."

"Wait. You hear that?"

"The river? Yeah—"

"No, be quiet for a second." Both brothers stood silent, straining to hear. "You hear that, right?"

Someone was playing guitar, barely singing or maybe even just humming along. It sounded both familiar and not, like an acoustic cover of a rap song on NPR. But also campground-y.

Ernie strained to hear and leaned in closer, like that might make a difference, same as leaning into driving curves or away from attacking enemies in video games.

Neil Young, maybe? Some slowed-down, over-the-campfire Nirvana?

They walked toward the sound, moving slow as if to not scare it away. The accompanying singing dropped in and out, sounding like lyrics remembered and forgotten. They kept walking, further than expected, the natural acoustics of the mountain and forest creating their own amplification. By the time they found the group of guys playing music, in the short time of walking from their own campsite to this one, the sun had started to set; the dusk light illuminated the scene as they approached. One of the guys asked for another beer, and another guy stood, pulled a couple of cans from the cooler he'd been sitting on, and tossed one across the circle to the first guy. He looked around to see if anyone else needed one, sat down again. Either nobody among them noticed the brothers, or they didn't think twice about them walking by. Ernie pulled his phone out of his pocket—no reception, still no messages—and realized it wasn't that late. Away from the cities and people, the streetlights and business lights and whatever other kinds of lights that seemed to always be on, night not only came faster than he was used to, but the dark was darker. Cleaner too, looking like it went on forever. It reminded him of growing up: spending full summer days outside, shooting baskets at his school past the end of the block or timing laps around the block with Benjamin. He was always sure he could stretch out the day a tiny bit further if only he willed it hard enough, despite every previous day's proving of the opposite. *Five more minutes*, he'd beg his parents, when they called that it was time to come in. *One more race around the block*, he and Benjamin would tell one another, sure they could do it even faster than the last lap. *One more basket*, he'd tell himself, wanting to end on four in a row, or five, or nine, or whatever his lucky number was that day, or a counted-down-from-5 buzzer beater from as far away as he could hurl the basketball with any semblance of accuracy, the attempted game-winning hero-shots getting longer with every year's worth of matured arm strength.

"What?" Scott called.

"Beer?"

Ernie shook his head, shaking himself out of another reverie, out of realizing that Scott was absent from all his long summer day memories, and why hadn't

Scott ever wanted to play, but then also shaking himself into realizing that he was shaking his head like declining the offer.

"Sure!" Ernie answered. "I mean ... Yeah. Please. Thanks!" Then, to his brother, "You want to have a beer with these guys?"

Scott shrugged, nodded. "Experience the road, right?"

They walked forward, and Ernie put out his hand to shake and "hey, man, how it's going" one of the guys, and the guy sitting on the cooler stood, took his hand, pulled Ernie in and wrapped him up in a giant bear hug. Ernie slapped him on the back and, up close, could smell the alcohol and pot, the combo creating a nearly visible, Pig Pen-like haze around him.

The guy stepped back, sized Ernie up like they knew each other but just hadn't seen one another in ages, taking him in like he was proud of Ernie, all grown up. He turned and looked at Scott, looked him up and down like checking him out, and when he finally found the words: "Holy fuck. You're even bigger up close. You're like ... like ..." He looked around at his buddies for help, but then thought of something. "Like that dinosaur in the rearview mirror in *Jurassic Park*. 'Closer than they appear,' right? Something like that!" He put out his hand to give the shake Ernie had tried to get. "Jeff," he said. "I'm Jeff. Come meet the guys, have a beer!"

"The second half of that joint is like two joints," the guy next to Ernie said. He'd already forgotten their names. The guy wore a flannel shirt, unbuttoned except for the very bottom button, and a countless number of hemp and bead necklaces that almost made up for his lack of undershirt, or maybe it was all one big necklace, Ernie couldn't tell. He thought it awkward, at first, that the guy was practically shirtless, and then wondered why he'd bothered to keep that one button done at all.

"What?" Ernie asked.

"The second half of that joint there in your hand," One Button repeated, walking Ernie through from the beginning, not sure where he'd lost Ernie. "It gets stronger the closer it gets to the roach, so that there is practically like two joints."

"What?" Ernie asked again, having heard him but still not getting it. "That doesn't make any sense."

Across from them, another guy kept nodding. Closing his eyes, nodding, opening his eyes. Agreeing with his face. He didn't say anything, but Ernie could hear him thinking, clear as if he were saying it aloud, "Yeah, yeah," or, "Fucking deep, man." He was white and had dreads. And then One Button started in again, or he'd been talking the entire time and Ernie had just been zoning him out, off in *Ernie's World*, or only a fraction of a second had passed and the pot had stretched out the moment, made it feel like an hour.

One Button continued, in depth, explaining how, as the joint got smaller, the pot wasn't traveling as far, so it got filtered less, so Ernie was inhaling more. Each puff therefore got the smoker slightly higher than the last. He looked like he would have diagrammed it on a chalkboard if he'd had one. Professor Hippie. For a moment, Ernie let himself consider and compare nicknames: One Button vs. Professor. One-B? The Professor?

One Button looked at Ernie, smiled and nodded like he could read his mind. The math didn't seem to add up to Ernie, how part of something could be more than its whole, but he also couldn't find a loophole in the argument. Ernie brought his left hand up to his mouth, next to where he held the actual joint, both hands and fingers making OK signs, miming like he was, in fact, smoking two joints at once, one in each hand.

"Where'd the rest of that chili go?" another guy asked. He didn't have anything specific about him. "We should offer some to the new guys. I bet Paul Bunyan over here is starving."

Ernie looked at his brother anew, like he'd completely forgotten Scott was there. He couldn't remember if Scott had been smoking too or if he'd waved them off. He seemed to be able to picture Scott *no thank you*ing, taking the joint from the guy on his one side and just passing it to the guy on his other, but then again he looked stoned out of his mind. Then again again, maybe Ernie was just so stoned as to make his brother look high.

"Gone," One Button answered. "We ate it."

"*All* of it?"

"'Gone,' I said. Told you we'd eat it all."

"Man, New Guy. You should have been here earlier. Should have seen this pot of chili, man. Though ... shit. I bet all your pots of chili look big with this big motherfucker over here." Scott smiled, raised his beer. "Still. It barely fit in the pot. We almost couldn't stir it. I was sure it was gonna spill over."

"S.T.," another of the campground guys said. "Surface tension." Like it was the one thing he'd learned and remembered from college, and everyone groaned, like he'd probably been saying it all night before Scott and Ernie got there. "Esssss Teeeeeeee."

Across from Ernie, Scott put an empty down at his side and grabbed another beer, there waiting for him between his feet, cracked it open. He held it in his hand, open and full, and stared at the fire. *Scott's World*, Ernie thought and laughed.

One Button noticed same as Ernie did, joined in the laughter. "So," he said. "Tell us something about this dude over here who's drinking all our beer." Ernie looked at his brother and wondered what to say. The previous life as a wrestler, the video game, the farm. Hell, at least one of these guys was probably a wrestling fan, would maybe even recognize the name Mr. Bison. Or if not wrestling, a video game fan? Would any of these guys be controlling his brother through some post-apocalyptic Old West a year from now? Scott smiled big at them, wondering with his eyes how his brother might describe him, but also maybe a little pleading to not. Or at least that's how Ernie read it. He wasn't sure any of that was his story to tell anyway; if Scott wanted to tell it, he could.

"Well," Ernie finally said, thinking of something. "In high school, when I was already in college but Scott was in high school, he got this hilarious bad haircut that kinda turned into a crew cut and then he just kept getting it cut like that for a while. He owned it, you know?" Ernie looked around the fire at everyone, making his point. "What'd you call it?" He looked across at Scott. "'The ol' high and tight'? But, not just a crew cut. Like, a flat top. He looked totally different." Ernie didn't say anything about how he'd been so much smaller, about how this was all still pre-metamorphosis, pre-Mr. Bison. Across the fire, Scott kept quiet, took another swig, and nodded along.

"I don't know," Ernie continued. "I didn't know anybody but, like, cops and dudes in the military who looked like that. Actually, I didn't know anybody at all. Cops and dudes in the military, in *movies*, I guess. He came up to visit me in college one time, and we were having a house party. I remember ... some of my roommates just could not let it drop that he looked like some kind of narc or something." Ernie thought back on it, couldn't remember the last time he'd recalled that Scott had come up and visited that time, that there was at least one moment in college when he'd tried to be brotherly. "He was really great about it actually. Just took all the teasing in stride, didn't really seem to be bothered."

Everybody kept quiet, waiting for more. Ernie looked around and shrugged, end of story. Scott just nodded—*yeah, yeah. It was true.*

One Button stood, put his hand to forehead in salute. "Officer Big Man. Please don't bust us, sir. You smoked too, man. That'd be, like, entrapment!" He stood stoic, straight-faced and holding the pose until finally folding in half in laughter. "I'm gonna piss, then turn in for the night. 'K, Officer Flat Top?"

Scott shrugged an OK, raised his beer in gesture.

One Button turned from Scott to Ernie and gave another salute, though less official looking. "Good night, Officer Big Man's brother."

"Night." Ernie half-heartedly saluted back, more a quick touch to the temple and then lazy wave. He looked around, wondering if anyone else—Dreads, Surface Tension, the other guy—would follow One Button's lead or keep hanging out, but it was just him and Scott left watching the smoldering fire. Everyone else had already turned in, Ernie guessed, and he wondered when that had happened, why he hadn't noticed, like when you suddenly realize everyone else has left and you're the last one still at the party.

Ernie stared at the fire, wondering what to do with it. Did they have a bucket of water nearby? Just throw dirt on it? He tried to remember what he'd done in the past, but nothing came to mind. He couldn't remember the last time he'd been around a campfire, couldn't remember ever having put one out himself. Couldn't visualize any specific pre-bed, fire-pit procedure. He closed his eyes for a second, thinking, and started to feel himself drifting into sleep.

"You nervous?" His brother's voice startled him out of it before drifting further. "Or ... not nervous. Anxious?"

Ernie looked at Scott, confused. "What do you mean? Why do you ask?"

Scott shrugged. "I don't know. You look it, a little, I guess." Ernie became more aware of the confusion on his face, but he didn't change expression. He realized his brother had read his thinking of what to do about the fire as something else. "I mean ... it makes sense," Scott continued. "It's understandable. I probably would be. Are you hoping we see Becca? Or ... hoping we don't?" Ernie started to shake his head.

Ernie stared at his brother for a minute, trying now to figure out how to just say that he hadn't really thought of it. Scott looked different than Ernie had ever seen him before. Because he'd never seen him high before? That was probably a part of it. But there seemed something more too. "Wait," he broached. "Are *you* ... what did you ask me? Nervous? Anxious?"

Scott gave Ernie a long, controlled stare. Trying to figure out how Ernie could tell, how he knew to turn it back on Scott. Wondering how self-conscious he'd been when he'd asked Ernie, wondering if the question had really been confession. "I guess I am," he finally answered. He made a thoughtful face and nodded his head, kept nodding. "Yeah, I guess I am."

"About the conference?" Ernie looked at his brother. "No," he answered himself. "That's not it." He looked at his brother, trying to urge a further confession, but also trying to read his brother's look and guess it himself. He was proud of himself for what he'd already guessed at and figured out. He thought about all the questions Becca used to ask him, wondered how many of them were more confession than question.

"That's a little it," Scott said. "I'm not really looking forward to all the attention. But also ... I don't know." Scott looked around the campsite, over his shoulder in both directions, looking for what, Ernie wasn't sure. He shrugged before continuing. "I got into some trouble in Detroit once." He paused like he was going to continue but didn't.

"What do you mean, you 'got in trouble'?"

Scott rubbed his face with his huge hands, looked around but not at Ernie. "That's just it, kind of. I didn't get *in* trouble. I didn't get arrested or anything. No one ever found out, and I left, onto the next town, the next match, and they never found me. I don't know. Nobody knows, I don't think. But it kind of weighs on me. I mostly just never think about it anymore. So much so, I'm almost surprised when something reminds me. But now ... going back to Detroit ..."

It hung there. Ernie wondering if Scott wanted to be pushed and so he was letting him down, or he'd gotten as specific as he felt comfortable and so appreciated Ernie's dropping it. He'd convince himself it was one, and then immediately, the moment he felt a sense of certainty, that moment itself was like a switch that had been flipped and he'd start following a trail of belief in the other direction.

"Shit!" Scott blurted out of nowhere, shaking Ernie out of it. "I never called Holly. I shoulda checked in, told her we'd stopped to camp."

"I don't have any reception," Ernie answered. "Or, at least, I didn't earlier. I don't know about you."

Scott nodded. "Oh, yeah. Right. I didn't either. That's why I didn't tell her. I think I thought we'd go back into town for some food or something and I'd be able to tell her then. Shit."

"What do you think we do with this fire?" Ernie asked.

Scott looked at the burning coals like he'd forgotten they were there and shrugged. "Just leave it. It should burn itself out soon. Practically has already." He stood up, tossed the empty beer can he'd been holding and fidgeting with onto the coals, turned and started walking away from the campsite, back toward their own.

Ernie stood, followed. Leaving the hippies' campsite, he realized again just how dark it was; he remembered his earlier recalling of Benjamin, their adventures growing up, his wolfman fantasies.

He stopped, stared far up into the sky until he forgot what he was staring at or looking for or trying to figure out. The less he actually tried to look at the stars, the more he could see: the sky opening up and stars spilling out everywhere, multiplying. He refocused and found Pegasus—the four bright stars of a body, the lines of legs and neck and head, the wings having to be imagined. He could never even find the Big Dipper, but he must have been paying attention in Astronomy long enough to learn something, or at least enough for it to remind him of playing *Kid Icarus*, sometimes with Benjamin, sometimes with Scott, though he seemed to have no memories of the three of them playing video games together. He remembered Kid Icarus's search for the three sacred treasures: Mirror Shield, the Light Arrows, the Wings of Pegasus. He was surprised at the memory, that he still had that info ready to pull up, in place of so much more important or seemingly easier to remember info that he'd forgotten throughout his life.

Continuing on toward their campsite, they could see and separate most of the other sites still awake by their campfires, or at least other campfires in the last processes of burning themselves out while their campers slept. It reminded Ernie of other family trips growing up, visiting museums or fisheries, those maps where you push a button on an index to see a tiny bulb light up near the corresponding city or river. One button lit up the drinking and music-playing campsite they just left; over there was the site they'd passed with a group of older guys sitting around their fire, mostly not talking, fishing rods leaned up against their van reminding him of the guys in *Shortcuts* who go fishing and find the dead girl; beyond them, the family of four: the parents who'd been trying to show the young son and daughter the perfect shade of brown to strive for with toasted marshmallow, the son seeming to most like it when his caught fire and went up in flame.

12.

"This is gonna be fun," Scott said, aloud but as much for himself as Ernie. "*In search of America.*"

Ernie wasn't sure what had prompted the claim, what made today any different than yesterday. Yesterday, they hadn't talked much, had mostly just driven in silence, but it had gone fast, all of a sudden they were up and over the Cascades, through Eastern Washington, already in mountains again in Idaho. It had been a full day but had seemed like nothing. Maybe day two was when *driving* turned into a *roadtrip*.

"In search of America," Scott said again, a little more enthusiastically. Ernie, still moving and thinking a little slower than normal, a little hungover. Scott, on the other hand, seemed fine. *More* energetic, if anything. Which seemed unfair—granted Scott was ... what, twice his size, but he was the drinker. Come to think of it, he couldn't remember Scott having a drink since he'd moved in. "Journey to the savage heart of it!" Scott continued, and Ernie shot him a slightly confused, *what the fuck* look. "Baptism by fire!"

"What?" he said, dropping his *the fuck*.

"You know ... baptism by fire. New adventures. Let's throw ourselves into the ... what's the word I'm looking for?"

Ernie shrugged. "I have no idea what you're talking about."

"Like ... a big oven. For glass blowing, or pottery, or ... furnace! We're throwing ourselves into the furnace and will just see what happens!"

"Isn't it '*trial*' by fire?"

"Is it? That sounds right too." Scott thought about it. "Maybe they're both sayings? Doesn't really matter. Baptism, trial. Same thing. The American dream, Ern!" He smiled big and goofy, and Ernie couldn't do anything but agree.

"Sure."

Outside, a long canopy of trees surrounded them. Like they'd been transported into the middle of a forest while not paying attention, while trying to figure out the right idiom for whatever it was they were embarking on. The drive was nothing but green, and Ernie surveyed all the trees, the wide open everywhere. It looked like somewhere Sasquatch might be able to hide, something he'd always thought about when little, not really believing but still keeping close watch out his window whenever driving through thick woods, on their way to or home from camping or fishing. His dad would be doing the same, for wildlife, deer usually, but a couple times they saw elk, and he'd stop the car, direct his sons' attention through the woods toward the animal. Even just seeing some deer, especially a big buck with antlers both ancient and otherworldly, seemed almost like magic, and the elk more mythic and magical still, making the leap to Sasquatch or a wolfman not seem all that ridiculous.

Ernie looked out at all that wilderness and pictured Benjamin as a wolfman—covered in hair, snarling, clawing the air, running through the trees and living off the land, or however a wolfman might live.

"Whoa!" Scott blurted, and for a split-second, Ernie thought maybe he'd seen it, Sasquatch, or maybe Benjamin himself. Then he feared maybe Scott had gotten preoccupied looking out into the woods, watching for movement himself, or maybe just zoned out, and was veering into the other lane of traffic and an oncoming car, or the other direction, off the road and into a head-on collision with a tree.

Ahead of them, and seemingly out of nowhere, the trees parted and everything opened up, bright and infinite. It felt a little like waking up. Like seeing a matinee and exiting the theater back into daylight after a lifetime of evening shows, the opposite of the surprise at how fast it had gotten dark the night before. Scott pushed down a little harder on the accelerator, his seat feeling a little more comfortable, the drive a little smoother, the SUV suddenly a little more like their own and not just something they'd rented for the drive. Ernie rolled down his window and dropped out his arm, caught the wind in his cupped palm. The air smelled like summer, the mix of evergreens and sun and blue skies.

Ernie recalled Scott's "search for America" and thought maybe he was right, this was it. They were doing it. He'd agreed to the trip not because of any desire to return to Michigan but just *because*. Because he had no reason not to, because it seemed like Scott wanted him to go, because why not? But wasn't this what roadtrips were supposed to be? Revelatory and epiphanic and life-changing and life-answering and everything else about life that he was searching for, everything he thought the farm might be able to be and was now believing a cross country roadtrip was *definitely* going to be. There was a simplicity to the moment—two guys driving, taking their time, without consequence. They had a schedule but one that afforded plenty of time and so didn't require rushing or stress. At least for the time being, Ernie had no job to hurry back to, and this kind of *was* Scott's job, he realized. A part of the job that was affording him not having to have a job, to be able to refocus his time and energy toward his impending fatherhood, making this a kind of *gap trip*, his travel between jobs, and Ernie got regretful for not the first time that he hadn't himself taken a gap year between high school and college. He got nostalgic for what could have been, and while Scott didn't *technically* take one either, his whole life had practically acted as one, and Ernie got, for nowhere near the first time, jealous, which then segued into resentful. But then, maybe actually for the first time, he caught himself—he squeezed himself around the idea and then released, letting it go, letting himself go. He redirected his attention back out the window, to the sun and the trees and the smell of roadtrip sweeping in the open windows and all through the car, and smiled. He felt either more like himself than he had in a long time or less, depending on what was actually his "self." Either way, he felt *good.*

"Oh. Hey," Ernie finally spoke up. "Probably goes without saying, but you ever want to switch it up, just let me know. I'd be happy to drive, give you a little respite." He paused. "Is that how you say it? Ree-spite? Rezpit?"

Scott shrugged his shoulders. "One of those. Something like that."

"You know what I mean though. A little break."

"Right. Thanks." Scott realized he hadn't considered the possibility. It could be nice to keep moving but not be behind the wheel. Getting to watch the road from the passenger seat, not have to worry about traffic or other drivers. "Thanks," he repeated. "I'm good now, but I'll let you know."

A few more silent miles down the road, Ernie reached out and turned on the radio. They were long out of the reach of any of the car's preset stations, if it even had any, and who knew what city someone may have set them for, but he cycled through them anyway, thinking one might share a signal with something local. The first five were nothing but static, then the sixth snagged something out of the airwaves and reeled it in, getting louder and more clean as it pulled. He rolled his window back up to be able to better hear, and recognized it.

"You ever play any roadtrip games?" Scott asked.

"What do you mean?"

"Like, you know how there's that saying, 'There are two kinds of people: those who like *this* and those who like *that*'?"

"I don't know what that means."

"Like, there are those who like these guys"—he pointed at the radio—"and those who like The Beatles. Everyone is one or the other, right? Stones or Beatles. You know, cat people and dog people."

"How's that a game?"

"I don't know. I guess not a *game* technically. Just something we used to do when sharing drives between gigs. We'd just try to find different either/ors. We'd come up with one and then try to guess which person the other was. Or we'd put everyone we knew into one category or the other. It just passes the time." He shrugged like he didn't care one way or another, it was just an idea, but Ernie could tell he wanted to play.

Ernie thought about it, listened to the song on the radio. "I guess I like Zeppelin better really."

"Sure. But they aren't an option. Not your *favorite*, but who do you prefer. Between these two?"

Ernie nodded his head along to Jagger crooning that he couldn't always get what he wanted. "The Stones, I guess?"

"Yeah, that's right."

Ernie wasn't sure what Scott meant. Was there a *right* answer? Right because Scott knew Ernie better than he did, knew that The Rolling Stones were his preference when he himself wasn't sure? Or *right* like Scott agreed? Like having the same answer was the *right* answer. He was a little surprised they'd shared any preference, having always assumed they were pretty much opposites. What if they never really got along not because they had nothing in common but too much in common?

"The Beatles."

"What?"

"I'm The Beatles. You knew that right? I was just saying it anyway, I guess."

That answered that.

"What else," Ernie asked, already a little into it.

Scott watched everything wash by outside. "*On the Road* or *Fear and Loathing*?"

"I don't know. I haven't read either."

"What?"

"You have? When? Don't people read those in school or something? You dropped out."

"Exactly. I think people usually read them *when* in school but not *for* school. I read a bunch in those years after I dropped out. Everything. All that shit that I feared I was missing out on by dropping out of school, I read on my own. I just spent that year working out and reading. You know ... training both body and mind, that cheesy bullshit." He smiled, beating Ernie to it. Knowing Ernie was probably thinking it, though probably wouldn't say it.

"Right. I guess *I* should have been the one who read them, if for school. But I was too busy reading the ... bullshit"—volleying the word back—"they made us read instead."

"Too bad. You read the wrong required 19-year-old reading. 'We were somewhere around Barstow on the edge of the desert when the drugs began to take hold,'" Scott surprised himself by still remembering.

Ernie waited for Scott to keep going, but that was it.

Scott was thinking, almost in his own version of *Ernie's World* but not quite. He'd tried to think of the next sentence, something about feeling lightheaded, and then bats, bats circling, screaming, divebombing the car. Then an inventory of all those drugs in the trunk, and then Scott was back to that *Dead Wrestler* website, all those deaths, so many drug-related, and the same sadness as when he was in the café swallowed him. Maybe he should try to use this video game as an opportunity to talk about ... drugs? Safety in wrestling? He hadn't ever really been one for a cause, but maybe this was why he'd been given this opportunity.

"I don't know," Ernie said. He knew Scott wouldn't accept it as an answer, but how was he supposed to decide between two unknowns?

"Yeah. I'm not sure either," Scott answered. "Probably too soon to tell. Maybe we'll table that one." He watched out the window, then started bobbing his head and bouncing his feet to whatever song had taken over from the chorus that had taken over for Jagger's remindering. He thought it was that one song that he always thought was Zeppelin but was actually some guy or band he could never remember, but maybe that was a different song and this was just another oldies classic that sounded familiar but he didn't really know.

Then the radio went to commercial, and Ernie cycled through the presets again, found nothing. He hit the scan button, let the numbers tick by until they grabbed a station, paused for a few seconds, then went ticking forward again until the next signal. He watched Scott watching the radio and could tell he was thinking. Trying to work out what he wanted to say before he started. The way the numbers clicked through reminded Ernie of watching a pledge drive, and then he thought of high scores and collecting coins in *Mario* and *The Legend of Zelda*, going to the fairy pond when low on energy and getting your hearts filled. He got nostalgic thinking about the game, all the time he'd spent playing it as a kid, and suddenly he was back in Benjamin's basement, working their way through Hyrule toward Gannon, still too young to be interested in girls or much else non-video-game.

"What about ..." Ernie started, and waited until Scott looked at him, curious. "Orange juice: with pulp or without?"

"With," Scott said. "Lots. Farmer style."

Ernie made a face. "What about peanut butter: crunchy or creamy?"

"Crunchy. Extra crunchy."

Another face—part surprise, part disgust, but not really either.

"What if ..." Ernie started, thinking of a wrinkle. "What if someone doesn't have a preference? Like, what if they don't even like peanut butter? Crunchy or creamy wouldn't really make a difference."

"Everyone has a preference. Sometimes people like to say they don't, but I don't believe in that." The authority with which he said it surprised Ernie. "Even if you don't like two things, you don't like one of them more than the other. Which do you dislike less?"

"What if you're allergic to peanuts?"

Scott sat quiet, thought about that. The radio kept scanning, pausing on a station barely long enough for them to try to recognize the song before again scanning to the next station.

"I guess they're the exception," Scott finally figured out. "Maybe there is always a third group: the exceptions, and they don't really count. Like a control group or the exception that proves the rule or something?"

Scott thought about it some more then nodded, pleased with his reasoning. "Some people might claim to be the exception, but they're really just indecisive. So I think that gets tricky."

"Sure," Ernie agreed. He wondered if Scott meant that as dig. *Some people claim ... really just indecisive.*

"I think there's something to this though. I think these either/ors are bigger than they seem. I think, if you analyze it, what someone chooses says a lot about that person. More than just a preference. I bet if you found the perfect series of combinations, they'd tell you everything you needed to know about someone."

"Like a personality test?"

"Exactly! Like a personality test. Like that ... Briggs Myers. Is that what it's called?"

Ernie shrugged. "I have no idea."

"Sure you do. You know, businesses sometimes make you take one, or you can do one online for free. Like you're an Introvert or Extrovert, Thinking or Feeling, all those letter combos. I don't remember them all. I think it was Briggs Myers. Something like that. Actually ... I guess that's exactly what this is." He was a little disappointed with the realization, that it wasn't simile so much as synonym. But maybe not exactly. Maybe there was something else slightly here. "For example," Scott continued, "there are two kinds of people: those who hit the scan button on a radio, then hit it again as soon as it hits a halfway decent station, and those who let it keep scanning through the channels, over and over."

"What if I was just waiting for you to stop it on a station. Being nice isn't indicative of a whole outlook on life."

"First of all"—Scott held up his index finger, like he was counting—"I didn't mean *you* you. I was just saying. I'm making this up as I go here. Second"—index and middle finger—"he who starts the scan must stop it, man." He laughed, realizing he'd at some point slipped into some kind of mocking-the-hippies-of-the-night-before voice. *Maaaan.* "And lastly"—for some reason, back to just the index finger—"being nice is totally ... what did you say? 'Representative of a whole life'? Totally."

"And if someone doesn't ever use the scan button at all?"

"See? You're totally what I was talking about! You're trying to be the exception or the control or whatever. But I don't think it matters if you actually use the scan button or not. If you *had* to, how would you use it. You know? Or, maybe it isn't even directly related to just 'scanning.' It's the way you listen to the radio—whether you hit the scan or keep hitting preset station buttons or just go through the stations manually, same thing. Do you not stop on The Beatles, even though it is better than … better than whatever stations keep getting stopped on before moving on?"

"It's been country mostly."

"Right, do you not stop on The Beatles even though it's better than all these country songs—"

"I kinda like country."

Scott shot his brother a look. "You haven't stopped it on any of them."

"I said kinda."

Scott laughed. "Don't get caught up on that though. Insert whatever you want. R&B stations, or political talk, or Top 40, or Christian radio. Same thing. Do you not stop on the thing that's good but you don't love, like The Beatles, because you're hoping the next station might be The Stones. Or Zeppelin. Or '90s rock."

"'90s rock?"

Scott smiled. "Or whatever. Same concepts apply."

"Like the campsite? Like how I said we should circle and look at everything instead of choosing the first great one that we ended up in?"

"Right. Though I hadn't even thought of that. But maybe that actually even proves this. Or supports it at least."

"And each of these either/or choices means something deeper?"

Scott nodded what Ernie thought seemed like too much. "I think we just proved that."

"Stones or Beatles?"

"Oh, totally. 'Street Fighting Man' vs. 'Let it Be'? That says it all." Scott paused, like considering his own statement. He agreed with that more than he'd even realized when saying it. "That might be all you need to know about someone. Probably tells you more than how they listen to the radio."

"Crunchy or creamy peanut butter?"

"More important still!"

Ernie laughed at that, and Scott smiled to have made his brother finally give in to the fun of it all. "Or you know. That one might just be preference."

They both went quiet, thought about Scott's theory on their own. Ernie pushed in the power knob, turned off the radio. Rolled his window down again.

Ernie looked at their atlas, tried to approximate where they likely were. There looked to be a town not too much further. The size of the dot on the map, he guessed, meant it should be big enough for at least a couple different food options.

"You hungry? Want to stop and eat something soon?"

"I could eat," Scott answered. "Wherever you want."

"I'm going to get, like, four burgers," Scott said. "Maybe five." Then, "Two kinds of people," as if the conversation had never lulled. Ernie expected something like "meat eaters and vegetarians," but instead: "Those who order a hamburger when at a hamburger joint—" Scott stopped, not only his idea but walking too, as if thinking about it was so important as to not be able to do two things at once. "Hmm. What's the other option? Chicken?"

"Nobody calls me chicken."

"What? What are you talking about? I didn't call you chicken. Burger or chicken *sandwich*—those are the options, right?"

"No, I was just kidding. You know ... 'What's wrong, McFly? *Chicken*?'"

"Sure," Scott said, though he didn't really. "Right. Anyway. I bet you're thinking of getting the chicken, aren't you?"

A part of Ernie wanted to *Are you calling me chicken?* Scott again, but he didn't get it the first time around, and so a second attempt would just be awkward. Which is part of why he wanted to, but he held it in. Further, he *was* actually but immediately reconsidered. What did chicken, as opposed to a hamburger, say about his "outlook on life"? He loved homemade burgers, getting them just right and slow-cooking on the barbeque, but almost never ordered them when out. Sometimes at a bar and grill, but never fast food. Becca never ordered a burger, bar and grill or fast food, but always loved and complimented Ernie's grilling, part of why he enjoyed making them so much. For the sake of the roadtrip and new beginnings, and maybe a little for the sake of spiting Becca, shouldn't he switch it up, go with the opposite of his impulse?

"I don't know," Ernie said. "I figured I'd look at the menu, then decide."

"Sure," Scott said and smirked. Ernie thought he could see him thinking, *those who know what they want as soon as they stop for food, and those who need to consider the menu.*

"What about chicken strips?" Ernie asked. "Or something like nuggets, if they have them?"

"Same thing. Burger or chicken. Doesn't have to be a chicken sandwich. Or maybe it's even burger or everything else. Like, if they have fish sandwiches, or whatever else. *Salad*," he added, almost disgusted.

Ernie stopped and bought a local paper from the vending box outside the entrance, thinking if his brother wanted to keep expanding on his theory and dividing the world in two, he could at least tune him out for a minute and read the funnies or do the crossword. Becca would have bought the *USA Today*, read the State-by-State page, so he opted for the local. They went inside, and, no one else in line, the register girl immediately asked if she could help them, if they knew what they wanted. Without needing to look at the menu, Scott repeated to her what Ernie thought had been exaggeration: "Four burgers please. And a large drink, large fries."

"I'll have the same," Ernie said, feeling rushed, too self-conscious to take the time to look up at the menu on the wall. "Except ... only two burgers. And medium for the drink and fries."

In the booth, Scott reached across and grabbed the sports section from Ernie and started reading full articles like he was a local, like he knew all the high school athletes personally. "You know, I actually normally get chicken. Or a salad!" Scott laughed at his own ridiculousness. "Never fries! This is probably gonna be the worst meal I've eaten in a while. Definitely. Unhealthiest-worst, I mean. But ... when in Rome! When on the road! Don't tell the video game guys."

Ernie looked at his brother, trying to tell if he was kidding or not. Did those guys care, did they want Scott to keep up some kind of Mr. Bison physique? Ernie wasn't sure. He skimmed the comics and the entertainment page, then flipped through everything else. They ate in silence broken only by Scott's occasional "hmm" grunt whenever he must have found something especially interesting or curious.

Ernie scanned headlines and first lines and flipped the paper around, mostly folding and refolding it into various configurations to take up the smallest space and make it as easy to read as possible while eating in the booth. He looked up and across at Scott, who looked oblivious to anything but his burgers and the sports page. Ernie made his own "hmm" grunt and brought his hand to his chin in what he thought was an obvious and universal sign for "ask me what I just read so I can tell you about it," but nothing.

Back down on the table in front of him, Ernie saw he'd finished everything he'd ordered without realizing it, some kind of pure hand-to-mouth hunger instinct. He looked down at his tray, surprised, then over at Scott, still fascinated at some local kid's recent heroics over the neighboring town's rival high school, or whatever he was reading. Ernie thought about how he'd probably never read a newspaper recap of a high school game, even when the kids had familiar names, had sat next to him in homeroom. He'd never been to a high school event, not when in high school himself, and not in any of the years since, not even to watch his brother play.

"Be right back," he said, and Scott finally looked up, smiled and nodded.

"'K," Ernie heard his brother say behind him. He was already standing, making his way to the trash. He threw away the wrappers and his empty cup and left the tray on top of the garbage, years of eating fast food having trained him to know where to put it. He went out to the car, grabbed the atlas from behind the passenger seat; he grabbed his phone from the door—still not blinking, still no messages—and put it back. Took the atlas back inside, spread it out on his half of the booth where his tray had been. Pretty early in the drive, Ernie had started to turn on the car's navigation, but Scott stopped him. "We don't need that," he'd said. "I brought an atlas. Reach back, it's right behind my seat. Navigation can be helpful, but the atlas is better. You can see it all at once, it's better. It's what we want." And Scott had been right: Ernie had already consulted it a handful of times on the drive, he liked the physicality of it.

Ernie found where they'd camped last night, traced his finger east for what seemed like the few hours' worth of driving they'd done, connecting last night to the small town he presumed they were now in. Ran his finger from one to the other and back again, not sure what he was looking for but feeling calmed by the back and forth.

Scott stopped reading, looked over at Ernie's fidgeting. He nodded. "That looks about right." He started to take another bite, then paused. "Hey. Lemme see that for a sec."

Ernie swung the atlas around 180 degrees, pushed it toward his brother.

"I don't know why I didn't realize this, but we're gonna drive right through Yellowstone. We gotta stop there, right? Now that we're professional campers!"

Ernie shrugged.

"And the buffalo! We can see the buffalo! It'll make a good story at the convention. Like it was meant to be. We can't be this close, and have time to spare, and not stop at Yellowstone."

"How far's that look?"

"I don't know. Tomorrow?"

"Yellowstone!" Ernie said, smiling big, excited. "I've never been!"

13.

Holly was going stir-crazy.

<I'm going crazy.> she texted Scott.

<Everything ok?> came back quicker than expected, almost immediate. She was pretty sure they were on the road. Maybe they'd stopped for food? Maybe Ernie was driving?

<Yeah, yeah. Just ... My parents :p> Holly felt a little bad as soon as she hit send. Her parents had come to help. *Were*, in fact, helping. And here she was, complaining. Here she was bothering her husband's roadtrip with her whiny complaint.

<Haha. Maybe a little time alone? :)> Scott replied, taking a little longer this time.

<Yeah, maybe. You two having fun?>

<Yep!>

Holly waited for a little more—what were they doing? were they stopped somewhere, was Ernie driving, where were they?—but didn't want to press.

A little time alone. She hadn't really considered that, despite it being the obvious answer. When they'd first moved in together, Holly had struggled with the change. She'd worried, at first, that it was a sign their couplehood wasn't meant to be; worried what it said about Scott, or herself, or *them*. They'd tried to be preemptive, to talk through the expected struggles as productively as possible, but the struggles had persisted regardless. It's hard to prepare for the unknown, Scott would assure her, when she'd get frustrated. When she'd ask why it had to be so hard, when she'd remind them both aloud that they'd *tried* to prepare.

In fact, they'd largely prepared for Scott to struggle with the change. He'd miss the road, the independence, his entire lifestyle, she was sure. Just the opposite, he'd assure her. I've gotten it out of my system. I'm ready for this!

And he had been. Holly herself? A little less, it turned out.

Holly remembered this now, this uncertainty they'd gone through, the struggle of navigating that uncertainty. She thought of the baby, their baby, *Billy* ... the complete and almost overwhelming uncertainty of approaching new parentdom, but reminded herself that they would struggle and navigate through uncertainty *together*.

One of the joys of their life together was just that, *being together,* but one of their discoveries was also the joys and necessity of time apart. Of being alone. It had taken them a while to figure this out, longer still to find the perfect balance, but they believed it was the secret to their marriage. To marriage period, they'd sometimes proselytize, while other times believing maybe each marriage had its own secret and this was just theirs.

She hadn't once gone stir-crazy at the farm since moving in, despite their lack of cable TV, internet, neighbors. Her parents *were* driving her crazy, but, she reasoned, it was less them, specifically, more a need to be alone, in general, to not be waited on, to not move through the house like someone in need of constant care and attention. This realization immediately made her feel better. Better that it wasn't the farm making her feel cooped up, or being pregnant, better about telling her parents she was going to go out for the day, *alone*, not because of them but because of her, a distinction she wouldn't share but one that made her feel less guilty about the decision.

"I'm going to go into the city," Holly called out from the living room. Her mom was in the kitchen, preparing something for dinner. Holly wasn't sure what needed to be done for dinner so soon after they'd just had lunch, but that was her mom. She wasn't sure where her dad was. Out walking with Billy maybe?

"You need one of us to go into town to get you something? Your dad can—"

"No, no. I'm good. I'm just ..." Holly paused. "I'm going a little stir-crazy, I think." She forced a laugh. "Thought it'd be fun to go into the city, maybe see Julie."

"Oh, how is she these days?"

"She's good. She's on maternity leave actually. Thought I'd maybe go get some pointers," Holly found herself saying, surprising herself.

"You want us to go with? I could be done here—"

"No, no. I'm feeling great. You guys stay here. Relax. Watch after Billy, make sure he doesn't get into any trouble." Another laugh.

"You sure?"

"Yeah, Mom. I'll be fine, I promise. I'll text you when I get there," she added, smiling, thinking of when she'd ride her bike to Elizabeth's when she was little, how she'd have to call her mom as soon as she got there.

Holly got off the freeway, already there. Their world had become so strange—they lived on a farm! they had a *buffalo*!—but also so insular. Holly realized she'd actually forgotten how close they still were to Seattle. The proximity was one of the selling points of the farm, a best of both worlds—the city still less than an hour away and at the same time a whole other world. But then, they hadn't been back since they'd moved. They'd talked about it, but the pull was less than they'd assumed. They had everything they needed, a calmer, slower life. Holly realized she hadn't once missed it since moving onto the farm, and yet, now, as soon as pulling off the freeway, she did. Visiting Julie had never been the plan, there had never been a plan at all, though she'd considered it once she'd blurted it to her mom. Then she got on the freeway, and heading north into Lynnwood held no pull. *Into the city*, she'd told her mom, and that was where she was headed.

She drove past Safeco, past … Seahawk Stadium. She couldn't remember the corporate name for it. Had never been to a football game. She thought of her dad taking her to games at the Kingdome growing up. Bonding over shared "the Mariners were horrible, and dear God so was that dome" stories were some of her strongest memories of her and Scott's early dates. She thought of taking her mitt to the games, she thought of the time all the children in attendance got to come onto the field after the game and run the bases. She thought ahead, to taking Little Billy to his first game. She pictured Scott arguing in favor of the Tacoma Rainiers, the Everett Aquasox. She thought of …

A horn honked, and Holly looked up, saw the green light turn yellow. She put her foot on the gas, sped through the light she'd apparently just sat through almost entirely. Maybe that's what happened to Ernie, she thought. Where he goes. Driving through Seattle, thinking back on going to baseball games with her dad, thinking ahead to games with her son … it seemed an easier slide than she'd previously realized.

She drove up and down blocks, cycling through memories. *Pike Place*, she thought, realizing feeling like a tourist here in the city seemed appealing. Maybe she'd get some fish to take home, they could throw it on the grill for dinner. Then she pictured herself walking through the crowd, herself and her belly, and it seemed less appealing. She kept driving, past what used to be the Lusty Lady marquee. She and her girlfriends had always talked about going in college. How funny it'd be, how they'd make a night of it. She tried thinking of any of the double entendres the place had used on their marquee over the years, but drew a blank. She thought how funny it had always seemed, walking through the Seattle Art Museum across the street—art, art, art, window, and through the window? A strip club.

That was it, Holly realized. She should go to the art museum. The same, or at least a similar, tourist appeal as Pike Place, but without the crowds, the chaos.

On the upper floor of the museum, a traveling exhibit: *The Rise of Sneaker Culture.* Throughout the exhibit, a gamut of tennis shoes, a near-history of track shoe development, Run-DMC's Adidas, a variety of Air Jordans, some early Reebok Pumps that Holly remembered so pining for when she was little. She didn't play basketball, didn't especially care about shoes, and they had been marketed almost entirely to boys, but something about them had grabbed her desire and not let go. Every time she saw a commercial, she thought they looked so *cool.*

Holly got out her phone to tell Scott where she was, saw she had three texts waiting for her from her mom:

<You get there ok?>

<Tell Julie we say hi!>

<Haven't heard anything from you. Just checking in to make sure you got there safe! You're probably just having fun, not looking at your phone. Let us know when you see this.>

She wanted her mom to know she was fine, she'd gotten to Seattle just fine, but didn't want to text her. Didn't want to check in. Didn't want to *have to*. And now, phone in hand but wishing it weren't, she didn't really want to text Scott either. Maybe he'd not reply right away—maybe he was driving again now, maybe Ernie still was but they were just enjoying their roadtrip and she didn't want to disturb him—and she didn't want to be the one checking in, the one making someone else feel like they needed to reply.

Holly returned her phone to her purse, thought of teaching. She thought of putting her phone away in her desk to minimize the possibility of distraction. She thought of her "The Body" deer scene lesson plan, one of her favorites of the year. One of her gimme days—it always went well enough to feel like a success, and she'd done it enough, felt natural enough guiding discussion, that it required no planning or prep work, and yet each class found something new to add every year, something small, but unique enough to their individual class to make it always feel fresh, exciting.

She was going to miss her students in the fall, she realized for the first time since asking her school about the possibility of taking a year off. A kind of sabbatical, she'd presented it as. There would be plenty she wouldn't miss, of course, but even some of those challenges, she would. Teaching both aged her and kept her young, she liked to tell friends whenever she found herself in the kinds of discussions where everyone had to talk and find something pithy to say about their jobs. The stresses were exhausting, endless; more often than not, it was like she herself was a student and one with never-ending homework. But some of those same stresses, the challenges underneath them ... they kept her young. The students found new ways to make her rethink what she'd previously not considered, they never let her get lazy or complacent in her thinking. Also, the aspect of teaching she believed to possibly be her own greatest strength was just talking to them like both their teacher and friend. She'd leaned too heavily in one direction when she'd started, belying who she was to try to be who she thought a teacher was supposed to be, and then swinging back too far the other way, overcorrecting and at times undermining her own authority, until finally finding and striking that balance, one of the aspects of her own life she was most proud of.

Looking around at the exhibit, Holly realized that, were she teaching in the fall, this exhibit would become part of her pedagogy. She'd tell her students about coming, would ask them stories about their own shoes.

Holly read the display case labels for the Reebok Pump, the Nike Air, the first Air Jordan. Each specified the year, the materials used, the shoe designer. She wandered from one case to another. Nikes with the waffle sole, the first Air Jordan with the Jumpman logo. There was a display case with Converse—the originals used for basketball, the first to be called "All Stars," the first to include Chuck Taylor's name.

She wandered through the exhibit, read more labels. The more she wandered, the less she read. The exhibit was interesting, though a little less so than she'd imagined. A little less than she'd hoped. She was maybe halfway through the history of the sneaker, wondering at her own disappointment. Was there something *better* she'd hoped for or just something *else*?

"This is my favorite, come look, come look!" A young girl had grabbed her hand, was pulling her toward ... toward whatever shoe was her favorite, Holly assumed. She wondered if this young girl read her as teacher and so she felt comfortable around her or was just generally so excited she couldn't contain herself, had to share her excitement with whoever was nearest.

The girl pulled her toward a case with what looked like almost any other hightop basketball shoe but spray-painted in gold.

"That all-gold shoe?" the girl said, like a question, but one she wasn't asking. "If that shoe," she pointed at the gold one, "had the spikes from that one?" and she pointed at another. "Oooooooooooh!"

Holly smiled, the girl's excitement infectious. "Those would be something special."

"I'd pay *anything* for that!" the girl said, and Holly couldn't contain her laugh.

And then, as suddenly as the girl had appeared, as out of nowhere as she was suddenly holding Holly's hand, pulling her to her *favorite*, the girl was gone, maybe showing someone else her other favorite, maybe onto a new exhibit altogether, maybe finally retrieved and corralled by a parent.

Holly felt disappointed in herself—disappointed she couldn't reach, much less sustain, the enthusiasm of the young girl; disappointed that, before the girl had grabbed her hand and tugged her across the room, she'd been considering her own lack of enthusiasm for the exhibit.

Suddenly, Holly realized what she'd been hoping for, whether she'd realized it or not. Probably she hadn't. The labels for each shoe gave a little info, a little context but, she realized, she wanted a bit more history. The whole exhibit was arranged in more-or-less chronological order, but she wanted, she was curious about, even more of a through line. *How* one shoe evolved into another. *Why*?

The *narrative of it*, she realized, and felt a quick almost pang at this tendency of hers to so often come back to that, but then a relief, a small sense of joy. Not quite to the level of the girl wanting one day to own a pair of spiked, all-gold high-tops, but a pleasure in figuring something out. She had been a little disappointed in the exhibit, and the root of that disappointment hadn't been obvious, but she'd found a solution instead of just letting it go unsolved.

That, perhaps even more than that it kept her young, more than her pride in the balance of her teacher persona, was what she liked about teaching: treating it like a puzzle. Figuring out the optimal order of events—daily lesson plan, building into a week, collecting into a full semester—so that it all flowed as smoothly as possible. Unlocking a way to talk about a book that would most connect to her students. Having a problem, struggling, considering different options, running into dead ends along the way, and then finally finding a solution. She was an English teacher, but it was the same feeling as cleanly solving a hard math equation. Putting that last puzzle piece into place, solving a Sudoku or Kenken, beating a video game.

How to Steal

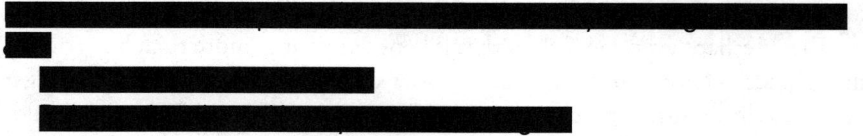

14.

"This is the one," Scott said, pointing from the passenger seat, Ernie having taken over after the burger stop so Scott could play lookout.

It was the first hotel they'd passed after exiting the highway, but Scott had urged to keep going, same let's-just-see-what's-ahead, just-in-case mentality that had made them loop through the whole campground of sites before returning to the first that had looked good just the day before, the same mentality Scott had been dissecting on the road before they'd stopped for food. "I know," he'd said, answering the look Ernie shot him. "This is different." He'd paused. "Or maybe it isn't. I don't know. Maybe sometimes wanting to know all your options before deciding is just an excuse to not make a decision, but other times it's an important part of the decision-making process." He'd thought about that, not knowing where exactly it came from, but it sounded smarter than he'd realized as soon as it was out of his mouth. He'd shrugged. And so Ernie had kept driving, past Quality Inn, Super 8, Best Western, Comfort Inn. Kentucky Fried Chicken, Applebee's. Red Roof Inn. Taco Bell. Ernie followed the road all the way until almost out of town, whatever town this was that felt like almost every other town they'd driven through or past. Far enough to be sure there weren't any more hotels beyond one more turn or over one more hill. Finally, Scott said, "That looks like everything. I think that first place was the one." Of course it was, Ernie thought, though he wasn't sure if the reaction was directed toward Scott, or himself, or where.

Ernie pulled into the parking lot, started to park in front of the entrance.

"No, no," Scott said. "Not here. Where would you park if we were actually staying here?"

"Not right here?" Ernie asked. They were stopped mid-park, the front corner of Sunny peeking into the spot, but the rest of her not following, still stuck in limbo. Ernie had given the SUV a name nearly as soon as he'd taken over driving, the name springing to him more like they'd made introductions than like he'd given it to her, though he hadn't yet said the name aloud, hadn't shared the naming with Scott.

"Not here," Scott agreed, shaking his head.

Ernie ran Scott's question over again in his head. Where would I park if we were staying at this hotel? He tried to imagine them staying here, on vacation together, or maybe some kind of business trip. Ernie had never been anywhere for work, had never had to travel to any kind of conference, only knew of "business trips" in the most abstract of ways. He flashed to thinking of his brother's old life, traveling from city to city, staying in hotels like this every night. At the time, he'd thought of Scott's wrestling as ridiculous, as an immature phase he'd grow out of (which, Ernie sometimes thought proudly, self-righteously, he had; never mind that it was now in essence paying for this trip, nearly the entirety of their current lives), but thinking about it now, he wondered if Scott hadn't figured out a few things he himself never had. Ernie had followed such a straighter line connecting then to now, believing that's what one was supposed to do, but where had that gotten him?

"Where would we park ..." Ernie said aloud, interrupting his own digressing train of thought, "if we'd checked in yesterday? Like, we went out for lunch and now are coming back to our room ..."

He kept his foot held down on the brake, keeping them parked where they were and closed his eyes to picture the scenario. What would we have been doing, what would Scott and I do if on an actual trip together? he asked himself, as if the idea were ridiculous, as if that weren't exactly what they were in the middle of at the very moment. Would this be the kind of town we'd make a pit stop in? This the kind of hotel we'd stay at? What was there to do in this town? Would we go out in the morning and just do ... touristy things?

"Drive past the pool first," Scott said, and Ernie put Sunny in reverse, went to find and drive past the pool, on their way to finding their actual parking spot. "Do a whole loop around the place, maybe even. Let's check it all out. But don't make it seem suspicious. Rule number three: know your surroundings."

Rule number *three*? Ernie wondered what these rules were—was there one big set of rules for everything or different sets for different situations? Was this rule number three for life or for parking at a hotel? What were rules number one and two? Had Scott already said and he'd forgotten? Somewhere on the drive between the farm and here, at some point over the fire, drinking and smoking with the hippies? Had he not been paying attention? Or could Scott have said "number three" to be funny, to not give it all the importance of being one of the first two?

Ernie drove past the pool.

"What are you looking for?"

"I don't know," Ernie said. "The pool? Where our room would be?"

"Do you have your own towel?" Scott asked. Ernie knew his brother knew they didn't. He shook his head. "OK, then. Do *they* have towels, and if so, where are they? What's the entry situation like: locked, open, do you need a room key, is there some way to subvert that?" *Subvert?* Ernie thought. "How many people are there? What's the sightline from, say, the front office?"

"OK. Yeah, sure," Ernie agreed, though unsure to what exactly.

"And?" Scott looked at Ernie, waiting for something. Waiting for what? "How's it all look?"

"Um ... good? Just a couple of people. The office was way up there, so I don't think—"

Scott interrupted with his laugh, grabbing his belly and smiling big. "Don't worry about that shit, Ern. You're overthinking it. You think some minimum-wage worker here gives a shit whether we swim in their pool or not? Just don't make it too obvious, don't rub it in their face and make them feel like they *have* to notice us, you know? Let's park." He motioned forward, vaguely, but Ernie suddenly felt oddly sure he knew the exact space. Like he could finally picture it: they'd checked in late last night, walked the long walk through the hotel to their room, got up this morning in time for the continental breakfast then went out to explore the town, had lunch at the local burger joint, drove around a little more, and now were returning for a nice afternoon swim. Instead of parking near the front door and walking through the lobby to their room at the far end of the hall, like they had the night before when checking in, he drove around to the back corner of the lot, next to the side entrance nearest their room.

"Perfect," Scot confirmed, and Ernie felt a pang of pride and then something like guilt for caring about impressing his brother. "Now, just get out some shorts or something and follow me."

"You gotta imagine we're staying here," Scott said, directing them toward the side entrance instead of back toward the pool.

There was an electronic room key reader to let them into the building, but it either didn't work or the door was left unlocked during the day; it opened without problem, and they were inside, walking down the hall next to each other.

"I thought you said no one would care."

"I also said we gotta make sure not to *make* them care. Someone sees us pull up, park, hop out of our car and go to the pool, it seems suspicious. It makes them feel like if they *don't* say something, they're being taken advantage of. Like we think they're too stupid to even notice.

"Here's the deal," Scott continued. He grabbed his brother, turned Ernie toward him and paused in the beginning of the hallway. "After I dropped out of college and moved to New York, I didn't really have any money. Ted, the guy whose farm I kind of worked on, he gave me a little bit here and there, but mostly he just let me stay with him for free, kept me pretty well fed. I had all this time on my hands—I helped on the farm, worked out, and read. Repeat. That was just about it. I tried to read as much as possible. Like I was telling you, Kerouac and Hunter, *Zen and the Art of Motorcycle Maintenance*, all that shit. So I'd go into town once a week or whatever and I'd go to the bookstore, this big Barnes and Noble that had just opened. And at some point, I realized, as often as not, when that security alarm would go off—which actually didn't happen very often—the cashier would just wave them through. 'It's probably just your cell phone,' they'd say, or they'd barely even say anything at all and just wave them through, tell them it was OK. They didn't care. People don't really care about their shitty place of employment, they care about feeling like they're being looked down on. That's number one." Scott held up his index finger, and Ernie realized he did this a lot, this counting thing. He wondered where it came from, when that started. "Then, the second thing I noticed or realized or whatever was I saw sometimes people would bring in their own books and ask one of the employees if that was ok. 'Do I need to leave this with you? Is it OK if I bring this in?'" Scott affected a voice for the customers asking questions and Ernie laughed at their ridiculousness, at how Scott obviously found them ridiculous. "I'm telling you, the cashiers always just waved them off, said it was fine. They didn't give a shit. So, one day—one of the days I actually had money with me, just in case—I found some book I wanted and then just walked around the store for a while, holding it in my hand as if it were already my book, as if I'd brought it in with me. Thinking, *I brought this in with me*. And I kept holding it like that, right out the door. Half-believing, myself, that I hadn't just stolen a book but was carrying out what I'd carried in, a book I already owned, something I'd bought weeks before, or had been given as a gift, or whatever, but also half-ready to apologize, to say I'd totally forgotten it was in my hand, ready to pay for it if anyone said anything, if anyone even looked at me with a hint of knowing what was happening." Scott looked Ernie in the eye for a moment, suddenly turning anecdote into lesson. "You see what I'm saying?"

Ernie looked at Scott in disbelief. His brother, Mr. Bison, book thief. How many different people was his brother? "I think so?"

"You gotta just believe it yourself, and most everyone else will too." Scott let that linger for a moment for both Ernie's sake and his own. Like his decision-making example from the car, it sounded even smarter said aloud than when it had occurred to him. "Actually, weirdly, learning that was one of the most important lessons I learned that year." Scott looked up toward the ceiling for a second, a moment of thought, then patted Ernie on the shoulder and turned, continued his way through the hall, toward the pool.

Ernie followed, trying to put himself in the frame of mind of his imagined self—bizarro Ernie that was hotel guest, walking next to bizarro Scott, also hotel guest, and also, apparently, famous wrestler, upcoming video game star, book thief. Just two hotel guests on their way to the pool. How would he hold his arms? Different than normal? How was he holding them now, was he moving different than normal? What about his stride—faster? Longer? Shorter? Would he pay more attention to Scott, or less; would they be talking; would he hum? Did he ever hum? And then they went single file to walk past the housekeeper's cart and Scott called "Good afternoon!" in to her and raised his arm in a lazy wave, and Ernie realized he was walking like a robot. *Don't overthink it,* he told himself. *Don't think about it at all. Just walk normal.* He looked at his brother—Scott looked so confident in his body, so comfortable with himself. Had he never noticed that before? Had he never before thought of it as something to notice?

Ernie reminded himself of his brother's story, thought of his combination of confidence and nonchalance and tried to move like that through the hotel hallway, his robot arms relaxing back to normal, his whole walk and posture slackening back into itself. Maybe trying too hard, maybe overproud of himself, he called to Scott, only a couple of steps ahead of him, "You remember the key?" Scott turned around and smiled. "Yep."

And then they were at the pool, and Ernie almost wanted to go back and do the walk again, now that he'd figured it out.

The pool gate was locked, but Scott reached over and unhooked it from the other side, no problem. They each grabbed a towel from the table where they were folded and waiting for hotel users and laid them out over two chairs on the opposite side from the entrance, circling the entire pool on their way to the dressing room to change. There were two women in the pool, each leaning against the edge farthest from both the entrance and where Scott and Ernie had left their towels, standing in what must have been about four feet of water. In the bathroom, Ernie went into a stall to change, while Scott just undressed and then put on his swimming trunks right there in the open. Ernie came out in athletic shorts and did a double take at his brother's trunks.

"Guess I did pack a pair."

They dropped their disrobed day-clothes on top of their towels on their pool chairs and Scott dove into the deepest end. He stayed under water for longer than Ernie would have thought, and when Scott resurfaced, he saw Ernie walking down the steps into the shallow end.

Scott made his way to the edge and beat Ernie there, leaned back into the wall and spread his arms out on the ledge. It reminded Ernie of the Jordan poster he'd had on his wall at one point in middle school. He hadn't thought of it in a couple of decades but could still perfectly picture it—black and white, MJ looking straight ahead, his arms extended and touching either side of the oversized poster, a basketball palmed in his right hand. *Wings*. He dropped his legs out from under himself and quickly submerged, rose to the surface and swam over.

"Thought you wanted to swim," he said, approaching Scott. He hadn't consciously thought it at the time but now realized some part of him had presumed Scott wanted to swim because he wanted exercise. They'd been on the road for a couple days, inactive. How frequently did his brother have to work out to sustain that bulk. Actually, he realized, it was possible Scott was going to the gym when he went in to town, but that was only once, maybe twice, a week. He realized his brother had been "working out" solely by keeping busy on the farm, building The Fence for Billy, working the ground, moving lumber from here to there. With that the case, the farm all seemed worth it anew, and he realized he missed it.

He pulled his eyes back from his far-off look where he didn't actually see anything at all and saw Scott looking at him, his arms stretched out, palms up. He remembered his question, and read Scott's *Wings*-like pose as, *And here we are.*

"But aren't we going to *swim*?"

Scott shrugged, closed his eyes, tipped back his head, his face up toward the sun. "This counts. I just wanted to get in a pool. It's nice out, we've been in the car all day. We've got some extra time, let's enjoy it. It feels good, right?"

Ernie nodded. He again let his legs fold into themselves and sunk under water. Staying under, holding his breath, he had the thought of it feeling like a baptism. What had his brother said? "Baptism by fire?" Like he was baptizing himself for the road? The rest of his life? He *did* feel kind of born anew.

What he remembered of his actual baptism was the water heater was broken. He remembered their father wearing white, same as him, both of them standing in waist-deep water. The room seeming like part bathroom, part sanctuary. He'd had Sunday School in that room, or a room like it, but he'd never seen the fourth wall opened before, a temporary wall that accordioned in on itself. The whole building was filled with these kinds of walls, opening or closing to grow or shrink rooms as needed. Opened, this one revealed the oversized bathtub they stood in for the baptism.

The room was filled with men, only men, all wearing Sunday best, Ernie and his father the two exceptions, in all white. Ernie didn't remember Scott being there, but because he wasn't, maybe he'd been too young, or he was and Ernie just didn't remember? His father led him into the pool from a starting place off behind a curtain, a kind of backstage. The eyes of everyone on him felt blinding, like stage lights or looking directly into the sun. Standing in the water, his father read from his Bible and a piece of paper folded in between its pages, and Ernie listened but also kept drifting off into worry that either Bible or loose papers were going to be dropped into the water. Ernie shivered, praying for it to go quickly so he could get out of the freezing cold water. He felt every goosebump tickling up his arms. His father read a section, paused, and the chorus of men answered. *Amen*, they said in unison, and *We do*, and whole paragraphs they all seemed to have memorized. His father called and they responded, back and forth, then he supported Ernie with one arm and held his son's head with his other and told him, *Fall back*.

Ernie resurfaced, ran his hands over his face, wiped away what water he could, and looked at his little brother. By the time Scott was Ernie's age when he'd been baptized, their family had left that church and with it the rite of passage that Scott would never follow in.

"See?" Scott said, smiling big. He again closed his eyes but kept his head still, didn't tip it back and up toward the sun. "Just enjoy it," he said, slowly and without opening his eyes or motioning in any way, almost like talking in his sleep.

"What happened to those girls?" Scott asked.

Ernie didn't think he'd been asleep, but not quite awake either apparently. Somewhere in that vague nowhere in-between, doing what Scott had instructed. Just enjoying it. *Relaxing*. Scott was looking around like he'd been in charge of keeping an eye on them, like he'd just realized he'd lost them.

Ernie looked back and forth, as if he were looking for them too, though he wasn't really. He hadn't realized they'd left, but he'd just as much forgotten they'd been there in the first place.

Ernie pushed himself away from the wall, bobbed back and forth some in the water. Pulled up his knees and treaded water.

"She was pretty cute," Ernie said, half-wondering if she actually had been or if he just remembered her that way.

Scott shrugged, and Ernie got annoyed. He'd really only said it because it seemed like what Scott was thinking and maybe wanted to say but probably wouldn't. He'd thought they might have this shared moment of attraction. Or: even if not shared attraction, shared moment of talking about attractiveness at least.

"I thought her friend was cuter."

The pool felt good but was getting boring. Ernie suddenly realized, alone in the pool and without the girls there, he did want to actually swim. Do a couple laps, get a little exercise. Or: if not swim, maybe get out and just lie in the sun, read a book. But even though it was just Scott, swimming felt weird with someone watching, and he didn't want to have to go back to the car for a book. He had a quick flash of wishing Scott weren't there, that he had the pool all to himself, that he was making the drive alone, though he never would have stopped at the hotel to use their pool if that were the case, though Scott was the reason for the drive in the first place. If one of them were making the drive alone, it wouldn't be Ernie. Really, he realized, he was kind of already ready to get back on the road. Something about it held some kind of pull on him, it felt comforting. Purposeful.

"Wait." Ernie suddenly stopped himself from bouncing back and forth in the water, pushing off from one foot to the other. "How did you know which girl I meant? How do you know I didn't mean her friend? Which one is *her* and which was the friend?"

"'Cause you didn't. I know. She was fine. Definitely cute. Just not really my type."

"But she's *my* type?" She was, from what Ernie had seen of her, from what he remembered. But it felt awkward hearing his brother say it, thinking of Scott as knowing his type, thinking he knew him.

"Wonder where the hippies are," Scott said. He was turned around, away from the hotel and toward the freeway that had brought them there.

Ernie had been able to hear it, the slight murmur sounding more like the ocean than traffic, but hadn't really realized the freeway was right there; or: he had but had forgotten, same as he hadn't noticed the girls' absence until Scott pointed it out, and then he couldn't not.

"Practically seems like we should see them driving past, doesn't it?" Scott answered himself.

"Yeah," Ernie added, though again not quite knowing what he was agreeing to. "Wait," he said again. "What do you mean? Were they headed in our same direction?"

"I don't know. Just seems fitting or something, doesn't it? We stopped to take a break, a little swimming pool pit stop, and it seems almost too coincidental for us to look out at the freeway and see their van driving by for it to *not* happen. Like we're on some weird race caper or something."

"*It's a Mad, Mad, Mad World*?"

"Right! Exactly! Doesn't it seem like that?"

"I don't think I've seen it, actually."

"You haven't? Actually, I'm not sure if I have. We didn't watch it with Dad? Seemed like a movie we would have watched with him, I thought we did, but I was too young to remember it, so that doesn't really count. I thought you might remember." Scott made a face, not so much like he thought Ernie was lying; he was just surprised Ernie hadn't seen it. He seemed to constantly be making references to movies, like that was how he saw the world, and was continually surprised when Scott didn't. Ernie turned and looked away, looked out at the freeway so Scott couldn't see his face in reply.

When Ernie looked back at his brother, Scott was mouthing something, and then Ernie noticed him counting with his fingers.

"How many Mads in that title?"

"How many did I say?"

Scott shrugged, shook his head.

Ernie said it again, "It's a Mad, Mad World? It's a Mad, Mad, Mad, Mad, Mad, Mad, Mad World?"

Scott laughed, showed Ernie his fingers. Seven.

"Too many?"

Ernie looked back out at the freeway, watched the cars drive by where he had been just staring off into that direction. If he focused on one car for as long as possible and watched only its progress, it seemed to be moving so much slower than when watching all of them at once.

It reminded him of watching the ceiling fans at home, the difference between watching the whole fan or just one blade. He kept going back and forth, tricking his brain—following one car from the beginning of his sightline to the end, then unfocusing to see them all at once, pretending it was one of those Magic Eye books or posters, having to cross and uncross his eyes to see the picture. "A sailboat *is* a schooner," he mumbled.

"What was that?"

"Oh. Nothing. Never mind." Ernie kept watching traffic, looking for and now even kind of expecting to see the hippies driving by. Waving their arms out windows at him and Scott like they knew they were there. Ernie realized the van he was expecting to see, insofar as he actually expected to see them, was The Mystery Machine. What had their van actually looked like? They *had* been driving a van, right? He couldn't picture it, only the fire, Scott sitting across from him. And One Button, shirt open, trying to explain something about one joint equaling two, or vice versa, or something like that. And Scott ... having said something about Detroit? About "getting into trouble" in Detroit? That couldn't be right, could it? Had he gotten more specific, but Ernie had been too drunk or high to remember, or had that not happened at all, and Ernie had been drunk or high enough to make up Scott having done something bad like he'd always secretly thought or wished?

"I don't think they said where they were going," Scott said, like that's where the conversation still was. "Maybe they were just camping?"

"Maybe."

Scott shook his head. "It seemed like they were *On the Road*ing it though." He looked at Ernie. "Didn't it?" Ernie nodded. "Wouldn't it be crazy if we did see them on the road? What if they actually are making the same drive as us? Caper finish line: video game conference!"

Ernie laughed, maybe the most he'd laughed in a while. "They didn't really seem like gamers. Like they'd drive across the country for a geeky conference—"

"*We're* driving across the country for a geeky conference."

"Sure," Ernie said. "We are. Different circumstances. I don't think those guys are the stars of one of the featured video games."

"A Phish role-player maybe?!"

And Ernie laughed harder still, coughed up a little pool water he hadn't been aware he'd swallowed.

They both turned their attention back to the freeway but didn't see any vans that looked familiar, neither like the Mystery Machine nor anything that jogged their memories of presumably having seen the hippies' van at the campground. At least one or two of the cars driving past must have been on long, maybe even cross-country, drives though. Maybe one of those cars was also on its way to Detroit, even if not specifically their conference. Or: somewhere in Michigan at least.

"You good?"

Ernie pulled himself away from figuring out which of those cars might be on the same path as them and looked at his brother. Asked *what was that?* with his eyes, his whole face.

"You good?" Scott asked again. "Dry off, get back on the road? We could lay out for a bit, sun dry and then ... *on the road again*," he added, singing it.

"Sure."

"We'll beat those hippies at their own race!" Scott added.

Their own race? Ernie thought. *Sure. Whatever.* "Exactly," he agreed. "It's a mad world out there." Scott smiled at him.

15.

The dog wouldn't stop barking.

"Seriously?" Scott said. "They can't shut that dog up?"

It was maybe the shortest-tempered Scott had been since he'd picked up Ernie at the airport. Maybe it was being away from Holly, maybe he was tired. Maybe being confined in a car with Ernie for the last couple of days had taken its toll, finally taxed his patience, maybe Ernie's own lesser brand of optimism had just worn off on him.

They were in some nowhere town in western Montana, or maybe closer to the middle of the state, Ernie had lost track. Montana was big. Tomorrow they'd wake up, make their way in to Yellowstone. They'd stopped here to call it a day, to make tomorrow an all Yellowstone day, losing none of their entry into the park to the dark. This exit had three hotels that all looked the same, nothing else. At least nothing they could see. Ernie wondered how anyone chose between the three, if each motel did thirty-three percent of the business of the people who pulled off at this exit and stayed here, law of averages, or if one somehow had an edge that was obvious to other travelers but not him. Scott had picked this one because he'd liked the logo on their sign the best. Thunderbird Inn. Maybe that was how everyone picked? Maybe this place was running away with the business, everyone else needing to update their graphic design budget, or maybe a whole renaming and rebranding process. Maybe that was how this small fucking dog—he could tell it was little by its little fucking yapping—in the room next door had ended up there? Ernie swore there couldn't have been more than half a dozen cars in that parking lot and the dog had ended up in the room right next door to theirs? The guy at the front desk couldn't have evenly spaced everyone out, every fifth or tenth room?

"Why don't they shut it up?" Scott kept going. "It's late. People are obviously trying to sleep."

Or maybe it was just the fucking dog, was what had so gotten to Scott.

"They must be out, right?" Ernie asked.

"You think? This late? With their dog left alone, just barking all night?"

"Have you heard anyone tell it to shut up? Any movement over there at all?"

Both kept quiet, listened for any non-barking activity. The barking stopped too, like the dog was also listening, all three now listening for the culprit together, or maybe like the neighbor had heard them complaining, had finally made her dog shut up. Because it had to be a her, Ernie presumed.

They didn't hear anything. Nothing at all, for just long enough to think they were maybe finally in the clear, long enough to start to slip off into sleep. And then again with the yapping.

"Fuck!" Scott pulled his pillow over his head. On the road, he used to travel with earplugs, for when they stayed in a noisy, partying part of town, or even just in case he split a room with one of the guys who snored. Most of them seemed to actually. But it had been so long since those days, when he knew exactly what to pack, for exactly how many days he'd be gone. He wished for a pair now.

"I'm gonna go complain."

"What?"

"Complain. I'm gonna go talk to the front desk. Let the guy know. I don't even think you're supposed to leave a dog alone in a hotel room."

"Seriously?"

"Yeah," Ernie said, shrugged. "I don't think so."

"No, I mean, you're seriously gonna complain? What's that even gonna do?"

"I don't know." Ernie shrugged again. "Don't you have to leave a contact number or something when you check in? Maybe he'll call them, make them come back or something. Or maybe he'll make them move rooms when they come back."

"We'll be asleep by then."

Ernie thought about that. "It'll still inconvenience them."

Ernie said it straight-faced, but Scott started laughing. Tried to hold it in, thinking too much laughter would wake him up completely—as annoying as the dog was, he was kind of right there, so close to sleep, but trying to hold back the laughter just made him laugh harder.

"That's kinda fucked up," Scott finally said, which made Ernie laugh some too, then yet another tired shrug. He stood up out of bed, started putting on his pants.

"Why are you getting up? Just call the guy."

"I think it'll mean more if I go in person," Ernie said, already pulling on his shoes. "I'm up. I'll go complain, show the guy how tired I look, how annoying it is." He looked at Scott, three-quartered his eyes closed like he could barely keep them open but couldn't quite keep them shut either. Put a little slack in his mouth, his shoulder. "I look tired?"

"You look like a zombie."

"Perfect! *I'll be back*," he monotoned.

"Zombie *Terminator*?"

"Something like that." Ernie smiled, Scott *finally* catching one of his movie quotes.

Ernie closed the door behind him, but then, instead of turning left and crossing the parking lot to the front office, he turned right, knocked on the neighbor's door. Maybe someone *was* in there? He tapped a couple gentle knocks, and the dog's barking doubled. Ernie could hear the dog at the door, scratching at the base of the door, trying to answer Ernie's knocking. There definitely wasn't anyone there. Or, Ernie supposed, they were now ignoring not only their yapping fucking dog but also someone knocking on their door. Him.

He moved in front of the window, growing less concerned with manners. Cupped his hands together on his forehead, around his eyes to see through the dark. The room had its curtains shut, but the secondary, see-through curtains, not the main ones. The room's bathroom light was on, giving enough light to make the whole room visible, and Ernie thought about how he could never remember what made a room visible at night—dark outside, but a light on in? Vice versa? Some other combination? Inside his own room, he'd assumed no one would be able to see in, but maybe that wasn't actually the case?

Ernie turned, made for the front desk. The parking lot was wet, and Ernie wondered when it had rained. He kept half-expecting to see someone else, another traveler, someone getting ice or something from one of the vending machines. Maybe even someone else going to complain about the dog. He readied to share a look with the person, his, *Really? Right? Can you believe it? I'm going to complain right now* ... all in a look.

The office was as empty as outside. Where was everyone? There wasn't any town to be out in. It all made Ernie seem even more out in the middle of nowhere than he was. Or: maybe exactly how out in the middle of nowhere as he was.

He stood, waiting. Looking around, like maybe the attendant was just somewhere he hadn't yet seen. Like maybe there was more to the room than a big, open box with a front counter and a desk with a computer for guests. There was a bell on the desk—no "ring for assistance" note, handwritten or otherwise, but obviously there for that purpose. Ernie wasn't sure why, but he didn't want to ring the bell. He didn't want to *have to*, didn't want to have to call for assistance, just wanted it to be there.

He leaned over the counter, looked at everything laid out—the maps for visitors, the notes for employees. The card reader to code the keys for which room. A legal pad, maybe half flipped over, with doodles—mostly arrows, triangles growing larger out to the edges of the page like a maze with only one path. Ernie thought of the scene in *The Big Lebowski*, The Dude scribbling on the piece of paper to see what had been written on the sheet above it, only to reveal a doodle of a naked guy with a huge dick.

He started laughing, caught himself before slipping into a *Lebowski* rabbit hole. Then, without really thinking about it, maybe just curious how it worked, if he could figure it out, Ernie pushed the "Set key" button, and the display screen, upside down from where Ernie stood, read, "Room?" Ernie pushed 1-2-9, and the display went blank and then flashed to, "Insert card." He pulled his own room key out of his pocket, quickly before it was too late, before the attendant came back from wherever he was, pushed it into the slot and just as quickly pulled it back out, assuming it worked the same as running your debit card at the gas station or an ATM now that they no longer held your card until the transaction was complete. "Card enabled." Ernie pocketed the card, exited the office.

Outside, Ernie scanned the horseshoe layout of rooms. Each had its curtains drawn or all the lights turned off. With the closer rooms, he could tell the difference; those furthest, including his own, he couldn't. They just looked dark.

He again started across the parking lot, following the same path he'd come but then turned a sharp left and kept to the walkway, made his way into the shadows going the long way. Scott had fallen asleep; or: was still lying in bed, cursing the dog and waiting for Ernie to return; or: was at the window, peering out, wondering what had happened to Ernie and watching for his return. If he was right up at the window but there weren't any lights on, would Ernie be able to see him?

Ernie kept making his way along the path of rooms until he got to the alcove with the vending machine with chips and candy bars—he'd already passed the one with pop and water, closer to the office—and saw it wasn't an alcove but a walkway to behind the hotel. Ernie walked through, checking it out. Were there more rooms back there, the place even bigger than he'd thought? Did these rooms he'd just been walking past have two doors, one on either side, front and back, or even some windows, a view out into their middle-of-nowhereness? Did his own room, and he'd not noticed, or forgotten? Was the attendant out back there, smoking?

Nothing. A view out into their middle-of-nowhereness, indeed, but from Ernie's view alone; the rooms didn't appear to have either back doors or windows. The back of the hotel was a solid wall of plaster from end to end. There was a shed that Ernie assumed held yard tools—trimmer, rakes, maybe a shovel. Maybe a lawnmower, though a place this big likely used a rider, and the little shed looked barely big enough to hold a push.

Near the shed, a pile of dirt. Neither shed nor dirt pile seemed to have seen any attention since who-knew-when. Or maybe the dirt pile was new? Ernie wasn't sure how to tell the difference.

Ernie continued forward, into the darkness—maybe to see if the shed was locked? to see what was in it?—then turned right, followed the wall to the corner of the building, all the way to another throughway at the corner. He wanted to think he hadn't noticed it there before, but he had, when they'd checked in, he'd just forgotten about it. Through the walkway was a corner room, then the room with the dog, then his own. He walked to his neighbor's room, without looking around to see if anyone else was now in the parking lot or if anyone had turned on their lights, without looking into the room itself, or even at the room's window at all, to see if he could still see through the sheer curtain into the room, and pushed his room key into the lock, pulled it out. He noticed as he was turning the door handle that it was quiet, the dog wasn't barking—almost aware enough of the quiet to wonder if someone had returned to their room, the dog finally asleep now with its owner home—but then he was already inside the room, closing the door behind him.

In the room, Ernie and the dog stared at each other, both seeming confused by the other, for half a second but what felt like minutes. Then the little dog lunged toward Ernie and opened its mouth to start barking, and Ernie was sure he'd never acted so fast in his life. Ernie knew it made no sense for there to be any interval of time, no matter how miniscule, between a dog opening its mouth to bark and the bark actually coming out, and maybe the dog actually was barking and he zoned it out, maybe he just didn't notice it in the heightened reality of the moment, or maybe the dog was lunging to bite and not getting ready to bark at all, thus the remembered visual of that open mouth, but he was sure he saw a bark on the dog's face, in its eyes, a look different than the look of a bite, like he could see the sound of the bark starting to release from the animal's mouth before he could even hear it, seemingly more like the logic of a comic book than that of real life, and in that instant, some barely measurable fraction of a second that Ernie would swear seemed to exist between visual and sound of the dog's bark, Ernie reached out and grabbed the lunging dog, and it landed perfectly in his hands, already wrapped around the dog's mouth, locking in the bark before it could be released.

Ernie turned and awkwardly opened the door, still holding the dog tucked into his arm, one hand still acting as muzzle, and carried it out back. He held it there in his arms and stared at that shed, at the dirt pile next to it. Then he flung the dog out and up into the air, sending it in an arc through the night. The dog landed, *cat-like,* Ernie thought, and looked up at Ernie, like wondering what had just happened, wondering if it should bark or lunge back at the man, wondering what to do now. It looked around, and next thing Ernie knew, it was running, toward the shed and then past it, out into the forest, the darkness of the night. A moment later, it was gone, completely disappeared.

Ernie stood silent, waiting to hear something. The dog running through forest, its renewed barking, someone behind him, a car in the parking lot, his brother wondering what he was doing. There was nothing but continued silence.

He walked back through the corridor, toward his own room. The neighbor's door, the door of the room with absentee guests and now absent of dog, too, was still open. He grabbed the door handle, pulled it shut. He thought about going back to the office, recoding his key back to his own room, but that seemed like it might take too long. The attendant might be back on duty, back from who-knew-where. Scott might start wondering what had happened, what was taking so long. Ernie knocked on their door, told his brother, into the door, "It's me. Ernie." He told Scott, or told the door, in hopes of Scott hearing, that he didn't know why but his key wasn't working.

He knocked again, a little louder, almost scared to wake his brother, even though that was exactly what he was trying to do, and then Scott opened the door. Scott didn't say anything, just opened the door, and got back in his bed.

"Thanks. I complained to the guy at the front desk. He kept apologizing but ... I don't know if he'll actually do anything." He shrugged but was unsure if Scott could see him in the dark room, unsure if Scott was looking at him, or even awake at all. "It doesn't seem to be barking now, does it?" Ernie tried. "Have you heard anything?"

"Nope," Scott said. "Been silent. Thanks. Good night."

16.

"You sound tired."

"I am," Scott answered. "You know ... long days, all the driving, crappy motel beds."

"It's been two days!"

Scott laughed. "Is that it? I'm getting old, I guess. Can't take the road like I used to. I miss you. Home. My own bed. *Our* bed."

"Well, we miss you, too," Holly said. "Me. Billy. Billy Jr." Holly rubbed her stomach, as if thinking of being pregnant made her confirm by touch, as if she were reminding their child to tell his dad he missed him. She'd recently taken to assuming they were having a son. She couldn't remember if she'd started thinking it before Scott had left but hadn't mentioned it or if it had sprung to mind in the mere days he'd been gone. She had to remind herself sometimes that they didn't actually know for sure yet, though most of the time she didn't even catch herself. "Your bed misses you, too."

"Billy *Junior*?"

Holly's turn to laugh. "Yeah, I started thinking of that as his name as a joke, now it just seems to fit—"

"*Him*? Do you know something I don't?"

"No, no. How would I even? Just intuition. Mother's intuition." She smiled, looked across the room at Billy. "What do you think of that, Billy? You going to like Junior? You okay with sharing your name?"

Billy had come at the mention of his name, had been standing just outside her office, in the hallway, as if peeking in on their conversation, and now, with her attention, he came toward her, laid down and rested his head on her foot. He did so delicately, as if knowing his own size, as if knowing he was getting to be too big for all this but was fighting the inevitability as much as Holly. He kept the bulk of the weight of his own head on the ground, resting just enough of himself actually *on* Holly to be touching, to let her know he was there, to convince her, *see, I can still rest my head on you and cuddle, I'm not* really *going to soon be too big to be in the house, to have to be restricted to only outside ...*

"How is the little guy?" Scott asked.

"The *little* little guy is great. I've been feeling great, everything's going smooth. The *other* little guy ... is quickly getting to be not too little."

Holly reached down, rubbed Billy's head as if she'd said something she didn't really mean.

"I don't think we're going to be able to let him in the house much longer though. Like, he's not going to *fit* for too much longer. He's already starting to rub on both sides, going through doorways. Not too long before he doesn't even try, or he gets stuck—"

"Or he takes out a wall."

"Right. I guess that's more likely." Holly looked down at Billy, frowned at him.

Scott pictured that for a minute, imagined the final extra growth happening overnight, over one of the nights they let Billy sleep in the house. Suddenly, in the morning, Billy being slightly too big to get back outside without doing damage to the house. It didn't happen like that, of course—all at once, overnight—but also, it kind of did, didn't it? There had to be some kind of singular breaking point.

"You letting him inside?"

"Yeah," Holly answered, a little guilty. "He's been keeping us good company, protecting the house. If you two had left a couple weeks from now, he'd probably already be too big and I would have had to sleep alone."

"But I wouldn't have left you two weeks from now."

"You know what I mean."

"How are your parents?"

"Oh, you know. They're my parents."

"That bad?"

"No, no. They're great. They love being here. I don't think they know what to think of Billy. Actually. I don't think they know what to think of why you're gone. I mean ... they're proud, but I don't think they get anything about the video game, or what a big deal it is, or anything—"

"Me neither, to be fair."

"That's fair," Holly answered, smiled to herself. "How's Ernie?"

"You know ..." Scott looked up and out the window, looking for his brother, though he wasn't sure where he'd gone. He was already gone by the time Scott got up—grabbing some pastries at the continental breakfast, just out on a walk? "He's Ernie. But ..." Scott rubbed his face, some of the sleep from his eyes. "He actually doesn't really seem tired at all. He seems ... the opposite? Well-rested, like the road is giving him some new energy or something?" Scott hadn't fully realized it until saying so to Holly.

"Good! That's good. Maybe he needed to get out of the house. Maybe he's excited to be headed home for a few days? Maybe he's happy to be spending time with his little brother!" Scott could hear Holly's smile, part *see, I told you so*, part happiness to hear Ernie was doing well, that they were getting along. *Bonding*, Scott could picture Holly thinking. "That's what I meant," she continued. "How is he doing being on the road? Not just if he's tired. How are you both, how are you two getting along? Are you bonding, do you feel like?" Scott laughed, pulled the phone away to laugh into the air and not directly into Holly's ear. "What?" Holly asked, when it finally sounded like her husband had reeled himself back in.

"Nothing. Yeah, we're good." The door clicked and Scott looked up to see Ernie balancing two coffee cups, one stacked atop the other, held between one hand and his chin, while he'd key-carded the door open and let himself in. "Everything's going great," Scott added so Ernie could hear him. "We stopped and went swimming yesterday, gonna head into Yellowstone for the day here in just a minute actually."

"Right. That's what your goodnight text last night said. Motel swimming?"

"Had to show him the ropes, had to walk him through the whole thing." Scott smiled across the room at Ernie. "He picked it up pretty fast."

Soon? Ernie mouthed, nodded to the door, outside, the road, onward ... Scott nodded back, held up a single finger.

"Oh yeah," Holly added. "Michael called right before you this morning. I picked up my phone without even looking, just assuming it would be you—"

"We're on our way!" Scott cut her off, a little sharper than he'd meant. "We'll see him in just a couple days!"

"Right. That's what I said. That you decided to drive, you and Ernie. That you were going to be in Yellowstone today, should be there in Detroit in just a couple days. He seemed surprised. But excited? Said he would call you."

Scott thought about that, what that might mean.

"He didn't say what about?"

"Nope, just that he'd call, he'd see you soon."

Scott nodded again, looked up at Ernie, who was antsy to hit the road. "I gotta go, Holl. Call me if you need anything? If anything changes?"

"I will. Tell Ernie I said hi."

"Give my love to ... *both* Billys?" Scott asked and laughed, and Holly said she would.

The entrance to Yellowstone came sooner than either brother had expected. They'd been even closer than they'd realized.

"Already?" Scott asked.

Ernie shrugged.

"I thought we'd grab breakfast somewhere first?"

Ernie shrugged again.

"You can get breakfast here," the park ranger offered and smiled big, like he'd just made these travelers' days, like why would you even consider eating *before* when breakfast could be a part of your whole Yellowstone experience? He handed Ernie a map of the park, pointed at the closest, best place to eat, the best places to camp, Old Faithful and the Old Faithful Inn and the visiting center. "You two staying the night or just passing through? Looking for camping or lodging recommendations?"

Ernie made a face, thought about that. He hadn't really considered it, they hadn't discussed either. *Let's do Yellowstone!* Scott had said. *Then we'll keep going on to Detroit from there*, and that had been that. Did "doing Yellowstone" mean staying the night or just passing through? Camping or using some of that video game money and getting a room, a suite-style room with all the amenities money could provide? Ernie started drifting, imagining a cabin, a lodge, a huge log cabin resort. He imagined a stuffed buffalo, a life-size buffalo watching over the lobby, old logging saws and mountain climbing equipment on the walls. He thought of Billy, home with Holly. He realized, for the first time, he'd thought of the farm as "home." And that he missed it. It and Billy, both. They hadn't really talked of Billy much thus far on the trip, even though the buffalo had been the entire impetus for the slight reroute to Yellowstone. Scott had mentioned after each of his conversations with Holly that she'd said to say hi and also that Billy was doing well, though missing them, and Ernie had thought it cute but also kind of ridiculous—that the buffalo would miss them, that Holly would be able to recognize that missing, that she'd become as attached to the animal as she had—but those thoughts were fleeting and quickly forgotten, having represented the entirety of his thoughts of Billy until now.

Ernie pulled himself back from thinking about Billy and the farm but only partially, back into the intermediary daydream of the log cabin resort, its rustic charm, a common area with a fireplace. Half in daydream, half not, like waking in the middle of the night and being aware you are dreaming while the dream itself continues, Ernie realized the lobby he was picturing was, more or less, the lodge at Mt. Rainier. He and Scott had visited often as kids, family dayhikes and weekend overnight camping trips, often stopping in the lodge for snacks. Their father treated it almost like a museum, a place to visit and read the placards on the wall, learn of the Mt. Rainier of the past. Ernie had always imagined staying there as something to aspire to; later, he'd realize they weren't camping *instead of* staying at the lodge because they couldn't afford it but because camping was what they did, was the purpose for being there in the first place, though later still in life he'd realize it was, of course, a little of both. At one point, in college, he'd taken a girl to Rainier for a daytrip hiking kind of date and they'd visited the lodge. He'd told the girl these stories, of visiting with his family, of his sentimental attachment to the place. Even at the time, he'd known that girl wasn't *the* girl, but telling her about it all, he let himself daydream of one day getting married at that lodge or maybe going there on their honeymoon, finally having the special occasion for the special place.

"Playing it by ear," Scott said, leaning down and across Ernie, answering the park attendant.

Ernie shook his head, a joke that had turned into subconscious habit that he'd do when Rebecca would say something to pull him out of his *sentimentlust*. He opened his mouth, starting to say something though not yet knowing what, likely just a note of agreement, but before he could figure it out, the attendant interrupted.

"Wait! Are you The Buffalo? *Mr.* Buffalo??"

"Mr. *Bison*," Scott and Ernie corrected in unison, though the guy was gone, didn't hear. He'd put up a finger and disappeared into his little park-entrance-stand, was back as quickly as he'd gone, holding a piece of paper. He looked at the paper, bent down to look into the car, across Ernie at Scott.

"Scott Isaacson? Wow, they said we'd recognize you if we saw you, but I didn't know that could be true since we didn't actually know who to watch for. Wow. You're huge! Sorry, I just ... you know." Like the guy at Home Depot, like the guy he'd worked with all those years ago when Scott had come through town and they'd all gone out for drinks, like countless guys who had reacted to Scott over the years, Ernie noticed this kid stand up a little straighter, roll his shoulders back a few degrees, push his chest forward ever-so-slightly, only all while not actually standing upright but folded over enough to keep his attention through the car, at Scott. It made it all even more awkward and noticeable than normal. "I mean ... it is you, right? Mr. Buffalo? Wait, of course it is. Mr. *Bison*, you said." Both Scott and Ernie had assumed he hadn't heard them. "They didn't tell us anything, just your name, to watch for you and your brother, that we'd recognize you when we saw you. You'd be the biggest guy we'd see all day, you'd probably be here early, they said." The guy nodded at himself, proud to have recognized Scott, like he won some kind of contest or something. "But ... what's the name mean?" he asked, and Ernie could see him thinking about it. "Just cause you're big like one? Wait! Is that why you're here? Because of the buffalo?"

"Hold on," Scott finally stopped him. "Slow down, hold on. What do you mean they told you to watch for us? Who? What are you talking about?"

"Oh! Of course. They just said to watch for you. The bosses. Said to send you to Old Faithful Lodge. Supposed to tell you there will be people to meet you there.

A whole camera crew, I think? They didn't really say, but that's what it looked like when I was there this morning. Like they'd just got there, were setting up ..."

"Michael," Scott grumbled.

"I think you're supposed to head straight there? Nevermind wherever I was trying to direct you. Actually, you guys were looking for breakfast, right? They'll have food there! Right, of course. That's actually the message I'm supposed to give you—welcome you to the park, tell you we're excited you're here, and to direct you straight to the Lodge, they'll be there waiting for you."

Ernie nodded, looked over at his brother. Look at you, Mr. Big Time. They're waiting for you. Scott shook his head at his brother, but then—

"Oh!" the attendant said again, like suddenly remembering. "Would you mind signing this for me?" He handed a second park map to Ernie, kinda motioned to him to pass it to his brother, Scott, Mr. Bison.

17.

It felt like being on a movie set.

Or: what Ernie assumed being on a movie set might be like.

One person in charge, a small handful of people the next level down who knew their roles but actually seemed to run things, and then those who didn't actually do anything but Ernie could tell thought they were in charge. Then everyone else—the actual workers, the people to whom this was solely a job. And, finally, next layer out, the growing number of spectators, most probably unaware what they were even spectating but they'd seen a crowd forming and so they joined it, curious what they'd see, what everyone else was seeing.

Ernie was somewhere between those last two groups, a kind of official spectator. As he watched it all, delineating the organized chaos into their groups and categories, he realized his current role was actually just where he'd always imagined himself being, in this scenario. He was surprised by his own realization that, when he had dreamed of this scenario, or something like it, this was in fact always the role he'd seen himself in. Not the star, nor the director or photographer or any other person in charge, but official spectator. Not one of the crowd, but not anyone with responsibility either, just close enough to watch it all, to walk around freely, where the other watchers weren't allowed, maybe the very occasional request for input and getting to add his two cents and let them take it or not.

Scott, meanwhile, looked wholly in his element. He seemed to know what to do before anyone told him, where to go before anyone directed him there. And then, when given direction, he seemed to know exactly what the direction meant, and then he performed it even better than expected.

"Right!"

And Scott held his right arm up in the air to his side and flexed. Fist and face directed at one another, smiling, stern-faced, smirking; then fist rotated out, same series of faces; then looking straight into the camera, same series of poses and faces again.

"Left!" And Scott went through all of the same.

Only, at some point, Ernie stopped even thinking of him as Scott; at some point, he'd so fully transformed into Mr. Bison, even cynical-about-wrestling-and-his-brother-as-wrestling-persona Ernie fully gave in to the show. It was the outfit, sure—buffalo fur vest, bare (and oiled) chest—but outfit alone, Ernie would have thought ridiculous. Outfit alone was what Ernie used to picture when thinking of his brother as wrestler. As *Mr. Bison*, ridiculous name that they'd conjured and thought awesome when playing video games together when little and that Ernie never understood how it persisted beyond their youth. He'd never considered the commitment to the role, the theater of it all. He'd thought of it as acting in only the derogatory way—his brother was *acting*, not really *wrestling*—never as what it seemed now—yes, his brother was acting because he was an actor, a performer, a star. Scott was barely even present in this Mr. Bison, and he was only posing for photos, not even in the ring.

Ernie watched, hypnotized. Mr. Bison was charismatic, he was a star. And big. Ernie felt it redundant to keep being surprised at his brother's size, but here it was twofold. First, it was the sheer size of this character being photographed. Not Scott, but Mr. Bison. The physical size, but also the aura, the personality. The way he drew all attention toward himself, and then reflected that attention back outward at everyone watching. The one-two realization, first that this actual bigger-than-life character was a person, and then that that person was his brother.

Ernie realized why Scott's size sometimes—when they hugged, when Scott did something physical that Ernie would never be able to do himself—caught him off-guard. When not here, in these circumstances, when not *Mr. Bison*, Scott actually shrunk himself. He kept his shoulders a little forward, rolled into himself; he dropped his whole head down into his neck, his neck down into his body, probably only fractions of inches, but enough to minimize. To not quite hide, but to at least not highlight, everything in reverse—neck outstretched, head held high, shoulders rolled back, Scott's whole body transformed into the living sculpture of Mr. Bison, all through posture and presence.

This is the version of his brother that had fans, this was why those computer programmers had remembered him all those years, why they'd built an entire game around him. This was the brother he admired ... but was also jealous of. Why did it all seem to come so easy for him?

"Break!" someone called, snapping Ernie out of his thinking about the moment and back into the moment itself. He watched Scott look around, looking for him, and then start in his direction.

Ernie watched his brother walk toward him and saw Mr. Bison melt back into Scott. Or: three-quarters Scott. The Scott that was also Mr. Bison, not the Scott who lived on the farm or who he was currently on a roadtrip with. As soon as the cameras were off, Scott was less *on*, but there was still an audience, there were still people watching him, and Ernie found himself watching too. Watching his brother, watching the people watch his brother. These shades of how Scott carried and projected himself were fascinating.

"You off in *Ernie's World* over here?" Scott asked, stopping right in front of Ernie.

Ernie looked up to see his brother smiling big, all teeth. Smile held over from the cameras, a little less melted back into off-camera Scott than the rest of him. *Ernie's World*? Ernie didn't think so. He'd always thought the phrase was for when he was zoning out, not thinking about anything at all. Sometimes he wondered if everyone did this, slipped into a kind of daze, but was less noticeable when doing so, or maybe more controlled, only letting themselves do so when alone, no one around to "catch them," to point it out, to tag it with a name. *Ernie's World*. But just now he'd actually been thinking, not blankly zoning out. He'd never before put so much thought into who his brother was, why he wrestled. He wasn't sure if he was surprised that he'd never before thought about it or that he was now.

He shrugged. "I guess so. Something like that."

"Food's provided," Scott said. "Whatever we want." And he smiled that big camera smile again, but then he laughed, his big barrel of a laugh. There was something about the laugh, something about the lack of constraint or control, that Ernie knew it was all Scott. Ernie wondered if Scott had recognized himself flashing Mr. Bison's smile and was laughing at himself or at the idea that food was provided, the ridiculousness of the whole day. Or maybe he was just laughing at his own mention of *Ernie's World*.

"You know," Ernie said. "I actually forgot Dad used to call it that. Becca called it *sentimentlust*."

"Like Dad's ..."

"Yeah. I told her that we teased him about his wanderlust, and she said I kind of did the same thing but with nostalgia."

"You do?"

Ernie shrugged again. "I guess. Kinda. Not exactly the same thing. I don't do research, collect nostalgia pamphlets." He laughed. "I guess ... I guess, sometimes, when I zone out, I tend to ..." He drifted off, thinking about what he meant. What he tended to do.

"You tend to?"

"I don't know exactly. Either thinking about nostalgia pushes me into zoning out, into ... *Ernie's World*." He laughed at using the phrase himself. "Or I zone out and then start thinking about the past and kinda get stuck there."

"You don't know which it is?"

"It's all kinda blurry to be honest."

"And that's what you were doing just now? Thinking about the past?"

Ernie thought about that. "Not really, actually. I was just thinking about ... you. Mr. Bison. This is probably weird, but I was kinda thinking about the differences between you two."

"That isn't weird. We're totally different."

Ernie looked at his brother, surprised. Surprised his brother agreed, surprised he knew. He'd thought he'd had such a unique epiphany.

"Sorry about all this." Scott threw his arm out, around in a sloppy arc.

"What do you mean?"

"*This*," Scott repeated, not as frustrated as at the dog at the hotel but close. He looked off in one direction, nodded his head. Turned to look the other way, did the same. "Wasn't supposed to be like this."

Ernie thought about that. He wasn't sure how it was *supposed to be*, that it was *supposed to be* any way. He echoed his brother's looking one way then the other, like he was trying to take it in, like he was thinking about it, though had no idea what he was taking in, what he was supposed to be thinking about.

"I think it's kinda great," Ernie finally offered. "Getting to see you in your natural habitat."

Ernie smiled but then noticed his brother's strained face, a grimace and shaking head.

"*Mr. Bison's* habitat," Scott corrected. "I guess. But that's why we're going to Detroit. The *farm* is my ... natural habitat, you called it? This drive was supposed to be ... it was supposed to just be a roadtrip. None of this. Not this bullshit."

Ernie looked around again, didn't really see the big deal. *Fuckin' Michael*, he heard Scott mumble.

"Mr. Isaacson?"

Both brothers turned to look at someone neither had seen approaching.

"Sorry," the guy not-quite-stammered. "Scott? Scott Isaacson? Mr. Bison?"

Scott gave a little wave, like *here*, like it wasn't obvious which of the two men was Mr. Bison.

"Mr. Burch at *Grantland* was asking if he could have a few minutes. For an interview?"

Scott shot his brother a quick look, then turned to the guy. "Sure," Mr. Bison answered, all smile, no hint of Scott's frustration, barely any hint of Scott at all.

Ernie wandered, weaving in and out of the crowd. Nobody knew who he was, nobody recognized him as the brother of the reason they were themselves there, the reason they were a *crowd*, but he knew. Ernie knew, and, he realized, he was carrying himself as such. As he walked, a lane parted for him—not a lane as wide as would have for Scott surely, not as wide as at the airport when Scott had picked him up, but a lane nonetheless. *Act as if*, Ernie remembered Scott telling him.

Ernie walked, observed. The groupings, the *layers* of people he'd recognized and subdivided earlier, it all reminded him of the bubbles of activity along the freeway. The cluster of gas stations, hotels, fast food places immediately off the exit, all thinning out the farther you got from the freeway, until finally an expanse of land seemingly unaware of its proximity to freeway, to activity.

Ernie looked for the densest collection of spectators, bee-lined for it. He presumed that's where he'd find Scott, the sun in this galaxy of activity. Instead, Ernie found cameras, lights, a set being set up or broken down, he couldn't quite tell which. The center of this cluster of spectators and activity was just the scene with the most literal activity. That made sense. He found a bench, stood atop it, and did a circle, looking in all directions. Nothing. He looked back at the group of people folding down tripods, backdrops. They were definitely breaking down. Because they were done for the day or just moving locations?

Ernie scooted his feet around in another circle, finally saw something. Was that them? He shaded the sun from his eyes. Yes, and now, seeing Scott, *Mr. Bison*, he was surprised he'd had even a second of uncertainty.

Ernie stepped down, made another path through the crowd that parted a little less for him now, more aware of its own chaotic dispersing as the scene seemed to be over than the man trying to walk through it with purpose. He wondered if Scott had recommended the out-of-the-way place. Maybe the interviewer, maybe even the interviewer's assistant, the guy who had come to retrieve Scott. Did reporters have assistants? Was this guy a reporter or just some guy doing an interview?

At the outer edge of the dispersing crowd, Ernie could see Scott more clearly than he'd been able to from the bench. Could see *Mr. Bison*, he corrected. His brother was sitting tall, somehow both sitting up straight and leaning back. All confidence, all power. All Mr. Bison.

Scott looked, saw Ernie approaching. Flashed him a smile—somehow half-brother, half-persona—then turned back to the guy sitting across from him, taking notes. As Ernie continued to get closer, he could hear his brother. Just as sounds, at first—his voice dropped an octave into character, all projection—then words, phrases.

Wrestlemania, Ernie heard his brother say. He smiled. *Tetris. Tyson. Roddy Piper. Rowdy* Roddy Piper? Ernie thought. He said it to himself, wanting to hear the words aloud. "Rowdy Roddy Piper? *Roddy* Piper?"

Then: *Mr. Shafer*.

Then: *Pony*.

Ernie stopped.

It all flooded back.

Petting Pony. Feeding the goat carrots he'd brought from home. Or: sometimes when he forgot, or they'd run out and hadn't yet made another trip to the grocery store, carrots Mr. Shafer gave him. Or maybe there was always a bucket there, waiting for him, always full of carrots. What Ernie remembered wasn't getting the carrot but holding it out. Watching Pony approach from wherever she was in the yard. The feeling of holding the carrot in both hands, his little hands trying to hold strong while Pony bit down, sometimes able to keep hold, but rarely. Laughing anew, every time.

And then the sadness when Pony moved away. Or, Ernie supposed, when Mr. Shafer moved away, taking Pony with him.

How his parents let him visit when the house was for sale, before it was sold, when it sat there vacant. Walking down the block and sitting in the empty yard, his first real sadness, first grief. He didn't remember Scott in any of these memories. He had trouble picturing Scott in lots of his memories, some of which he was sure his brother was in fact there for, but he didn't have *trouble* picturing Scott there in the yard with him, so much as he specifically remembered him not being there. Specifically remembered being there alone. Scott had been too little, too young to go with him. Certainly too young to have gone by himself.

Part IV:

HOW TO TELL A STORY

Vernon's World

Vernon drifts off into a waking dream. Another world.

Or he *slips*.

Or he *falls*.

He's unaware of the transition, the in-between. It's only before and after.

Or maybe the in-between is the interesting part. Maybe the in-between *is* the world.

He's unaware of what causes the drift, the *slip*, the *fall*. What gives him the nudge. It's only here one moment, there the next.

Or he's aware of the cause, he feels and recognizes himself starting to shift from here to there, and allows it.

Or he not only allows but encourages it.

Or maybe it's conscious? Purposeful? He introduces the idea into this mind and then follows where it takes him?

18.

Back on the road, back to silence. Back to there being ... *something* between them. A wall, tension. Ernie wanted to say something but couldn't. He was trying to be ... better. Not himself. Or, not *not himself*, a better version of himself. Address things where his normal impulse would be to not, to bottle everything up, to bury it. He felt like he'd made a breakthrough, telling Scott, realizing and telling himself, that this was part of why he and Becca had broken up. That it wasn't because Bulleit ran away, it wasn't because of work, it wasn't because Becca fell out of love. Or: not entirely because of these things anyway. He'd been blaming symptoms instead of causes but was now trying to talk about things, trying to get better at taking responsibility. But he couldn't make himself, couldn't figure out how.

Ernie watched out his window, and Scott watched the road, and they drove. Miles on the odometer clicked by, added up; the scene in the movie with a sped-up clock or a calendar flipping through days, *months*, noting the passage of time. They kept quiet, left the radio off. Listened to the car's rattle, the hum of traffic outside and the road below, the silence between two people in a car. Ernie tried to think of something to say to start a conversation but kept finding himself drifting off into thinking about silences between people instead. The landscape was somewhere in that grand wash between forgettable and memorable, the sky somewhere between blue and gray—enough clouds in the sky to call it cloudy, few enough to claim blue skies.

"You always go home again," Scott said.

"What?"

"I don't know," Scott said. "I was just thinking. We're headed back to Michigan after you came back to Washington. I was just thinking about the idea of home, I guess. What it means, where it is. It all seems circular or something."

Home is where the heart is, Ernie thought, before cringing at himself, at being cheesy. He wondered if he'd actually cringed, if Scott had noticed, or if it had only been in his mind. A mental cringe. But then he thought about where his heart was, where he actually thought of as home. Were they on their way to his home? Did he really already think of the farm as his home, as he'd thought of it the day before? Because he so liked the farm? Because he and Scott were finally bonding? Because he'd grown up in Washington, and so always thought of it as home, no matter how long he'd lived in the Midwest?

"I thought the saying was, 'you can *never* go home again'?"

"Yeah," Scott answered. "That's the saying." Ernie could see Scott looking like he was thinking about it. "But ... I don't know. I think that's bullshit. You can go home again all you want, all the time. You probably do. You know? I don't mean *you* you. Everyone. 'You,'" he said, letting go of the steering wheel and putting air quotes around it. "You always go home again," he repeated. "I guess I don't know about *always*. The trick is, it isn't home anymore, right? If you're going *back* to it—"

"Right—"

"And do you really want to see what it's become anyway? Wouldn't you rather leave those memories intact?" Scott thought about it for a moment. "Assuming they're good memories, I guess. Maybe it should be 'you *should* never go home again.'"

"Right," Ernie said again. "That's *why* the saying is you can *never* go home again. What you just said. It isn't 'home' anymore, it's changed, all that."

"Yeah. Maybe." Scott rubbed his chin, nodded. "Seems more complicated than they want to admit though, don't you think?" He went pensive.

"*They*?"

"It's like that saying. 'You can never step in the same river twice.' Who said that shit? Some Roman philosopher or something, right? I never quite knew what to do with that."

"Same thing!" Ernie snapped, starting to get worked up. This was the version of his brother that drove him crazy, that he could get so frustrated with. "That's what I mean. It just means—"

"No, no. I get it. I know what it means. I'm not a moron."

Ernie stopped himself from making a joke.

"But I feel like there's more to it. I had this theory once. One of those theories you come up with when you're on the road, sleeping in a different motel every night, spending long hours in the car by yourself, just thinking."

Ernie realized he'd never really considered the actual logistics of his brother's time wrestling.

When he had thought of it all, those thoughts had been limited to the ridiculousness of it and then something of a jealousy at the unfairness of it all. That Scott got to sleep in, he had no real responsibilities for most of the day, he could do whatever he wanted. Ernie didn't think about all the alone time, the lack of the stability of a *home*. He certainly didn't think of his brother driving from city to city *thinking*.

"It was something like," Scott continued, "if you think you think you can step in the same river twice, you aren't all that smart, cause the river's changed—"

"*Right!*"

"But! There's more. At the same time, if you think you can't, you're full of shit." Scott laughed at himself. "Step in that river all you want. Again and again. Jump around in that shit. Don't overthink it. Don't be a jackass. You know?"

"Just do it?"

"Exactly. If you want to get all Nike about it." Scott laughed at himself again, proud of his own quick thought. "Anyway. Sorry about Yellowstone. That was kind of some bullshit."

Scott's version of it being bullshit wasn't the same as Ernie's. Ernie thought about the night before—lying in bed, unable to fall asleep, looping back over it all in his mind. *He* was the one who'd had the relationship with Pony. Why had Scott borrowed it as his own story, his life? *Stolen* it. Without asking. Without even telling him, without warning.

"I need to get out of the car and stretch a little," Scott said, roadblocking Ernie just as he'd thought he had his opening. "I have an idea."

Summer, no students anywhere, it barely felt like a college campus at all. There was an overwhelming quiet, a heavy *lack* looming over the place. It seemed almost like a ghost town, like an empty movie set of a college campus. Ernie wondered if this was what life with his brother was like, everything seeming like a movie, everything painted with and holding onto a patina of the unreal.

Across campus, they found the one building open and with any real activity. The bookstore. It looked the same as the campus they'd walked across to find it—familiar but not, like a movie version of a university, and then all shifted a degree or two. Scott walked in and right up to the first person he saw behind a desk, asked where the gym was, which building. The student employee said something that sounded like gibberish, and then Ernie realized it was probably some school-specific acronym. Ernie turned around, scanned through the store, not looking for anything but thinking something might jump out at him.

Scott turned to Ernie, waited for him to notice the guy had stopped talking, stared at him until Ernie realized he was being stared at. "You catch that?"

"What?"

"His directions. Where we're going."

"What? No. I stopped paying attention. I don't want to go to the gym," Ernie said, like it was obvious. "What are you talking about? I don't have any interest in their gym."

"We've been cooped up in a car for a few days, I thought it'd be fun. Stretch our muscles a little bit."

Ernie laughed at that, the idea of *their* muscles. "I didn't really think we'd been 'cooped up.' We were just at Yellowstone all day, the pool." Ernie paused. "Was that just two days ago?"

"Yeah, that happens. You lose track of days on the road." Scott stretched. "Maybe I'm just tense from yesterday. I hate all that shit, the photos, the … attention."

"Really?" Ernie answered before meaning to.

"You couldn't tell? I thought maybe I seemed miserable yesterday."

Ernie had thought just the opposite. His brother had been hypnotic, had seemed to always know exactly what to do, where to go. He'd thought he was getting a peek into Scott being in his element.

"All that shit wears me out. What do you do when work drives you crazy?"

Ernie thought about that. Lie awake in bed and stew, he thought. He hadn't really thought of work in a while. Had already more or less completely given himself over to this life on the road and life on the farm before that.

"You had moments where work drove you crazy, right?" Scott asked.

"Of course. It almost never wasn't driving me crazy. But that's office-job shit. I mean, you know. That's like what you do now, right? Or, you know. Before … all *this*, I guess." Ernie realized he didn't actually know what his brother's job was. Or had been. Had he quit? Just taken a year off? That was Holly, he was pretty sure. He remembered them saying something about a sabattical. Had they *both* taken a year off? "That's different from … being a wrestler."

"Sure. Of course it is. But … what's that one quote? The very first line of one of those Russian novels? 'All happy families are the same, unhappy families are different'? Something like that?" Ernie shrugged. "Where was I going with that?" He looked at Ernie, who was of no help. "Something about jobs. They're like the inverse of Tolstoy's families. All boring jobs are alike; fun jobs are each fun in their own way?" Scott thought about that, nodded at his own theory. Ernie wondered if it had come to him right then or if Scott just said it and nodded at himself like it had; Ernie wondered how many times Scott had said some version of that idea to someone before, wondered if, in fact, it had been someone else's saying, something else Scott had stolen as his own.

"Anyway. Getting off track. What do you do when work gets under your skin? Or Becca? Or whatever. How do you let off steam?"

Ernie shook his head, raised his shoulders up into his neck. "I kind of don't."

"You don't know?"

"I mean, I don't do anything. Not 'I don't know what I do.' I just bottle it up. You know that. I'm the quiet brother, I hold everything in."

"Fuck, Ernie! You gotta let that shit out. It'll kill you."

Ernie looked at his brother like *You think I don't know that?* but couldn't actually say it aloud.

Scott got stern. "I'm serious, Ern. You gotta let go of that shit before ..." He drifted off. Ernie looked at Scott, not quite looking like himself but not like Mr. Bison either. He looked more serious than Ernie was used to seeing him look, more ... solemn. Regretful maybe. Ernie searched and rolled over in his mind ways to ask him what he meant, or if he was okay, or what he was thinking about, but then Scott was shaking himself out of it, also something Ernie didn't think he'd ever seen him do before. He'd started to notice Scott rubbing off on him; it hadn't occurred to him that the reverse may be happening some too. Had shaking himself out of *Ernie's World* rubbed off on Scott unconsciously or was it another borrowed affectation?

"Let's go to the gym. Let get this shit out."

"I don't know. I'm not disagreeing with you. I just ... I don't think the gym is where I 'get my shit out.' That seems more your outlet."

Scott laughed. "Fair. But I bet they have a pool. Or a sauna or something. A climbing wall, a basketball court. You don't have to ..." Scott switched into his mock-bass impersonation of someone doing an impersonation of their assumption of him and did air quotes, "*Work out.*"

"You don't think you have a to have a student ID or anything?" Ernie said, switching tactics. "If they're even open."

Scott made an incredulous face. "I'll just walk in like I belong there. Same idea as the pool."

Ernie thought of his brother striding in with the mentality that he belonged there. Like he was a student—a summer student?—and laughed at the idea. "Because you look like a college student, you think?"

"A nontraditional student, back to finish his degree, sure. I never graduated. I could go back to school."

"Sure."

"Or a teacher maybe? Teachers get to use university gyms, right?"

Ernie laughed again, shook his head.

"They don't?"

"Oh, I don't know. Just. You don't look like any teacher I ever had." He thought back to his own teachers, could barely remember the name of a single teacher he'd had in college. Had it all been that forgettable? Maybe Scott had had the right idea: drop out, go the "school of life" route. Ernie couldn't remember a single teacher he'd ever had, and meanwhile they were in the middle of a roadtrip being paid for with Scott's "school of life" royalties. "Yeah, I don't know. Maybe you just tell them who you are, play the famous card?"

"Fuck that. That's Yellowstone all over. We were supposed to have a relaxing day in the park, not a day of photos and having to be Mr. Bison for everyone. The whole reason I stopped here was to let go of that, not have a bunch of summer school kids watch me work out. I bet they just let us walk in. Some student working the counter during the summer cares if we walk in to work out? He looks at me and says something?"

That caught Ernie off-guard. Scott rarely referred to or hinted at his own size, rarely if ever seemed self-aware of how intimidating his very presence could be. "Cares if *you* just walk in to work out. I don't want to be a dick, but I'm out. I'll walk the campus, I think."

"You sure?"

"Yeah. You work out, and I'll give myself a tour. It'll be fun. We can meet back up in ... an hour? Here? The bookstore?" Ernie thumbed back over his shoulder at the bookstore behind them.

"Hour and a half?" Scott answered. "I'm gonna run back to the car, get a change of clothes. Probably try to take a quick shower after too."

"Perfect."

Ernie zigzagged through building walkways, the quad, down a few paths that looked to be hidden shortcuts but probably everyone who went to school there knew about them. Some of the paths and buildings reminded him of going to school and for small moments, he felt almost 20 again, everything seeming new, the whole world still out ahead of him, and then he'd make a turn and it would look nothing like his own experience, shaking him out of his nostalgia, back into the present. He made his way to the other end of campus before realizing he'd gone so far, found himself at the football stadium, and then was surprised to find it open, that he was able to walk in and right down onto the field.

Ernie hadn't been on a track since high school, and it felt relaxing and beautiful, big and overwhelming all at once. He'd always loved sports fields of any kind—something about them seeming both purposeful and bigger than their purpose.

At some point, in junior high he thought he remembered it being, Scott went through an athletic version of a growth spurt—he didn't grow three inches in four months, that actually came a couple years later, and this was a decade before he disappeared for a year and reappeared with his wrestler physique, but seemingly all of a sudden he could throw balls faster and farther; playing homerun derby in their grandparents' backyard or one-on-one basketball in their driveway was no longer a contest, despite the age difference in Ernie's favor. Scott shrugged it off, was modest to the point of it driving Ernie crazy, and Ernie stopped playing sports altogether. Didn't try out for baseball the next year, stopped dreaming maybe the basketball coach would drive through their neighborhood, see him sinking long three-pointers from the mailbox and beg him to join the team. Instead, he threw himself into fandom: checked the newspaper box scores every day, became addicted to *SportsCenter*.

Ernie looked out at the field, the grass seeming almost impossibly green, the track around it appealing in a way that surprised him. In high school, despite having given up on playing sports, and hating the running days in gym most of all, Ernie liked to sneak out of the house at night and run through the neighborhood. He dreaded his gym teacher's weekly "It's a beautiful day to run!" every Friday, but that seemed almost part of its appeal at night. The risk not only of getting caught but of getting in trouble for sneaking out to do something he didn't even really like. He didn't have a car, or any friends who would also sneak out, to drink in the fields or hang out at Denny's, drinking milkshakes and eating breakfast after midnight, or whatever the cool kids were doing. He didn't have a girlfriend. He didn't have anywhere to go, any reason to not stay in bed, but he'd wait until he couldn't hear their parents anymore, until he saw the lights flick off under the slit below his door, and then slowly get back up out of bed. Slide his feet from bedroom to back door, careful for the creaks he'd noticed and made note of during the day, and grab his Walkman from where he'd left it in the garage the night before.

Ernie loved the way his neighborhood looked and felt at night. The silence and stillness. He always underdressed, liking to start cold, shivering almost, then warming up as he ran, the cold in the air washing over him. In the dark, he could see inside the houses with their lights on, watch people doing whatever they did. It reminded him of dioramas at museums their parents took them to as kids, or the shadow boxes he'd done as projects in class. "Little frozen universes," a teacher had called them, the phrase sticking with him for all these years. Ernie remembered the Thunderbird Inn, was surprised he didn't recall these little frozen universes then. He wondered how that dog was, if it returned to the motel and was there waiting for the owners when they returned, or if it kept running. Maybe it was living in the woods with Benjamin, the Wolfman and his sidekick. He wondered what the dog was doing, what Benjamin might be up to, what about all those girls he'd had crushes on in junior high and high school? How many high school sweethearts were still together, how many girls who he'd had a crush on had already gotten married and divorced?

Without thinking about it, Ernie was jogging along the track. He felt like an athlete, here on such a nice *real* track. He wasn't dressed to run—jeans, bulky, flat-soled Adidas that he stopped to tighten and retie—but he was all the way across campus from the car, and a trip back and forth, any obstacle at all that gave him enough time to actually think about what he was doing, would only ruin the moment.

He found himself now glad it was summer—glad for the campus being empty, glad for the beautiful weather. If there'd been anyone else on the track, anyone within eyeshot at all, he might have felt self-conscious. That was another reason he liked running at night—he wasn't being timed, he wasn't in competition with anyone else, he wasn't being watched or compared to anyone else. There was only the joy, the purity of the moment.

And then, as soon as Ernie recognized what had until then only been subconscious, as soon as his mind conjured the words *purity of the moment* instead of just feeling the moment itself, the joy drained out of him. He was suddenly aware of his uncomfortable-to-run-in shoes; his jeans stuck to his legs. He remembered why, even after he'd transitioned to boxers in high school, he'd kept a couple pairs of briefs, just for running. His feet hurt, in inappropriate running shoes, and his legs hurt from being jolted into action after years of nonuse. Running had always been best, the reason he'd ever enjoyed it at all, as much as he could say he'd ever enjoyed it, when it washed everything else away.

In high school, running through his neighborhood after sneaking out of his house, Ernie made bets and rewards for himself. If I run up the hill, around the two blocks past the Hansons', and back down before the song ends, Jennifer will tell me she likes me. If I make it to the train tracks without having to stop to walk, Katherine will ask me to the next dance. If I run my whole course for the night without once having to stop and rest, Amy will be there waiting for me, arms open, ready for a kiss. The end results of these bets not happening never seemed to make them less inspirational; that was the girls' faults, not his own. He was always careful to word his self-bets to not put the burden of action or initiation on himself.

It was always Katherine asking *him* to the dance, Jennifer telling *him* she liked him, never the other way around. Ernie knew his limits, didn't want to bet himself into action, into something he knew he couldn't do. But, really, running was the best when, after making one of these bets with himself, he didn't actually think of the girl he'd used for inspiration. He didn't think about *what might happen if*, or the pain in his legs or side, or even the music he was listening to in his headphones. It was best when he didn't think of anything at all. He always thought this was what was meant by a runner's high, by being in the zone—nothing affects anything else, everything is a tunnel of action and motion and the brain turns off, or goes into overdrive, and everything happens as it should. Every shot ball swishes through the net; pitchers can pinpoint any corner of plate they want or hitters make perfect contact with pitches that should have fooled them; he can run for longer periods than he'd normally think possible. Maybe Scott was in his own zone in the gym right now, lifting more weight than he had in a while, doing even more reps than was his goal.

Instead, right now, trying to not think of anything at all, Ernie was too conscious of trying to think of nothing. He was thinking of everything. He was already winded. His side ached. He could hear himself breathing so loudly it distracted everything else. He made himself sprint the straightaway before taking a break and could, stride by stride, feel a blister forming on his left foot, his shoe and sock rubbing into his skin. It felt like a needle, a thumbtack pricking into his heel with every step. A V of sweat soaked down from the collar of his shirt and, lower, a circle of more sweat in the middle of his chest, a running exclamation.

Into the next curve, Ernie let up, started walking. He couldn't remember the last time he'd run like that. It felt good and horrible at the same time, and he remembered why people liked to run and also why he'd always hated it. He walked the next lap, cooling down, taking deep breaths, holding his side. He thought of Scott, his brother's years spent wrestling. Making almost no money, living in cheap hotels when on the road, a series of cheaper apartments when staying in place, filling in the gaps between places on friends' couches, who knew where else. Scott hadn't ever said as much, but there'd been enough small hints for Ernie to be pretty sure these presumptions were at least close. He was less sure if what he pictured was pity—those hard times, all that hard work to barely make a living—or jealousy—the glamour of being twentysomething and living on the road, on friends' couches, not having to work for The Man. Scott himself was almost as mum about the specifics of those years as their Uncle Paul had been about the war. Ernie couldn't remember the last time he'd thought of Paul; he wondered if Scott ever did, if they'd maybe even reconnected over the years.

A dust of rain appeared, raising goosebumps on Ernie's arms. It felt refreshing, like standing under a mist machine at an outdoor summer concert. Ernie thought of running through sprinklers in their grandparents' front yard with Scott. He thought of the rain washing away his sweat, pictured the two separating like oil and water, unable to mix. He thought of Travis Bickle, wishing a heavy rain down on his city, something to wash away the dirt and scum.

Ernie thought of Benjamin. Before Wolfman, before he'd discovered girls, before he started thinking of them as something to run *towards*, Ernie's inspiration had been *away*. In elementary school, he and Benjamin would run through the neighborhood. At night, after long days playing outside, after staying out too late, the sun having set, they would have to run home in the dark. Earlier in the day, they would tease each other to get the other running—*Suzie is chasing you! Brenda looooooves you!* But at night, there was more danger, they had to run faster. They ran through the neighborhood, through a block of backyards, calling after one another—*Freddy Krueger is right behind you! Leatherface!!* Neither was yet allowed to watch these movies, but they'd heard things, could imagine the bad guys. They'd seen the movie posters and video box covers, knew these were names to be feared, names to run from. They ran faster than they'd ever run before, faster than they would ever run again. Faster than anyone else ever.

Ernie thought of the quarter-mile in front of him, made a bet with himself: If I can sprint this next lap, without stopping, without slowing down, I'll confront Scott. I'll ask him why he stole my story, why he didn't tell me. I'll ask him why he thinks we grew apart, why we needed him to get a windfall of video game money and buy a farm for us to reconnect.

Ernie put his head down. He closed his eyes, opened them and looked up, and there was nothing in front of him but track. Nothing else existed, everything else had been washed away, dry-erase-board clean. He wasn't running away from anything or toward anything. He forgot about everything, forgot how his foot and legs and side hurt, forgot about the dog, the Thunderbird, forgot Scott was off lifting weights or doing whatever, forgot about confronting Scott, forgot Scott was even on the trip with him, forgot he was on a trip at all, forgot he hated running, and just ran.

19.

Ernie felt Scott approach, though only realized the feeling after the fact, after Scott lay down on the grass next to him. After he'd opened his eyes and turned his head to make sure it was indeed his brother lying there next to him.

Ernie, all running afterglow, smiled at his brother, returned his head skyward but kept his eyes open, squinting. He pulled his hands out from under his head, visored the sun out of his eyes with them. "I ran a few laps," he finally blurted, not necessarily wanting to but surprised Scott still hadn't said anything.

"Nice," Scott answered. He paused. "Probably a good idea. Smart. Definitely better to be in shape and ready for when the zombies attack."

Scott looked like he'd been waiting for this, for Ernie's continued response. Big smile on his face, he knew he was being coy. He reached down to his side, then held up a big paperback of collected comics—a line of zombies, their empty, blank eyes looking directly at Ernie, ready to swarm and overtake them there on the football field; in the background, a splintered and blood-splattered family photo, all smiles from happier, presumably pre-zombie times. A big crease down the middle—Ernie assumed Scott had folded it in half, but it also made it look like his brother was himself in something of a zombie apocalypse, had been carrying this book around with him in his back pocket, his only form of entertainment. Ernie didn't even like to dog-ear pages, couldn't imagine folding a book in half.

"I haven't read a comic in forever. Since we were little. Remember O'Leary's?"

"Sure."

"Man, that place was great."

Ernie waited for his brother to elaborate, wondered where he was going with it. Sometimes Ernie wondered if he had more of a fondness for nostalgia than others or just talked about it more; was it a greater predilection or was he just quicker to work it into conversation? He didn't really remember Scott ever bringing up their childhood, playing video games, or with *G.I. Joe* or *Star Wars* toys.

"And?" Ernie finally prodded.

"What do you mean?"

"You asked if I remembered O'Leary's. I thought maybe there was more story there."

"Nope. Just that it was great. Picking this up reminded me of going there, I guess." They returned to silence, looking up into the sky, Ernie with his hands shielding his eyes, Scott holding the book open above him, shading his whole head.

"Actually," Scott said, and Ernie wasn't sure if he was surprised there was more, or if Scott was confirming what he'd assumed all along. "You know what I remember about Dad taking us there? Just walking around and not really knowing anything about comics. We didn't know who any of the writers or artists were yet. Or ... I didn't at least."

Ernie closed his eyes, rubbed his face. He pictured walking through the biggest comic book store he could imagine, unsure what he was doing, almost lost. "Nope. A little later, I guess."

"Right. You connected to a couple of the guys, collected them for a little while, right?"

"Yeah," Ernie said, surprised Scott remembered.

"Right. And I guess I moved on before I even found my guys. But those first few times especially. We didn't know anything, we just walked around, picked up a couple random things that looked cool. I remember every time we went I'd try to buy one issue of something I'd heard of, *Spiderman* or *Batman* or whatever, and one I hadn't. Something new or weird or whatever."

Ernie again waited for his brother to keep going, but the pause held longer than expected. That was either all there was to it, or Scott was reminiscing now.

A cloud passed in front of the sun, and the temperature dropped 10 degrees. Even with his eyes closed, Ernie felt it get darker. He wondered if it was a singular cloud, something that would just as quickly pass and keep going, or a whole sky of them. He didn't want to open his eyes yet.

"How was the gym?"

"It was great actually."

"No problems?"

"Nope. I'm telling you, people believe what you tell them."

Ernie let that hang in the air before asking, "What'd you tell him?"

"Oh, nothing. Told him ... *with my body*." Scott laughed. "I just walked in. Stood up straight, gave him a quick nod, then quickly looked past him, out to where I was headed."

Ernie thought about that, nodded. He pictured it happening, his brother approaching some undergrad working the summer shift at the gym, Scott standing up a little straighter as he walked, taller, almost unfolding himself or expanding. As he worked his way through picturing what Scott had described, he realized this was the first he was aware of Scott being aware of standing up straighter, making himself bigger. In Yellowstone, when Ernie was able to describe to himself what about his brother looked and seemed different, he assumed it was instinct—there was a crowd, pictures being taken, Scott was in character, and it all presumably just ... *happened.* The entire display had been unexpected, this recognition of Mr. Bison as character, but even still, Ernie didn't think of Scott's intention, his awareness of this creation.

"You?" Scott asked.

"What?"

"You ran a few laps?" Scott said. "How was it?"

"It was ... it was great too actually," Ernie said, almost surprised at his own answer, the pain in his side, his foot, his entire dislike of running already fading. "I can't really remember the last time I ran. A few weeks every couple years or so, I guess, whenever I try to get in a little shape. I haven't run on a track since high school. And I hated it then. But this felt good. It was fun. Something about how nice the track is made it ... I don't know. Better? Just made it seem ... fancier?" It sounded dumb as he said it, but he let it linger there.

"That makes sense." Scott sat up, pulled his left knee up, tucked his right elbow behind it, his left arm out behind him, and twisted himself to his left. Ernie heard his brother's back crack three times, and then Scott did the same in the opposite direction.

Ernie sat up too, wrapped his arms around his pulled-in legs, didn't try to crack anything. "You know," he said. "It's funny. I hated running in gym, but in high school, I'd sneak out of the house at night, after you and Mom and Dad went to bed, and I'd just go running through the neighborhood—"

"Sure."

"Isn't that weird?" Ernie paused. "Wait. What do you mean, 'sure'?"

"You know. Sure. You snuck out and went running."

"You knew?"

"Did you think I didn't?"

Ernie looked at his brother, wondering if Scott was fucking with him. He didn't think he was.

"Do you think Mom and Dad knew?" It wasn't the question he'd meant to ask—he'd *wanted* to ask how Scott knew—but it was the question that came out.

Scott shrugged. "I don't really think so."

Ernie thought about that. He looked down at the grass, pulled a handful of blades out of the ground, a handful more.

"What are you thinking about?" Scott asked. Ernie looked at him. Surprised at his brother's question, surprised he looked like he was thinking about anything.

"Why'd you tell that reporter guy about Pony?"

Scott's turn at surprise. "What do you mean? Because he asked?"

"No," Ernie said. He picked at the grass between his legs. Pulled out handfuls, threw them out in front of him. "No. He didn't. But that's not what I mean. Not why did you tell him. Why ..."

"I didn't—"

"That's *my* story." Ernie stopped pulling grass, stopped fidgeting, turned to look Scott straight in his eyes. The question was forceful, focused, but his eyes showed that he was hurt too. "My memory. My *life.*"

Scott shook his head, looked his brother in his eyes.

"Why is it part of your story? Your, like ... your fucking *origin story.*"

"What do you mean?" Scott asked.

"You didn't go visit Pony! Did you *ever* even meet her?!"

Scott thought about that. "One," he said and held up his index finger.

Again with the fucking counting, and already Scott was filling in number one. "Yes. I remember Pony. We would go see her together!

"Two. I don't know. It's just part of ... what did you call it? My *origin story*? Exactly, actually! Holly made up most of it actually. Made it up, wrote it, put it together, whatever. I wasn't Mr. Bison because of M. Bison and Wojnarowicz's 'Buffalo' or any of that. I just liked buffalo, man. I thought they looked cool, I was big, it seemed like a good name. Holly gathered all of these stories—from me, stories I'd told her about you, some of her own life. She put it all together, turned a cool name into a *character*. She's probably half the reason this video game exists.

"Three: I didn't *ask* you because I didn't even think of it, but also I never thought it would turn into anything. I never thought I'd be interviewed. I never thought I'd be the star of a video game!

"But also, while we're at it—" Scott held up his hand with all four of his giant Mr. Bison fingers stretched out, and, for a flash, Ernie forgot where he was, what they were talking about. "Four: It's not really any different than your Benjamin story, right?"

"What Benjamin story?" Ernie was confused.

"You know. The whole Wolfman thing. 'What do you wanna be when you grow up? I'm gonna be a Wolfman!' *I* told you that. It was like this game we'd play. I told you I wanted to grow up and be a Wolfman and you'd say you'd be The Invisible Man. Sometimes Benjamin would play too. Before he moved. He could never decide though. Sometimes Dracula, sometimes Frankenstein. There was someone else too, right?"

"The Mummy," Ernie answered before realizing it.

"Yes!"

"Creature from the Black Lagoon!" They both started laughing, picturing Benjamin's Creature impersonation.

When the laughter wound down, Scott looked at his brother. "Have I not told you all this? Like when we came out and visited? How Holly and I met?"

Ernie held his arms out to his sides, looked around. Like, *try me*. Like, *we don't have anywhere to be.*

20.

I had a match, up in Everett.

This was just after Mom died. I moved back. Or ... not really moved back. I came back for a few months, was the idea. I didn't even really know why, it just felt like I should. Like, I should help Dad or something, I guess? I sublet a room in a house, went over to Dad's a lot.

One night, I was out at the bar. I didn't really want to get drunk with Dad, but the house where I was staying was depressing as shit. It was close enough to downtown that I could walk though. I could go out, get drunk, not have to drive. It was kinda nice. If you call an excuse to drink too much nice.

My rent was month to month. I wasn't really sure if I was going to stay in town or, if not, how long I would stay. I didn't really know the circuit out there. It didn't seem like there was much of one actually. If I stayed, was I going to try to help build one? Was I going to have to get a real job? Doing what?

At the time, I liked to tell myself I liked going to the bar to sit and have a beer and ponder all those questions, but probably I was just going to get drunk. I was avoiding pondering those kinds of questions.

Anyway. This one night. It was March Madness, there were a couple games on different TVs. I don't remember who or what round it was. I didn't really care about watching. But I liked that they were on, I liked pretending like I was watching. This particular night, I'd noticed this cute girl in a round, corner booth. She was really into the game. She was with a couple friends. I kept looking over, checking her out, I guess. Kinda trying to figure out the relationships between them. A boyfriend and her brother maybe; or a boyfriend and a third-wheel friend? I couldn't tell. And then I'd look back at the TV, so I wasn't just looking like I was checking her out or like I wanted to fight or something. I don't even look like that, I don't think, but guys see my size, see me looking anywhere near their direction, that's how they read it. Sometimes they'd lean one way or another, and she and one of the guys would look like a couple, but then other times they just all looked friendly. I couldn't tell what was going on. She was cheering the most of any of them, was really intently watching the game, getting really excited for certain baskets. It was adorable. She was magnetic. She didn't seem to notice me looking at her, didn't seem to notice me in the bar at all, but I had to keep reminding myself to look away, to keep my eyes on the TV.

I didn't do a very good job. She finally noticed or finally made it known she'd noticed me—noticed me checking her out or just noticed me watching the game by myself or maybe both—and called me over.

"Hey, you. Come join us. Don't just watch the game by yourself, come watch it with us. We've got room for you."

One guy scooted out of the booth, moved around to the outside of the other guy, made room for me on the edge next to her.

I tried to act like I didn't really want to, like I was good, no thanks, but I didn't want to be rude, they had made room, so, fine, I'd join them, though of course this was the best-case scenario. I grabbed my beer, took it with me to their table. Soon as I sat down, I finished it, kinda nervous, not sure what to do or say, and one of the guys picked up their pitcher from the table, topped me off.

"Who you like?" she asked me, still not taking her eyes off the TV.

"Oh, I don't know," I said or something like it. I tried to tell her I didn't really have a team, just liked watching the game. I tried to make some kind of argument about how that made the games more fun to watch, less stressful; I didn't get caught up in rooting for one team or the other, could just enjoy good basketball.

"Agnostic," she said, and I'll tell you, I was in love right there. "I don't really get it myself," she added. "Believe or not, you know, but whatever."

We watched the game, made a little small talk. Gonzaga won, Holly bought us a round of shots to celebrate.

We started talking, and it was so easy, so natural. I told her all about wrestling, the road, Mom, Dad. How I was back in town, not really sure what I was doing.

She was in grad school to become a teacher—her dad had been a high school English teacher, it was what she'd wanted to do since she could remember. I didn't know anyone who'd actually known what they wanted to do when they were little, who actually grew up and continued down that path. That whole idea seemed like a myth or something.

At some point, both of the other guys left. I didn't even notice. Don't know if they left together, at two different times, what. Holly and I immediately felt in sync. There was another game on, and Holly would look up at the score every now and then, but mostly we were just in our own little bubble.

"See, I don't get it," she said again, at some point. "If you weren't here, I'd be paying more attention to the game, but I don't really care, like I did for that Gonzaga game."

"Isn't that kinda nice? Not feeling so stressed over it."

"Not at all! The stress is part of what makes it fun. It gives it stakes." She looked

at me. That smile! "Don't get me wrong, I'd be getting pretty into it ... but it's not the same."

"You would be?"

"Yeah."

"If I weren't here?" I'd never before so fished for a compliment, reassurance.

"Or maybe I'm just talking to you 'cause it's a shitty game."

I looked up, and it was a blowout.

She told me about her classes, what she liked about teaching. How she knew it was what she wanted to do. All her ideas for classroom exercises and homework assignments and activities that she couldn't wait to try out in the classroom, once she was done with all her own classes, though she liked those too.

The game ended, the bar slowly emptied, the bartender called last call, we got a last call, the bar closed.

"So ..." she said. "You gonna invite me back to your place or what?"

I hadn't even got that far, hadn't thought ahead at all.

But I tell her we can walk there, so we do, and we fool around some, but mostly we just stay up all night, talking. She asked me all kinds of questions I'd never really thought about before—about wrestling, about leaving school and moving to New York, about our parents, about you, about our relationship.

Then, in the morning, she gave me a kiss goodbye and was gone. Just like that. I don't even know how, she just disappeared. I don't know if she called a friend, or a taxi, or walked, or what. It felt like ... I'll tell you, it felt like an emotional one-night stand. That's the cheesiest shit ever, I know, but that's what it seemed like. I'd told this girl, this woman, shit about me I'd never even thought about before, much less told anyone, and I knew more about her than just about anyone, but I didn't know her name. I swear, that night, the next morning ... I felt like I knew this was the girl I wanted to marry ... and she was gone.

Fast-forward, Dad's back on his feet or whatever, I feel ready to get back east, back to the circuits I knew, the promoters who knew me. I'd mostly not really wrestled in those couple months, but I met enough people to put together one, like, exhibition show before I leave, and who shows up? Holly! She knew my wrestler name of course, I'd told her all about Mr. Bison. I didn't know if she'd even gotten my name or not, but she knew Mr. Bison and somehow saw a flyer. And so she came, brought those two friends from March Madness. But I was getting ready to move! I was moving in like three days!

But we traded numbers, and after that we talked almost every night. I'd call her from whatever shitty motel I was in and I'd tell her how the match had gone. But she started doing this thing ... she started weaving all these stories I told her into a ... well, into a story. A narrative, she called it. It was fun! Like we were building this thing together.

Why buffalo? Why Mr. Bison? Tell me a story about when you were a kid. Tell me about something you and Ernie did growing up. Tell me a story about someone you look up to. Why that person, why that story?

She'd ask me all these questions, and I don't know if she was taking notes or not, if she just remembered everything, if she was asking because she was curious or specifically because she knew she was putting it all together for me, but over time, she'd built this whole story. Some of it was me, some of it was you. Some was totally made up, some was her. It was great, hearing her take this, like, this raw info I gave her and hearing her mold it into something. Something about me!

The Legend of Mr. Bison, she called it.

21.

Holly sat on the couch, restless. She wanted to go out into the field and curl up into a ball with Billy and sleep, but then she heard her father's voice in her head. He's a wild animal, he said. What if something happened to you, to the baby? The voice felt so real, she felt herself getting frustrated at his ... not forbidding but warning. Wild animal my ass, she thought. Billy came and went in and out of the house, they let him fall asleep at their feet. Billy is my animal. This is my house. Just because you're here helping doesn't change that, doesn't give you the right. It made her want to all the more, but at the same time, she didn't want to get into it. Whether or not her dad would actually even say anything, his imagined caution felt so real, the possibility didn't feel worth her energy.

She rolled from one side to the other, frustrated now at her father. She knew, without having to turn on the TV and flip through channels that she didn't want to watch TV.

She got up, went to her office. She laughed, seeing her notebook sitting there on the middle of her desk. *The Year of the Buffalo*. Every time she saw it, it felt silly—*it*, the notebook; *it*, this whole year of pregnancy and sabbaticals and video games and a live buffalo. She didn't really know how to keep a diary, so she'd started taking notes. Making lists. Some were practical, others joke-y.

How to Tie Your Shoes
How to Pass the Days When Pregnant and Not Working
How to Make Yourself Smile
How to Brush Your Teeth
How to Floss

One of her favorite lesson plans was when she divided her classroom into groups and had them write instructions. She'd bring in peanut butter, jelly, and bread and ask them to write instruction for how to make a sandwich. At the end of class, she'd try to follow their instructions, putting the jelly on the wrong side of the bread or scooping the peanut butter out with her fingers if the instructions didn't make clear otherwise. Or bags of marshmallows and toothpicks and ask them to build a simple structures and paired instructions and then swap with each other, see how close they could get.

The lists starting as mostly little instructions for Junior, but more and more they became lessons Scott had shown her over the years, more remembrances of their courting than instructions for their son.

How to Throw a Baseball

How to Punch

How to Forget

She flipped back through her last handful of pages.

How to Wink

How to Take a Punch

She stared at *How to Steal* and felt weird. She took her Sharpie and scratched it all out.

When they'd first started dating, Scott loved showing Holly his wrestling moves. Or maybe she loved being taught and he obliged. She asked lot of questions—*Why fold your leg like that? How hard do I slap the ground?*—teaching him how to teach her. It was a way for one to understand the other—Holly getting a glimpse into Scott's world of wrestling, Scott seeing how much Holly loved the teaching and learning processes, imagining how great she must be in a classroom. One of Holly's girlfriends in college had had this theory: *Seeing someone in their element, seeing them do what they are good at, is incredibly sexy.* Holly had found the observation so obvious she'd thought "theory" was overselling it, though it had stuck with her. She thought of it often with Scott. He'd wrap an arm around her, show her how to bend, where to move. It was sexy, Scott showing her how to do this thing he was so good at, but it was also incredibly seductive. *Is it sexy like this in the ring?* she'd tease. It was all so close, so intimate. *It doesn't work quite like this in the ring,* Scott would answer, and then lift her in the air, take her to the ground. Wrestling as foreplay.

Holly had sometimes joked she should help Scott write a book. Part instruction manual, part personal story. He'd teach her how to do the things he'd largely taught himself, and she helped craft his story, his persona. *Why buffalo*? she'd ask. *Why the name, Mr. Bison? Why wrestling, when did you know, how?* She loved taking these little stories of his—his anecdotes, the lessons he'd learned on the road—and figuring them out. Putting them together like a puzzle, making them more than what they were.

She went back and squinted, reread through her own scratching. Flipping back and forth between what she'd just scratched out and a new, clean sheet of paper, she rewrote the list.

Rule number one: People don't want to feel like they're being looked down on.

Rule number two: Act as if ...

Rule number three: Know your surroundings.

Holly stared at the rules. They felt helpful, interesting. Maybe they weren't how to steal. *How to ... Get What You Want*? ... *Be Confident*? She jotted those down, though they still didn't feel right. She'd come back to it.

She'd zoned out a little staring at the page and thought of Ernie. *Ernie's World*, Scott called it. When he said it, it sounded a little judgmental or dismissive, but she liked the idea. This whole dream world to be able to escape to.

An idea!

Holly closed the notebook, went almost darting out of the room. In the spare bedroom was a giant Tupperware box of all her old Nintendo games and the system itself, miscellany. She'd moved it with her from her parents' house to the dorm to each subsequent house, apartment, this farm, though she hadn't opened it since college.

She carried the full box back to the living room, dropped it in front of the TV. Removing the lid felt almost like opening a just-excavated locked treasure box. Covering the top, acting almost like second lid, was her folded Power Pad. She wondered if it still worked, if it might be appropriate exercise during pregnancy. Under the Power Pad, a tangled ball of cords—original controllers, NES Advantage controller with turbo buttons she could lock down for running and swimming in *Track and Field*, Zapper Gun, *Power Glove*. Then, the lowest layer, Nintendo subsoil, the games themselves. The gold box of *Zelda* jumping out from all the gray, then she started scanning titles: *Metroid*, *Goonies II*, the *Rad Racer* she'd traded R.O.B. for after getting it as a Christmas present but finding it frustrating, though she kept the game it came with, *Gyromite*. She kept digging, found *Super Mario Bros. 2*. She remembered it being one of her favorites though couldn't remember why, other than the option to play as different characters. Her parents often teased her that playing video games was for boys, which she thought was ridiculous, though it was true, none of her girlfriends ever really liked to play, and almost all of the games she played were *about* boys, but that was part of why *SMB2* was such a favorite.

She could play as Princess! She could save the world, not have to be the one who required saving.

Holly plugged the system into the back of the TV, almost surprised she was able to, that TVs hadn't advanced beyond having this connectivity. Every other new piece of technology seemed to need a new power cord, a new cord to connect one electronic to another.

She blew on the end of the cartridge, instinct despite it having been almost twenty years, pushed it in, was surprised again when it came on, seemed to work just fine. She selected Princess, started playing ... her impulse had been right, this was exactly what she'd wanted to do, the perfect mix of doing something and nothing.

How to Take a Punch

Don't brace.

Or, more honestly, both brace and don't. It's counterintuitive, it sounds contradictory, seems impossible maybe, but there in the middle of the two, the fine line between this and that: the sweet spot.

Same as throwing a punch, same as forgetting, same as everything: don't force it. Allow it. Go with it. Don't get punched: take the punch.

You'd be surprised too how much you can take. How hard a punch. The body is tougher than you think. It'll shake off more than you think it might.

Or it doesn't. The body can take more than you think it can until it doesn't.

22.

"Let's stop." Scott's voice sounded odd and surprising, cracking the long quiet. Overloud and like someone else's. He looked at Ernie, like, *right?* and stretched, as much as he could without punching into the window or blocking his brother's view of the road.

"Food or bathroom?" Ernie asked and wondered when he had slipped into such shorthand. When had full sentences become too exhausting or even unnecessary? And which of those two relationships – exhausted or familiar – had they slipped into with one another? Both?

"Who was the actress in that *Gas Food Lodging*?" Ernie asked.

"What?"

"Was that what it was called? I just thought of it, because of the exit signs. Did you ever see it?" Ernie remembered a guy he'd met in college who had so loved that movie, had fallen so in love with the actress in it, that he'd up and moved to New Mexico. Or Arizona. Wherever the movie was set.

"I never saw it though."

"But you've heard of it? You know what I'm talking about. That indie actress who was in a bunch of those movies."

Scott shook his head, shrugged that he had no idea. "Neither," he said. "I don't need anything. I just think we should find a place for the night. Make an evening of it."

"Here?" Ernie made a show of looking around, one side to the other, out his window then across and out Scott's. There was nothing. Ernie wondered why he hadn't said anything 10 miles back, 20, when they were at least somewhere near something, near civilization, or why he didn't wait for the next series of *lodging, next exit* billboards. But he hadn't really said anything since the story about meeting Holly. He'd finished the story, then they'd walked back to the car, and they'd started driving. Not in awkward silence necessarily, but in silence nonetheless.

"Sure. Seems as good a place as any. Better. I bet we can find a cheap room somewhere out here in the middle of nowhere. And a *real* bar, not some college kid bar posing as a dive. We need ... one of those places that's been around forever and never even had a landline."

Ernie looked at him.

"You know. So the women – the wives and girlfriends or whoever – couldn't call and ask if their man was there."

"What are you talking about?"

"You know. Used to be a place like that just outside our town. Dad would go there, Mom sent me a couple times to see if he was there. She never sent you?"

Ernie shook his head.

Scott grunted a *huh.* "Or she'd call the place next door – I forget what it was. A laundromat? A cobbler or tailor or something old-time-y like that? She'd call up old Habberdasher Joe—" Scott laughed at his own joke, let it keep going until it wound itself down, not even trying to get back to his story until the humor of the idea, or the visual, or the word itself, wore off. "And ol' Joe would run over next door and check and see. I even bet he'd just leave the phone there on his counter, Mom waiting on the other end for him to come back with his report."

Ernie was only half listening. Why hadn't their mom ever sent him? He was the older brother, if anything, the memory should be his, not Scott's.

"Now that I think about it," Scott continued, "seems kind of like an old movie." He was picturing something black and white, a Frank Capra town, probably an uplifting tale of salvation or triumph by the end.

"Sounds depressing."

"Right. That too. Depressing, but, you know. An uplifting tale of salvation or triumph by the end."

Ernie looked at him, like, what are you talking about?

"There," Scott said.

There? Ernie wanted to ask but didn't want to release the doubt in his voice so clenched his teeth and cinched his lips, nodded in agreement.

"That's what we need. That's the kind of place I knew we'd find out here."

The parking lot was dirt and would have looked like a random, empty lot save for a couple of pickups and what looked to be an either stretched or lowered Chevy Caprice wagon, or maybe they just look like that, and a few railroad ties to denote spaces. The place itself looked familiar, the kind he'd driven past on various roadtrips, through Roy, Washington, or Hebo, Oregon, Truckee, California, and wonder who ever even went there. The only sign that this wasn't closed down was the bright neon Stroh's sign next to what must have been the front door. If there were any windows, they were in the back, where he couldn't see them.

Ernie remembered Scott asking about *On the Road*, remembered telling his brother he hadn't read it, which was true, he hadn't, but he knew the gist. The idea. He'd seen *Easy Rider*. What had Scott's either/or been? *On the Road* or … what had it been? Kerouac or …? Hunter! *On the Road* or *Fear and Loathing*, he was pretty sure. He'd told Scott he hadn't read either, but he'd seen the movie. Why hadn't he said that at least?

Scott point-A-to-B'ed from door to bar, Ernie followed a step or two behind, trying to draft off his brother's confidence.

"Shot of bourbon," Scott called the moment he'd planted himself onto a stool, signaling with pointer finger, arm only barely raised off the table, and *hey, man* head nod, enough to call it a signal, but barely.

"Back?"

Scott smiled big, like, *yes*. Like, *I knew this was the place*. "You know it," he said.

"And you." The guy looked at Ernie.

"Same."

"Man," Scott said, turning to Ernie. "Bartenders nowadays don't know how to tend bar."

The barman put down a shot glass in front of each brother, cracked open two beers at once, one in each hand, and placed them behind the shots. "Not you, man," Scott clarified, and then his big, kinda-but-not-quite goofy smile. At first Ernie thought he was nervous or covering for himself, trying to sell the bartender that he meant no offense, or somehow already drunk, but then he recognized the expression from a few times earlier in the trip and realized Scott was just happy, he was showing joy and gratitude for the bar in general and the drinks in front of him and a good bartender specifically. And then, for no reason that seemed obvious, Ernie further realized where and why that smile of his had seemed familiar—it reminded him of Benjamin. It was the Wolfman's smile.

"Maybe you're going to the wrong bars," the barman said.

"Maybe," Scott answered. "I don't really go to bars at all anymore, but maybe. That's possible."

The bartender walked away, to ask if the guy sitting at the other end of the bar needed anything, or to chat with his regular, or just to get away from the out-of-towners. Ernie pulled his attention back to Scott, saw him with his shot raised, waiting. He picked up his own, went to cheers.

"What are we cheersing?" Scott asked, pulling his away.

"I don't know." Scott stared at Ernie, waiting for him to know. "Your video game?"

Scott shook his head, made a face.

"Being on the road?"

"There we go. To roadtrips!" Scott raised his glass high. "Roadtrips and beer-backs. Dying arts." He tossed back his shot, and then his smile turned into *what the fuck?* "Whoa, whoa! Don't put that down. You can't put it down without drinking after we cheer. What the fuck?"

"Sorry." Ernie drank the shot.

"That's better. Putting it down is bad luck, Ern. It, like, negates the cheers. A goocher, man. A reeeal goocher."

Ernie laughed, big, loud. He surprised himself. All trip he'd been quoting and referencing movies and Scott never seemed to catch it or know what he was talking about, and here finally was one of this own.

"Honestly," Scott said, ignoring Ernie's reaction. "Never been out drinking before?" He grabbed his beer and drank, back to his normal face and normal composure, like nothing had happened. Like he hadn't just scolded his big brother. "Where was I?" He repeated his slightly raised arm with extended finger signal to the bartender. "One more?" he asked, like a question, like the *please* was implied, then, back to Ernie, "Right. Beerbacking. Lost art, I say."

Ernie nodded in agreement, *sure, sure, that's interesting, I know what you mean*, though he didn't. He did his own fair share of drinking, but not like his brother, he now realized. Not in bars across the country, not as vocational perk.

The bartender came back, asked, "Two more?" Ernie had only barely touched his beer but answered, "Sure. Another round." He finished off his beer in one long pull to make room for the new one, and Scott was already holding up his new shot for another cheers. Ernie put down the empty, tried to keep his face straight, picked up his shot and went to cheers again, and, this time, Scott said, "to lost arts," still impressed with their impromptu stop or stuck in the beginnings of a drunk repeat mode, a scratch in his record, and then they cheersed and tossed back their second shots and as soon as Ernie slapped down his glass, already he felt it, the quick one, two, three of the drinks.

"Know what else?" Ernie said, wanting to blink his eyes wide like he could wake himself out of already feeling drunk, but holding back the urge.

"What else?"

"Another lost art," he said. "Bagging groceries." Ernie didn't know where the idea had come from or why it was coming out. "Every grocery store now, they either have all those self checkouts and you have to do it yourself, or the cashier is doing it. All those bags attached to that little baggie merry-go-round, that Lazy Susan thing, and the cashier's putting stuff in wherever. You get bags with one or two things in them, refrigerator items spread out all over the place. They used to get all your groceries in the perfect number of bags, all Tetris style."

Scott hadn't said anything, and Ernie stopped, wondering where the rant had come from.

"I don't know," Ernie downplayed. "Like you said. Lost art."

"I agree," the bartender said, reminding them he was there. "Most places don't have baggers anymore. I know exactly what you mean."

"Fuckin' A," Ernie agreed.

"Where you guys from?"

Before Ernie could speak up, Scott answered, "Out west."

"And on your way—"

"East."

"Very ... specific."

"Don't ask, don't tell, right?" Scott said and smiled a little conspiratorially. Ernie couldn't tell if he was hinting that they were up to no good and shouldn't say too much or why he was being purposefully vague. He kept expecting Scott to laugh and say he was just kidding, tell some version of their roadtrip history and destination; wondered if he'd tell of the conference in Detroit, the whole video game story, or make up something else, come up with some other possible destination, or a different reason for them to go to the same. It all seemed like a pretty great drinking-in-a-random-bar-in-the-middle-of-nowhere tale. Instead, Scott kept quiet, let the vagueness hang there and the bartender, who had maybe been waiting for the same thing, finally walked away, thinking who knows what.

They kept drinking, backing off the shots and sticking to cheap beer, with the occasional *one more shot* mixed in. *One more*, Scott would urge. Or *one more?* Even through the darkened bar, it was clear the sun had set, day had turned to night. Ernie wondered, a couple different moments throughout the night, where they were going to stay, why they hadn't planned ahead and figured that out before all this, all these drinks. Now they were past driving-level drunk, and neither had any idea where they were. Instead of voicing any of that though, he'd answer *sure*, or even work in his own occasional *another round?* Or signal to the bartender without having to say anything.

"You ever hear of this guy, the Georgia Rambler?" Scott asked.

"No. I don't think so. Is that ..."

"What?"

Ernie wanted to ask if it was a song. It sounded familiar. But he thought it either obviously was or obviously wasn't. He feared he'd sound dumb either way. "Nothing," he said.

"He wrote this newspaper column. Down in ... well, I guess it must have been Georgia. Obviously."

Ernie realized he'd been thinking of "Midnight Rambler." He was glad he'd cut himself off before saying it.

"I don't remember who told me about him. Or maybe I heard about him on the radio or something. NPR? Anyway, I read a bunch of his columns online, while bored at work, and they're pretty great."

Ernie wasn't sure if he'd meant wrestling work or more recent *work* work. He knew his brother liked to go to cafes while on the road wrestling, get online and do he-didn't-know-what, same as he sometimes did now. Was that what he meant? Or just the regular kind of bored-in-the-office work? Also, he listened to NPR? Every time Ernie thought he had his brother figured out, Scott did or said something to make him feel guilty for thinking he'd had Scott figured out.

"They're these great pieces about everyday people. Like, somewhere between town gossip and *This American Life.*"

"Alright."

"Anyway. I guess his deal was, every day, or every week or whatever, however often he did his column, he'd drive to a small, neighboring town and just go to some little place, a bar or ice cream joint or laundromat or whatever, and he'd ask people who the most interesting person in town was. Then he'd either track down that person and get their story, or he'd just kind of collect stories there from those people, you know, in the deli or wherever he was."

Ernie looked his brother in the eyes, wondered what had made him think of it. Just the fact that they were in some small-town bar? He wondered if Scott realized he was likely the most interesting guy in the bar in any bar he was in. And then, as he thought it, Ernie wondered if he'd previously ever realized that about his brother. He was sure he had, but would he have admitted it? Ernie could *feel* himself thinking about it. The idea swam around in his head. Which is when he finally realized just how drunk he was. Which is when he realized he really had to piss.

"I'll be back. Bathroom break." He overconcentrated to walk as straight a line as possible to the back corner, where he assumed the bathroom would be, and it was. There was one urinal and one toilet, a set-up he never fully understood as for one person or two. He left the door unlocked and stood in front of the urinal, his arm out, resting on the wall in front of him, leaning into it and holding himself up.

When Ernie returned to the bar, Scott was surrounded by a group of three or four guys, Ernie couldn't quite tell. They looked like they were just talking, and then, out of nowhere, the guy swung his fist through the air. Scott didn't quite duck but leaned back and turned, leaving the guy to stumble forward at the absence. Ernie could see Scott look at the guy's friends like wondering when they were going to restrain him, walk him out of there. Instead, they laughed, called their friend names.

"Nice dodge, pussy," the guy said when he recovered from the miss. Scott finally saw Ernie, gave him a look and nodded to the door. *Time to go.* "You can't just take the punch like a man, you gotta dodge it like some kind of faggot."

Scott shot his look at the guy now, gave him a glare. Ernie didn't think he'd ever seen that look before. Not with that intensity certainly.

"You gonna hit me back, or you some kind of hippie?" the guy kept urging. His friends were still laughing at his miss, laughs that he redirected toward doubling down on trying to prove something against Scott.

Scott took a breath, and Ernie saw that look that had come over him melt away. He shook his head. He looked over at Ernie, motioned for him to pay the bartender. Pay their bill so they could leave before this escalated much further.

"You just gonna bob and weave and dance around like a little faggot," the guy kept going. His friends were still laughing, at his miss, his namecalling. The whole thing. Laughing at what they got to witness, laughing that they didn't have to be involved themselves.

The guy went to swing again, and it all looked so slow to Ernie. He thought about people describing intense moments as "like they'd happened in slow motion," he thought of action scenes in movies that actually happened in slow motion. He wondered if that's how it always worked for fighters, for any athlete. How hockey goalies make saves when he could barely keep his eye on the puck, how baseball players were able to hit pitches that seemed too fast to be able to respond to. He remembered Scott teaching him how to punch, his surprise at Scott saying how much arm strength was leg strength. Like a pitcher pushing off the mound, the straight line and direct correlation of ballspeed all the way through the body, down to the foot on the rubber.

Ernie watched the guy pull back his hand, his whole arm, so he could swing it out and around, one big arc, but everything about it looked sloppy. Ernie could see the guy's hand was fisted all wrong, almost no part of his body seemed to be working in concert with any other part, his whole body leaned forward with and into the punch, no part of him planting for support, like he'd learned nothing from missing and almost falling on his previous attempt. The guy might have been in his fair share of barfights, beating up other guys that also didn't know what they were doing, but Ernie was pretty sure that he'd never played baseball.

Scott again leaned, bent at his neck, but seemingly into instead of away from the guy's punch. Ernie wondered what had happened, had his brother read the swing wrong? When even he himself could tell where it was coming from, where the guy was hoping to land it. Was Ernie seeing it all even slower than his athlete brother?

And then a noise, but unlike anything Ernie expected. More thud than slap, a crunch, a ... crinkling? Before Ernie could process the sound, could find the right description, it was already covered by a yell. It started low but stretched itself and got higher, grew from yell to scream and filled the room, and then Ernie realized it was the other guy on the ground, not his brother. The guy was curled into a ball on the floor, his hands tucked into his body, his whole body tucked into himself. His scream had tapered off, was now coming out in hiccupped spurts. It seemed, to Ernie, like he wanted to say ... something, but language had left him, all he had were cries, throat sounds.

Scott looked at his brother. "We should go."

He looked back at the bartender. "Sorry."

The bartender shrugged. Ernie thought he might add that the guy was asking for it, but he stayed silent like that. Ernie turned from bartender to the guy's friends, wondered if any of them might say anything, but they seemed in shock. Speechless, standing still.

"We're good?" Scott asked. "You paid?"

Ernie nodded.

"Alright." Scott thought for a minute, nodded. "Alright," he said again and headed for the door.

23.

Ernie had asked if Scott wanted him to drive, though why he thought he might be more sober than his brother, he wasn't sure.

"Not just drunk," he'd reminded. "You just got punched. In the head. I can drive, really."

"I'm fine," Scott had said. "If anything, the hit sobered me up. I can get us a few miles down the road, no problem." And sure enough, he'd gotten them a few miles down the road, where they'd found another cluster of freeway pitstop hotels.

Scott asked the woman checking them in if they had a fitness room. Or maybe a pool and hot tub.

"Both!" The woman smiled. "But ..." She looked behind her at the clock on the wall. "Both are closed until morning. They open at 10 a.m., and there's continental breakfast from 7 till 10." She smiled again.

"Thanks." Scott took the two room keys on the counter, turned and made his way for the elevators.

Ernie had stood there, motionless, speechless, through the whole transaction. Still unsure what had happened. Unsure how or why they weren't telling this woman about the whole thing, not that it was any of her business, but how was the story not leaking out of them? He didn't want to say anything if Scott didn't; he was doing all he could to not say anything. It was Scott's story, Scott had to at least initiate it.

"Let's walk."

"What do you mean?"

"The fitness center is closed. The pool and hot tub are closed," Scott said. "I'm too amped up to sit here and watch TV."

"Walk *where*? We're in the middle of nowhere."

Scott shrugged. "We can buy some shitty snacks at one of those gas stations and walk along the side of the road or whatever."

Ernie looked at his brother like he still wasn't sure.

"*I'm* walking." It was more forceful than Scott usually talked to Ernie. Frustrated, almost parental. "You can stay here, I won't be gone long. I just need to move, I think. Get rid of some of this energy."

"No, no. I'll go. Let's walk. Was it cold out?"

Scott looked at his brother, shook his head. Like he was still frustrated but playfully so now. He cracked a smile. "Nah, it's nice. It'll feel good."

"I forgot!" Ernie threw his arms up into the air, pulled up his shoulders and smiled wide. He thought he was being equally playful but then suddenly could see himself as if outside himself and remembered how drunk he was. He'd forgotten that too.

He looked at his suitcase, like trying to figure out if he needed anything from it. He looked back at the door, nodded, made an exaggerated *after you* arm out, bowing motion.

Scott led the way, to the stairs at the other end of the hallway instead of the elevator they'd taken up, through the lobby, outside. He looked to Ernie like he had a purpose, like he knew where he was going.

Ernie wondered if his brother had been here before. Maybe when traveling, when on the road wrestling? Was this the kind of town that might host a match? Might Scott have stayed in this very hotel before, drank at the bar they'd just come from even?

Then he remembered Scott walking through the hotel in ... Montana, had that been? Had that really only been three or four days ago? It already seemed like weeks, months. A lifetime ago. He remembered it like a totally different version of himself, following Scott through the hotel toward the swimming pool. Following his brother not too unlike he was right now, so, he supposed, maybe not actually that different of a version of himself.

He remembered Scott's story of swimming in hotel pools all across the country, his story of stealing books somewhere in New York. Ernie realized his brother probably hadn't been in this town before, this was just one of his skills, his superpower. *Believe it yourself, and most everyone else will too*, Scott had told him.

"So," Ernie finally tried. He let it sit there for a moment, still following Scott through the hotel parking lot, toward the main street of another small town off the freeway in the middle of nowhere. "What happened back there? What ... *happened*?"

"What do you mean? The guy punched me."

Ernie stopped walking, waited for his brother to notice. When Scott finally turned around to look at him, Ernie was just looking at him, head tilted down, eyes angled up. *Right. I saw that he punched you.*

"Look. The guy was being a dick. He wanted to fight. Actually, you know what. He didn't want to fight. He wanted to land a punch. He didn't want to fight, and he didn't want to take a punch. He wanted to hit someone, he wanted to hit *me*; he wanted to prove he was as strong as he thinks he is. He wanted to surprise himself at how hard he could hit me, and then he was already looking forward to acting like it hadn't been a surprise at all."

"All that? You could tell all that?"

"More or less." Scott cracked his knuckles, all four of his left hand, then only two in his right. He braided his fingers together, turned his hands inside out, stretched out his arms. It looked to Ernie like he'd been the one who'd landed the punch, not taken it. "I told you, those guys are all the same. Almost always one in every bar. Sometimes you diffuse the tension, sometimes you just leave."

"And sometimes you let them hit you?"

"Usually their buddies will stop them before then, or you just leave. You let the guy think he intimidated you out of the bar, whatever."

"But *sometimes you just let him hit you?*" Ernie repeated. "In the *head*."

Scott shrugged. "Usually they'll swing for your chest, knowing it's kinda fucked up to hit someone in the face. Or they'll swing for your head, knowing you'll just move and dodge it. Which he did, and I did. And, almost always, that ends that." Scott stared out down the road, off into nothing. "But then he swung at my head *again*. Like he expected a different result? So I gave him a different result." Scott laughed a little at himself.

"But ... it didn't hurt?"

"A little. I've got a little headache. It hurt that guy a lot worse." Scott laughed again, a little more awkwardly this time.

"Oh, shit!" Ernie remembered. "Like fucking *Gladiator*!"

"With ... what's his name? Russell Crowe? And ... River Phoenix's brother."

"Joaquin. But, no. Before that. It was this boxing movie. Did we see it together?"

"I don't think so. I don't remember."

"I don't actually remember it that well. But at one point ... I can't remember if the whole movie is about bareknuckle boxing specifically, or if that's just one scene. Brian Dennehy is like a trainer, or ex-champion, or both or something? I remember one specific fight scene where they are boxing without gloves and whoever is boxing goes to punch Dennehy in the head, and he turns his head down and into it like you did, and ... I think it breaks the guy's hand!"

Scott nodded.

"Do you think you broke that guy's hand?!"

"Probably." Scott paused. "Though I wouldn't say *I* broke his hand. I think *he* broke his hand. If it is indeed broken." Scott paused again, looked to Ernie like he was considering whether or not he thought it was broken. "You see how he was holding his hand?"

"I did!" Ernie said, excited that he had. "It was all wrong!"

"See? I told you most people don't know how to punch, right?"

Ernie made a fist like his brother had taught him, held it up for Scott to see. Scott smiled, nodded, and Ernie smiled back, proud. Ernie looked around, saw nothing in any direction. There was their own hotel, among the cluster, behind them, but further than he would have thought. How long had they walked, how far? Was there really nothing else here? A small, makeshift freeway-exit town, and then nothing?

"You think he would have broken it if he'd known how to punch?"

"*If* it's broken."

"Right. You know what I meant."

Scott shrugged again. "Probably."

Ernie looked surprised.

"It's gonna hurt like a motherfucker either way. Might result in a broken hand either way. It would have hurt me a lot more if he'd known what he was doing though. Still might have broken his hand, but I'd be in a lot more pain now at least." Scott thought about that. "Not that he knows, either way. He's probably comforting himself right now thinking how my head hurts as bad, or even worse, than his hand." Scott laughed at that. "Course, I wouldn't have let him hit me if he'd known how to punch."

Ernie again stopped walking, thought about that. Thought about everything Scott had taken into consideration, all in that moment where he himself had just stood in awe. He'd never himself been punched, never even been in the presence of a barfight. He'd seen a couple macho back-and-forths, but his brother was right. It was always just posturing, waiting for someone to break it up before it got started.

"Seems crazy," Ernie said, "you thought through all that so quick. It seemed to all happen so quick."

"I didn't really think it through. I didn't stop and think about it. That's just what it sounds like now. I just reacted. It's instinct."

Ernie had both hands up in the air in front of himself, making fists. Thumb in, thumb out; wrists bent, wrists locked into flat lines. He didn't throw a punch but held them there, like *ready*. Ready to spar, ready to throw a punch. Or maybe ready to block one that came his way. Practicing how to hold his hands, his arms; how not to. He finally turned his attention from his fists suspended in the air to his brother.

"You know how I showed you how to punch. Taking a punch is the same. You should know how—and be ready—to react to your own punch when it lands.

That's part of it, and you gotta know how to take a punch too. Brace yourself and tense your muscles, like locking them into place. Lean into it even, so it connects before it's supposed to. Make it hit you while it's still gaining power, not when fully realized. Try to take a punch before or after it's at full strength. Tense your muscle and lean into it, like a block. The block itself can be its own counter, even before returning your own punch. Or—" Scott punctuated his speech, like to grab Ernie's attention, though he already had it. "Or: you roll with it. Take the punch but turn with it. Slacken your body, let it go loose. Relax your muscles."

"What do you mean?"

"You've heard of people getting in car accidents, right? How the drunk guy will come away less injured than the sober one. Because they didn't know better, because their body was relaxed."

"OK, sure. That makes sense. I guess. But ..." Ernie trailed off. "How do you know? Lean into or roll away?"

"Practice. You practice until it's intuition. Until it's all action and reaction. People think wrestling's fake, like we don't know what we're doing. Like it's all choreographed or something. Which ... one, wouldn't that be impressive enough? Two, it's constant acting and reacting. You gotta know what you're doing ..."

Scott trailed off, was staring off into the distance but not at anything. Ernie had noticed it once or twice before, Scott looking a little like what he assumed he himself looked like when drifted off into *Ernie's World*. Ernie watched his brother, expecting Scott to shake himself out of it, maybe even make a joke about *Scott's World*. Instead, Scott's only movement seemed unreal; looked like he was slowly shrinking. He still looked large, though less so. More lifelike, more *regular.* Tired. Ernie thought he looked a little like he'd just lost a fight, not won one.

"It's why I finally stopped wrestling," Scott finally said.

"What do you mean? I thought you met Holly."

Scott shook his head. "No. I kept wrestling long after we met. It sounds more romantic like I quit just for her though. Holly likes to say she likes the *narrative* of that. Maybe I would have at some point." Scott thought about that. "Probably. I mean, I would have had to have stopped at some point. I just ... I wasn't good anymore. I stopped getting matches. Or the matches I was getting were bullshit. But it was my fault. I couldn't sell anymore."

"What do you mean? Couldn't sell tickets."

"That, too, I guess. One leads to the other. Or they're the same thing. I don't know. I couldn't sell the moves anymore. At first, I just started pulling punches and kicks. Literally, not like the saying. Like, I was literally pulling them. I'd throw too weak, or I'd stop before connecting. A guy can't sell that he's being hit if the hit stops before even getting to him. And then it spread. It's like a virus. Like when a hitter is in a slump or something, I bet. I started pulling punches, and then I stopped being able to sell getting hit." Scott looked down at the ground, kicked some dirt and rocks around. "I don't know. Maybe I wanted to get hit."

Ernie waited for Scott to continue, felt sure there was more waiting. He again looked around. He couldn't remember the last time a car had passed. What time was it? He had no idea—no idea when they'd left the bar, what time they'd checked in to the hotel, how long they'd been walking. It was dark, had been dark that whole time, but how long was 'that whole time'? He thought to get his phone out of his pocket and check, but he didn't really want to know. He didn't want to disturb the moment with the light of a phone, and it didn't matter if he knew what time it was. Maybe he had some missed messages, maybe not. Maybe something from Becca, but probably not. He realized he couldn't remember the last time he'd looked at his phone. He'd forgotten about it, given himself almost entirely over to the roadtrip. Back in Washington, on the farm, his life had quieted, slowed down, and now he'd carried that slowness onto the road. It felt good. *This* was life, he realized. Living on the farm, building planters and a fence. Spending time with his brother, his sister-in-law. A buffalo. And now being on the road with Scott, being in it together. Roadtrip partners.

"You guys had a dog, right?"

Ernie was more surprised by the plural than either the question itself or that it had seemingly come out of nowhere. He hadn't thought about Rebecca since they'd been on the road, maybe even longer, but he knew that's what Scott meant by *you guys*. He'd thought *of* her, just a moment ago, about the idea that she probably hadn't texted, and also generally, insofar as they were Michigan-bound, but he hadn't really thought *about* her. Not her as a part of *them*.

"Bulleit," Ernie said, the easiest way to answer.

"That's right! Bulleit." Scott scrunched his face, tried to think of how he knew that. Had Ernie talked about him, showed pictures? "Pitbull?"

"Part bulldog, yeah. She was a mix."

"Right, her. Sorry."

Ernie didn't remember Scott saying 'him,' but thought he'd probably just missed it. He shrugged it off. "Did you know pitbull isn't actually even a breed?"

"What do you mean?"

"'Pitbull'"—Ernie made air quotes in the air—"isn't a breed. It's kind of just a catchall for a certain kind of look of a dog. Big head, cropped ears, bulky. I think there's a couple of other specific distinctions, but I always forget. That's what they told us at the ..."

"Shelter? She was a rescue?"

"Kinda ... Yeah. Basically." Ernie left it at that. "We rescued her. Took care of her. It's crazy how quick you become attached. How quickly you already can't imagine a life before. And then ... She ran away."

"That's right. I do remember you telling me that," Scott said. "How hard was that?"

"Really hard." Ernie saw something out of his periphery, a light, and then as quickly as he'd realized it was headlights, the car was already approaching them, just as quickly passed. Would probably be on the freeway soon, heading to who-knew-where. "Like ... it affected us. I mean, I guess we were having problems, but I don't think I realized it. It seemed, at the time, like Bulleit running away caused our problems, but of course it just made us address them." Ernie thought about that. He wasn't sure he'd realized it as honestly as he'd just said it, or if he had, he hadn't actually put it into those words, even for himself. "Or: not address them, I guess would be more honest. It highlighted for us that we weren't addressing them?"

Scott nodded. "I can see that. I mean, I think. That makes sense. I never had a dog."

Ernie made a face of surprise before he realized it. "Really?" Scott shook his head, and Ernie thought about that. They hadn't had a dog growing up, Bulleit had in fact been the only dog he'd ever had. It seemed, he realized, like once you've had a dog, crazy to believe that you ever hadn't. That anyone ever hadn't.

Another light, *pair* of lights, appeared out of Ernie's periphery, into his line of vision. Two cars wasn't really *traffic,* but it almost seemed like it after so long with none. Had they crested that invisible line between late at night and early morning? Ernie looked at Scott, expecting him to be watching the car as well, but he was staring further off into the distance again. Ernie watched him like that for a minute or two, Scott never noticing, looking deep in thought. About how he'd never had a dog? About how pitbull isn't really a breed?

"There's Billy," Ernie finally said.

"What was that?"

"Billy. He isn't a dog but ... seems kind of more like a pet dog than, I don't know, a cat? A hamster? I had a hamster when I lived with Gina for that year. *We* had a hamster. But that seems to barely count. I forget about it usually."

"Right. Exactly. Billy."

Scott didn't say more, and Ernie looked at his brother, curious what he'd meant. Exactly what?

Scott cracked his knuckles again, then noticed himself doing it and looked down at his hands, made himself stop. He rubbed his hands together, thumbed at his palms, trying to keep himself from cracking them more.

"When I was traveling around, sometimes we'd go out drinking, but that shit like tonight would happen as often as not. Not to mention, when you're doing it all the time, one city after another, it's cheaper to just buy a few six packs or a bottle and take it back to your hotel room." Scott rubbed his left arm with his right hand, then switched. Ernie hadn't seen him so fidgety before. "Sometimes we'd get together in someone's room, sometimes guys would just drink by themselves. Sometimes ..." Scott drifted off, looked away. Continued under his breath, to himself. "Sometimes guys did more than just drink apparently."

Scott looked at Ernie, remembered where he was.

"I liked to drink and wander the town. Usually we were in *town*-towns, though sometimes little outposts like this. I liked to have a couple drinks and then go walk after the matches. I guess that was the impulse tonight."

Ernie wasn't sure where his brother was going. He brought up the story to explain why they were walking?

"One of those nights, I was out walking ... somewhere outside Detroit? Or, I don't think it was that close to Detroit actually. Somewhere in Michigan. Grand ... Grand Valley?"

"Grand Rapids?"

"That sounds right! Grand Rapids always really liked us actually. Always really came out and supported us."

Scott drifted off again, but different than before. Ernie hadn't quite known the other driftings had been to somewhere bad until he saw this one as comparison. Now his brother was picturing crowds, fans. Scott looked at Ernie, saw him waiting for more story, and the image disappeared.

"Anyway. The match went great, and I went back to the hotel. Had a few beers, a few swigs of Beam. Watched some TV and decided to go on a walk ..."

A few seconds passed, minutes. Ernie wondered if they were going to stand in silence like that until the sun came up.

Finally, Scott said, "Do you know the worst thing you've ever done?" He looked at Ernie.

"The actual worst thing?"

"Yeah. When I ask that, do you know immediately? What jumps to mind?"

"Masturbating when I was little?"

"*That's* the worst thing you've ever done?"

"You asked what jumped to mind! I don't know, but that's what did. The guilt drove me crazy!"

Scott nodded. "Right. The guilt ..." More silence. "Overwhelming guilt, and for something everyone does. Probably not the worst thing you've ever done, but it's what jumped to mind because the guilt was so strong and because there's no one, single thing you've done that's that bad."

Ernie thought about that, tried to think if he could come up with anything worse. Something with Becca probably. But that was more tendencies, patterns. Not really a worst thing, but regrets. Definitely not a single worst thing.

"The trick to a good punch, to *taking* a punch," Scott said. "To a magic trick, a good pitch, almost anything—is to not just know how to do something with your whole body, but to know it with and through your whole body. So it all feels natural, it's instinct—"

Ernie kept thinking about Becca. A single worst thing? *Technically*, he'd cheated on her, they were still married but separated. He didn't really think that counted. Then suddenly, he remembered the dog at the Thunderbird Inn. Had that been the worst thing he ever did? He'd broken into someone else's room. And then just let a dog loose out in the wild? The memory surprised him; remembering it felt more like watching a movie than his own actions just a few nights before. He thought about telling Scott—as a better answer than he'd given, as confession. Would this count as a *worst thing*?

But then, already, Scott had moved on. The moment seemed to have passed.

"Once something is known to the point of being instinct, how do you unknow it? You know?" Scott looked at Ernie. "How much practice does it take for a musician to play a song at a different pace? How many pitches can a pitcher throw at 70% speed before letting loose with one or two, out of habit, without thinking about it?"

Scott took a deep breath, exhaled slowly. Started again. "I was out walking, and I looked to my left, down this kind of alley, and there was this guy down there a ways, maybe a block away. He was yelling, but I don't remember hearing him before I saw him. In my memory, I saw him, and he was yelling, but is it possible I actually didn't hear him? Once I heard him, it was so loud, so unignorable. He was yelling at this dog ... *His* dog, I guess, but he seemed like such a horrible person. He was yelling at this dog, this dog that was cowering from him. This dog was curled up, leaning away ... I remember seeing it brace every time he started yelling anew, but maybe it was just one, constant brace and cower, and it was just sitting there, curled up. And it was this big dog. A pitbull, I think, actually. I don't know, maybe it looked like Bulleit even ..." Scott suddenly seemed out of breath. Like he'd told this monologue all in one breath, like monologue as round of a fight.

"I don't know why I said that. It just ... This dog ... and then the guy swung down and hit it!" Scott shook his head, put his hand on his neck like giving himself a massage. "I just stood there, staring in disbelief. I couldn't believe it. He yelled something at the dog again and then swung down and hit him again."

Scott finally looked over at Ernie, saw his own disbelief echoed on his brother's face.

"I was in shock, and then I yelled at the guy. 'What the fuck are you doing?' or something, I don't even know. And this guy, he yells at me to mind my own business. I started walking toward him, and he looked like all those drunk, overconfident assholes in bars, all these guys who want to pick a fight to show how tough and manly they are. Except he was picking a fight with his dog. And now he was telling me, 'I thought I told you to mind your own business?' as I walked toward him, like that would make me go away. So he could go back to beating his dog? Like that wasn't my business. I walked straight at the guy and swung and landed the hardest punch I've ever thrown."

Ernie's eyes bugged out, he couldn't help from smiling. He kind of looked his brother up and down, like he was trying to measure how hard of a punch that could be. This giant of a man, and not just that, but a giant who knew how to punch. Knew how to throw a punch, but also knew how to restrain himself.

"The guy swayed and buckled, and then collapsed. I think as much out of surprise that I'd actually hit him. I'd skipped everything that usually leads up to the actual hit. But then, I looked over at the dog, and something like a flash came over me. I saw a flash of this guy hitting his dog, and I got down on top of the guy and hit him again. I just kept hitting."

They both stood silent, the story standing there with them.

Ernie wasn't sure what his brother was telling him. Or: he was sure but struggled to accept it. He must have heard wrong. He wasn't sure if he wanted confirmation or not, but then he thought about all the questions he'd left unasked over the years—questions for Scott, for Becca, his dad, himself. He had to make himself ask, pushing it out like actual, physical exertion. "What do you mean?"

"Just that. I just kept hitting. I hit him until my arms were tired and I couldn't hit him anymore. I finally rolled off him and then just kinda lay there on the ground for a while, exhausted, until finally I felt the dog nuzzle my face. It seemed right then, his wet nose against my cheek, pushing my face, like he wanted to wake me up. Like he knew what I'd done for him and he was making sure I was OK, or thanking me, or telling me we should go. Or something. I don't know. Maybe he'd nudged the other guy too, and he'd never reacted. I don't know. But I stood up, and I'd punched that guy until I couldn't feel my arms anymore, but seeing the dog replenished me or something. I picked him up and carried him all the way back to the hotel in my arms."

Ernie nodded. In awe, in wonder. "And then what?"

"I took him with me, to the next town. I took him to an animal rescue, told them I'd found him like that. I kind of wanted to keep him, but he was pretty beat up. I didn't know how to take care of him, how to make him better. I was on the road, he needed attention. I hope he was alright. I like to think he was."

"No. But. What about the guy?"

Scott shook his head, scrunched up his shoulders.

"Was he ...?" Ernie couldn't even say the word. Couldn't conjure it, couldn't make himself say it out loud.

"I don't know. I don't think. He wasn't when I left. But ... Honestly? I don't know."

Ernie stared at his brother. At one more incarnation of his brother. All these versions of Scott and he felt like he barely knew any of them. Over the last few weeks, he'd finally started to get to know and understand one, and then another would emerge.

Ernie thought about Becca. He thought about flirting with Steph the night Bulleit ran away. The electricity between them as he laughed and smiled at her story, the way she smiled back, and he was sure they were sharing this moment. He thought about Bulleit, how he and Becca took her in, took care of her, doting and pampering and treating her like their baby, and then he thought anew about leaving that gate open, the absentmindedness that had always been there but that Becca had been pointing out more and more as their relationship declined. He thought about how he'd noticed that decline but never said anything. He thought about the night, weeks later, after Becca told him she wanted a divorce, that he and Steph went out for drinks and ended up back at her place. He thought about how that had made everything awkward at work, an awkwardness at work to echo the awkwardness he'd been wading through at home for weeks, and then how Holly's call had come at just that moment, providing an out, a distraction, an escape, a new beginning. Ernie looked at his brother and asked again, to himself, not saying it out loud but almost feeling as if he had, *What about the guy?* He thought about what his brother might be capable of. He thought about his brother's question. *What's the worst thing you've ever done?* He thought about how his answer had been doing what every young boy does, and then he thought about how, instead of discounting that answer, instead of scoffing at this nothing compared to what he was trying to work his way up to sharing, *confessing*, Scott acknowledged understanding Ernie's guilt. Ernie thought about how, whether the guy had deserved it or not, Scott's guilt must have weighed on him after unleashing the full power and force of Mr. Bison on him. The guilt and the not knowing. He thought about how other, closer brothers might have confided this to each other years before now. He thought about what it might have meant to have been there for Scott when this had all happened. And then Ernie thought about how, after graduating college, Scott had called him. He thought about how that must have been right around when Scott dropped out of college, how he'd probably been looking for advice or encouragement or support, or just someone to listen. He thought about Scott asking him, before they stopped at that university gym, what he did to let off steam. He thought about Becca pointing out how he bottled everything up. How that was unhealthy. He thought about what it might mean to not. He thought about all that, and thought about it, and thought about it ...

Next thing Ernie knew, he was on the ground. He didn't remember collapsing or letting himself down or falling, he didn't remember how it had happened, how he'd gotten from there to here, but he was lying on the soft, gravelly shoulder of the road and crying. He couldn't remember the last time he'd cried this hard. Maybe never? It felt surprising, but also good; a little embarrassing, but also freeing. A relief. And then Scott was lying down next to him, taking Ernie's hand in his. Ernie wondered if he should say something, or if Scott was going to. Instead, he felt Scott squeeze his hand, and then, looking to his side, he saw Scott was crying with him.

24.

The room was dark. Lights-off, middle-of-the-night, bottom-of-a-cave dark.

Ernie strained his eyes, trying to see something, anything, and then when he stopped trying and let himself just relax, his eyes finally started to adapt. Pupils dilating, stretching to take over his whole iris, trying to see in the total absence of light. Bit by bit the room started to become almost-visible, and with it, Ernie's memory of the night before—lying on the side of the road with Scott, the two of them holding hands and crying together; finally standing and pulling each other up, brushing themselves off; walking back toward their hotel in silence, a silence that felt so crisp and clear, like his entire being had been run through some kind of cleansing cycle; getting back to their room and then already in his bed; falling asleep faster than he maybe ever had before, as simple and easy as a flip being switched. Ernie pushed the blanket and sheet back, looked down at himself and saw the blurry outline of his body but still nothing distinguishable. Patting himself down, he felt he was still wearing the t-shirt and jeans he'd been wearing the day before. He clicked his feet together and was almost surprised he'd managed to get his shoes off, although he couldn't imagine ever actually getting into bed with them on.

"Scott?" Ernie looked over at Scott's bed, but he didn't stir.

Ernie looked at the nightstand between their beds, found it odd he couldn't see the alarm clock. Reaching his arm out, he started patting the table, feeling for where he thought it should be. He felt a shirt, pulled it toward him. The crash of the clock hitting the ground startled a gasp out of him before he realized what had happened, and Ernie instinctively looked back at Scott, ready to apologize, but Scott still hadn't stirred. Though everything was a little more visible than it had been moments before, his eyes continued their adjusting, and the room had lit up with the softest red glow of the clock. Leaning over, Ernie looked down to the ground where it beamed the time back up at him. 9:13. *A.m.?* Ernie wondered for a split second in surprise, even though p.m. made no sense. He wondered when they'd gotten back to the room. One? Two? *Three*? Maybe. How had they slept in so late? How was it still so dark? Was it this dark in the middle of the night? Did hotel rooms get this blacked out? He couldn't remember. Ernie looked toward the windows and now, with the room finally starting to come more and more into view, saw two coat hangers floating in the air. A magic trick? What the fuck was going on? No, they weren't floating. They were coat hangers with clasps to clip onto pants. That's what Ernie thought they were for anyway. Now those clips were holding the blinds closed, not letting in even the littlest hint of daylight. It was ingenious. Another of Scott's tricks from the road? He should write a book! Ernie surprised himself, thinking. Some kind of how to! Ernie looked at Scott one more time and saw why he hadn't stirred before now. He wasn't there.

Part V:

HOME IS WHERE

How to Build a Character

Think about their motivations. Their goals.

Picture the distance between who they were and who they could possibly be. Think about it as actual distance, a literal picture. Draw it if it helps. Write it out. Talk through it with someone.

Let go of who they actually are. Let yourself let go of who you think they are. Make them who they want to be. Let them become who they want to be.

Build the world around them from there.

25.

Holly stood in front of the wall of glass, clipboard dangling at her side, and stared out across the campus. "The Farm," she'd taken to calling it. She liked the sound of it, the way it called back to their farm in Washington. Others around the company had picked up on it, started using the name as if it were official nomenclature. "The Farm," setting itself apart from everyone else in the valley and their *campuses*, their *compounds*.

Mr. Bison Farms? Holly wondered if they might someday christen it. *CP Games Farms*? *CPG Farms*?

Holly squinted, slowly, more relaxed than a squint, like paused somewhere before sleep. She let herself drift into something verging on daydream. She could see the field one day full of buffalo, a whole herd. She could imagine a normal day, buffalo becoming part of her lunchbreak, part of what relaxed her; perhaps a rumor would get started, going around the office that watching the buffalo was inspirational, was part of how she got her ideas, when and how she figured out the solution to whatever problem had been plaguing them.

After Scott called her, told her he was home. Asked if she could pick him up at the airport. Said, *no hurry ... I couldn't do it ... I missed you. I'll tell you all about it later ...* After she got everything together, told her parents she was running to the airport to pick up Scott, and hustled out the door before they asked any questions that she didn't yet know the answers to. After she pulled into the clusterfuck of cars at Arrivals and saw her husband standing out among the chaos, looking like the giant she'd fallen in love with but almost forgotten or taken for granted in the years since, and especially in the week since he'd hit the road with Ernie; after Scott jumped in, pushed the passenger seat as far back as it would go, helped direct her out of the moving mass of everyone coming and going, and then told her everything on their drive home. After he told her about the hotel pool, Yellowstone, the bar fight, leaving the hotel and walking along the side of the road like he'd used to in the old days, finally telling Ernie about ... everything.

Everything? Everything. After he told her all about the note he'd left Ernie, the explanation that, now that he'd told Ernie everything, he felt done, he wanted to be home, he didn't want to be this Mr. Bison for a convention center of people, but he hoped Ernie would go in his stead, would be his proctor ("that's the word you used? *Proctor?*" "Haha, yeah, I don't know where it came to me from ..."), would tell stories, talk up the game, become a character! After that triggered something in Holly. After everything clicked into place, all at once, the puzzle that she didn't even know she was putting together suddenly fully revealed in front of her eyes. After they got home and she showed Scott her notebooks, after she reminded him how together they'd built this *Legend of Mr. Bison*, after she showed him how she'd been playing through her old NES *Super Mario Bros. 2*, after she connected all the pieces for him and laid it all out, describing her vision, her idea as it had all clicked into place for herself. *Go West 2: Vernon's World.* After Scott called Michael to tell him about the idea, and before he could get out much more than the title, Michael told him all about what a discovery Ernie had been at the conference; he'd come alive, he'd embraced this whole persona, somewhere between a heightened version of himself and the character of *Mr. Bison's brother.* After Ernie called and Scott put him on speakerphone and he told Scott and Holly more or less everything Michael had already told them, but they didn't interrupt him or cut him off, just let him tell his story, basking in the glow of his performance.

After everything thereafter, Michael offered Holly a job on the CP Games campus in California after she took as much maternity time as she wanted; Ernie signed divorce papers and moved to Washington to live on the farm and take care of Billy until he decided what to do next; Scott settled into his new life as a stay-at-home dad, one more new persona.

Holly's phone vibrated again. She was excited to tell Scott about the idea she'd just had. How Vernon would get to the dreamworld. Or maybe how he travels through it? She wasn't sure which, but she knew the visual. The item. Magic shoes!

Holly closed her eyes, let herself picture it all. Mr. Bison and his little cartoon brother or any number of other playable characters putting on these all-black, spiky, magic shoes, letting them walk on clouds, traveling through this magical dreamscape.

Holly opened her eyes, returned to looking out at the fields. Back to mentally placing a couple buffalo here, a few there. It was going to be quite the sight. It already felt like home.

Acknowledgments

Biggest of thanks, first and foremost, to Dan Hoyt. For asking if I had a manuscript and saving it from the graveyard of my hard drive, to working on it together with his publishing class to make it so much better, to being generally and always so encouraging and enthusiastic and supportive.

Thank you to all my friends who read versions of this over the years — Dave Housley, Jensen Beach, Jac Jemc, Caleb Curtiss, Leesa Cross-Smith, Tom Williams, and especially my "Dramaturgy Bros" writer group buddies, Matthew Kilpatrick and Russell Brakefield, who read versions of this more times than anyone should have to read their friend's manuscript. I am no doubt forgetting a few who read and helped and encouraged along the way, for which I apologize. The road to publication for this book was so long and windy, I've probably blacked out chunks of time when I was working on it, else I probably wouldn't have been able to keep moving forward.

I read a handful of books about buffalo over the years, sometimes as "research" but more often than not just for fun, and pieces of each likely worked their way into this: *Why They Call Him the Buffalo Doctor* by Jean Cummings, *A Buffalo in the House* by R. D. Rosen, *American Serengeti* by Dan Flores, and *American Buffalo* and *Meat Eater* by Steven Rinella.

Thank you to my family—my parents and brother but also extended, biological, and friends who I think of as such. I have been blessed with an embarrassment of riches with a life filled with people who are loving, encouraging, hilarious, ego-building, motivating, supportive, and basically all the other good adjectives too.

Thank you, finally, to you for picking this up. It means a lot.